The Christmas Café

The Christmas Café

A NOVEL

ELIZA EVANS

G. P. PUTNAM'S SONS
NEW YORK

PUTNAM
— EST. 1838 —

G. P. PUTNAM'S SONS
Publishers Since 1838
An imprint of Penguin Random House LLC
penguinrandomhouse.com

Trade paperback ISBN: 9780593544563
Ebook ISBN: 9780593544570

Printed in the United States of America
1st Printing

Book design by Ashley Tucker

This book is dedicated to the Hedrich family.
Thanks for the inspiration!

The Christmas Café

One

"SIT." SYLVIE WEST DESPERATELY WAVED AN ORGANIC UN-cured pepperoni training treat at her one-year-old pug-chihuahua rescue puppy. "Come on, schnookums. Sit for mama."

Uttering a delighted growl, Crumpet went into a sly downward dog position, his teeth still clamped around Sylvie's favorite Christmas-themed bra. Considering it was a double D, it was a wonder the eight-pound pooch had managed to stealthily snatch it off the bed and make it all the way across the room by the time she'd turned around. As usual, Crumpet had deduced that Sylvie was getting ready to leave for work, and the puppy wasn't going to let her go without a fight.

"Two treaties, then." Sylvie upped the ante in her negotiations. Seeing as how she was already behind on holiday preparations at the Christmas Café, she didn't have time for yet another power struggle with her furry toddler this morning. "Now drop it. Drop the bra."

Another playful growl rumbled from Crumpet's throat, and she swore the puppy's furrowed eyebrows raised as if posing a silent question. *What're you gonna do about it?*

Welllll . . . she didn't know exactly. *Maintain eye contact*, the trainer had told her. *Make sure the dog knows you are the authority figure.*

Right. She was the authority figure around here. Or at least she was supposed to be. But every time she gazed into her pup's innocent, slightly bugged eyes, she turned to mush. Before she'd fallen in love with him at the shelter eight months ago, poor Crumpie had been neglected and abandoned. Left for dead in a box on the side of the highway. The first time she'd seen him in the pen, he'd cowered in a corner, resting his little chin on his paws and gazing up at her with the most forlorn expression. Coaxing him out of his shell had taken months—and a whole lot of gourmet treats. And now that he was living his best life, she didn't want to crush the dog's spirit. Even if it meant she had to sacrifice her good bras.

"Yip!" Crumpet gave the bra a good shake.

"You're going to rip it." Sylvie sighed and glanced around her cramped bedroom. The fluffy comforters and pillows had seemed like a good idea at the time, but now all the homey comforts she'd added gave Crumpet too many places to hide— he loved to wedge himself underneath the antique church pew under the window . . . or between her upholstered tufted headboard and the wall. And of course her door was open a crack, which meant she couldn't make any sudden moves or her beloved little wiggle butt would tear all through the house like a Tasmanian devil and probably chew her bra to shreds.

"You want a chewy stick, then? Or a cookie?" She'd baked a new set of Christmas-tree-shaped dog confections to sell at the café over the next three weeks. "I'll give you *two* cookies if you drop the bra right now."

At the mention of cookies, both of Crumpet's perked ears twitched.

Ah yes, she and this puppy had a lot in common. They would both do pretty much anything for a cookie.

"I baked them fresh last night," Sylvie taunted. "Remember? They're in the kitchen." She shuffled a step in the direction of the door, but the motion set Crumpet off. The dog bolted out of sight, her bra trailing behind him.

"Great." She rushed from her room down the narrow hallway in time to see Gramps walking in from the front porch with the newspaper. "Close the—"

Crumpet streaked across the room at Mach speed and sailed over her grandfather's plaid slippers on his way out the open door before she could finish the sentence.

"No!" Sylvie raced to her boots and shoved her feet into them.

"I'll go after him," Gramps offered, lumbering to the coat-rack.

"That's okay." The last thing she wanted was for her seventy-nine-year-old grandfather to take a fall out there on the ice.

She frantically snatched her winter jacket off the couch. Who cared that she was wearing her Christmas flamingo pajama pants? Who cared that her red curly hair had likely tripled in size overnight? Her baby could get hit by a car! She had not rescued her little Crumpie Wumpie just to lose him like this.

Sylvie tore out the door. "I'm coming, Crumpet!" A blast of frigid mountain air muted the shout.

The sun had only started to peek above the snow-capped mountaintops to the east, highlighting the very farthest edges of the horizon with a soft pinkish glow. Most of the prairie-style bungalows on her street were still dark. "Crumpet!" She slogged through the fresh powder that had fallen overnight, searching the ground for footprints.

"Yip!" her puppy yelped from a house three doors down. "Yip! Yip! Yip!"

"I'm coming, baby!" Sylvie's boots skidded on the layer of ice under the snow as she veered to the left and blazed a path through her neighbor's yard. Honestly, if anyone in Silver Bells did happen to see her tromping around in her pajamas at dawn, they probably wouldn't be surprised. Growing up here, she'd managed to develop quite the reputation as . . . quirky.

"Yip! Yip!" Crumpet's delighted barks grew louder as he pranced and bounced, tossing her bra through the snow. Just her luck she'd ended up with a dog that loved bras more than tennis balls.

"This isn't a game," she called, slowly approaching. "Now sit! Stay!" Since those commands didn't even work inside the house, they likely weren't going to do much when her dog had gotten a taste for sweet freedom.

"I'm not kidding, Crumpet." She'd gotten close enough now that she could almost grab him. "Easy. Let's go home."

"Yip!" The dog assumed his favorite *come and get me* position—butt in the air, tail wagging.

Oh, for the love . . . Sylvie lunged, but Crumpet ducked out of reach at the last second—still managing to hold on to the bra—and darted into the street.

"No!" Stuck on her knees, Sylvie flailed to get up, managing to find her feet just as a car turned onto the block. "Stop! Oh, God! Please stop." Waving her arms, she sprinted into the road between Crumpet and the SUV, huffing and puffing.

The car came to an abrupt stop in front of her, and the driver's door swung open. "Are you okay, miss?" a man called.

"I'm—" Sylvie's jaw dropped when he climbed out of his car. The angled winter sunlight highlighted his tanned face and chestnut-colored hair, which had exactly the right amount of length and wave to make him appear both stylish and easygoing. Even from a distance she could tell his eyes were a sapphire blue . . . or maybe she only hoped they were because with his classic Hollywood jawline and the vintage wool coat he wore, otherworldly blue would complete the fantasy.

She pried her gaze off of him and glanced down at her pajama pants. Seriously? She was out here in her PJs with her hair a red storm cloud, and the universe had decided to send a Marlon Brando look-alike to the rescue?

She *loved* Marlon Brando. Her Grams had loved Marlon Brando too.

"Do you need help?" The man stepped away from the SUV. "Are you in trouble?"

"My dog," she said weakly. "He got out . . ." Before she could continue the explanation, her sweet, loving, butterball of a puppy trotted past her, lugging the bra along, and proceeded to jump up on the man's leg, begging for a scratch behind the ears.

Crumpet also had a thing for good-looking men. Another quality the two of them had common. Except, Sylvie wasn't quite as smooth as the dog in her greeting. "I'm so sorry," she sputtered, trudging closer to him. "I was chasing my puppy all over and I thought you were going to hit him." And, oh lord, now she was getting teary because even with all the hassles Crumpet had brought into her life, he was her best buddy besides Gramps and what would she do without him?

"I didn't even see the little stinker." The mystery man lifted the dog—along with the bra—into his arms and carefully untangled the undergarment's strap from Crumpet's teeth. "This must be yours?" The blue of his eyes—yes, they were actually blue—deepened with obvious amusement.

"Yeah." Right about now Sylvie was wishing she'd grabbed her beanie and scarf so she could've hidden her tomato-red cheeks behind layers of wool.

"Very festive." The man gave the bra an appreciative glance before holding it out.

"Thanks." She took it from his hand and quickly stuffed it into her pocket. "I don't know why I bother buying him toys at the pet store when he only plays in my bra drawer."

Mystery Man had a nice laugh—crooning and gravelly . . . sexy, Crumpet might say. And Sylvie would have to agree.

"He sure is a cute little guy." He gave the dog a good scratch behind the ears while Crumpet tried to lick his chin.

Sheesh. At least she exercised a little more self-control than her dog. You didn't see her trying to lick him. Yet. "Well, I'm sure you have places to be." What with his chiseled jaw and glowing smile, this man definitely had someone waiting for him somewhere. Sylvie held out her arms to take the dog back.

"Actually, I'm not sure where I'm headed." He carefully nestled Crumpet into Sylvie's arms. "I'm jet-lagged so I woke up early. Thought I'd go in search of some breakfast. Do you happen to have any recommendations?"

Ah, a tourist. Perfect. She relaxed a little, knowing she'd likely never see him again. Not when she planned to be attached to her oven at the café for the next two weeks. Besides, he looked like he'd be spending his holiday on the slopes nearby. "Nothing's open around here until seven." This was Silver Bells, after all. Not some big city where everything was open twenty-four seven. "But I'd highly recommend the

Christmas Café. They have the best breakfast in town." It never hurt to put in a shameless plug for her employer.

"The Christmas Café." A dimple winked out from behind the man's smile. "Sounds perfect. It was nice to meet you . . ." He lifted an eyebrow.

"Sylvia. Or Sylvie. Or Syl. People tend to call me one of those three most of the time. My grandmother's name was Sylvie and the same thing happened to her . . ." *Uh-oh*. Her babbling reflex had kicked in.

"What do you like being called?" Mystery Man asked, gazing at her intently like he really wanted to know.

"Oh. Uh . . ." She'd never really thought about it. "Sylvie, I suppose."

The man nodded but his gaze never left hers. "Nice to meet you, Sylvie. I hope I'll see you around town."

"Oh, definitely not." Sometimes her mouth tended to work faster than her brain. "I mean, it's not that I wouldn't want to or anything, er . . . not that I really want to either, but I'm really busy around the holidays so I don't really get to see people because I'm super busy and I just don't get out much." If her social skills were any indication, she obviously didn't see many people. "Anyway. Nice to meet you." Still cradling Crumpet in her arms, she whirled and slogged through the snow to the sidewalk before any more awkwardness could come out of her mouth.

"Merry Christmas, Sylvie," he called before getting back into his car and driving away.

"Merry Christmas." She watched the dark SUV disappear around the corner. "You saw him too, right?" she asked her dog. How often did a good-looking, kind, and jovial Marlon Brando look-alike randomly show up in life? "Never. That never happens." Maybe she should leave the house wearing her Christmas flamingo pajamas more often.

"Yip!" Crumpet licked her chin and gave his best puppy dog eyes as she carted him into the house.

"You were very naughty," she told him gravely. That was about all she had in her discipline skills toolbox. "I'll give you a cookie if you promise to never steal mummy's bra again." Sylvie kicked off her boots and set the pup gently on the floor.

"Yip! Yip!" Crumpet spun in circles.

"Musta taken you a while to catch him." Gramps looked over the top of his newspaper from the kitchen table, which used to sit in the dining room at the house he'd shared with Grams for over five decades. Steam swirled from the extra cup of coffee he'd set out next to his.

Boy, did she need coffee. "He almost got hit by a car. It was horrible." Sylvie dug Crumpet's cookie out of the plastic container she'd filled last night and then joined her grandfather at the table. "But the driver stopped and helped. He turned out to be pretty nice, actually."

"I saw 'im out the window." Gramps's deep brown eyes twinkled. "Sure looked like you two were havin' a *nice* conversation."

"He was having a nice conversation." Sylvie handed her dog the treat and then wrapped her hands around the mug to warm them. She really had to get to work, but nothing beat a cup of strong hot coffee after a spontaneous frigid morning jog. "I was being my typical self."

She cringed remembering the way the man's brows had pinched when she said she would definitely not see him again. "Why can't every man be as easy to talk to as you are?" She squeezed Gramps's shoulder. "Or maybe I'm the problem."

Why couldn't she be more like her older sister, who was so well-spoken? Or charming like her brother? Yes, she realized that being adopted meant she didn't share their blood, but you'd think they would've rubbed off on her over the years.

"Any man would be lucky to talk to you," her grandfather insisted stubbornly. "You're a gem, Sylvie. And don't you forget that."

"Thanks, Gramps, but this gem needs to get to work." She rose from the table and carted her mug to the sink, Crumpet at her heels. The kitchen at the Christmas Café gave her the perfect hiding place. There she could simply turn on her music and bake. She only had to talk to the waitstaff, the line cooks, and Abe, the goat farmer who delivered the milk, butter, and eggs she used in her confections. "I'm going to make my spiced eggnog scones today, so you'd better come by."

"I'll see if I can clear my schedule," Gramps muttered, and then went back to reading his paper.

A pang settled beneath her breastbone. Grams had been gone for two years, and Gramps still wasn't any better at being social than Sylvie was. "I'm sure Chuck and Dean would love to meet you at the café later this morning," she pressed, giving his white tufted hair a pat on her way past the table. "I'll set aside some scones for you."

"All right, all right," she heard him mutter as she made her way down the hallway.

Seeing as how her bra was still wet from Crumpet's adventure, Sylvie rifled through her drawers until she found something suitable and then got herself ready in record time. She'd made it within five feet of the front door when Crumpet started to howl.

"I know, I know." She swept the puppy up into her arms

and smothered him with kisses. "Maybe I'll bring you with me tomorrow, but today is just going to be too busy." She crossed the room and set him in Gramps's lap. "Be good!" Before those little howls could pull at her heartstrings, she snatched the tub of freshly baked dog treats off the counter and rushed out the door, half walking and half ice skating to where she'd parked at the curb last night.

Crap. Fresh snow blanketed the entire car, which she might've noticed earlier if she hadn't been so busy saving her dog's life. Muttering to herself, Sylvie opened the door and shoved the cookies inside before digging through five layers of discarded to-go coffee cups she'd meant to bring to the recycling bin to locate the window scraper.

"I love white Christmases. I love white Christmases." She repeated the mantra to herself while she maneuvered around the car, brushing and scraping. "I love—"

Her feet slid out from under her and she couldn't catch herself before she landed on her butt in the slushy street.

"Are you kidding me?" She might love white Christmases, but all this snow and ice could kiss her frozen ass.

"Good morning, Sylvia." Marion, her neighbor, waved from the sidewalk. The sixty-year-old woman was geared up head-to-toe for her morning power walk—purple snow pants, silver puffer jacket, giant ear muffs. Marion didn't miss a morning of power walking—rain, snow, or shine. And Sylvie couldn't even brush off her car without taking a tumble.

"Good morning, Marion." She gingerly got her legs beneath her and pulled herself up using the car for support.

"Have you heard the news?" The woman effortlessly walked across the ice to get closer.

"Nope. Haven't heard any news today." She had a theory

about Marion's commitment to power walking—being the first one out and about in the morning meant she got to share all of the gossip she'd accumulated since the day before.

"The Holiday Channel is filming scenes for a movie here over the holidays!" the woman blurted. "Apparently they were looking for the most festive town in all of America to shoot these scenes and they chose us!"

"Right. Claire told me about that." As the distinguished mayor of Silver Bells, her older sister had droned nonstop about her *important* calls with the movie's producers. "I guess it's not much of a surprise." Every year Silver Bells went all out to live up to its Christmassy name. Sylvie swore most of the town's annual budget went toward the holiday decorations and events. The bylaws required every business in town to dress up their façades with garlands and lights and red velvet bows. And silver bells, of course. And then the town hosted everything from a Christmas lights parade to a Christmas ball—all within the next two weeks leading up to the big day.

"I can't wait to watch the movie. Maybe some of us will be extras!" Marion adjusted her earmuffs.

"Mmm-hmm." Sylvie had never actually watched a movie on the Holiday Channel. She preferred the classics, especially around Christmas. But she was determined to think before she spoke for once.

"This is going to be great." Marion started to march in place, as though to burn extra calories without pausing her gossip. "It'll really help all the businesses in town. Especially the Christmas Café. I know things have been tough this year."

"Tough?" Sylvie momentarily forgot about her wet jeans. "Things at the café are fine." At least she assumed they were.

Her boss hadn't mentioned anything to her about things be-ing tough.

"That's not what I heard." Marion started to swing her arms and power walked her way back to the sidewalk. "Any-way, have a good day!"

"Yeah, you too." Sylvie slid into the driver's seat and tossed the scraper over her shoulder.

Forget her cold, wet jeans—if the café was in trouble, she had bigger problems.

Two

MARION BAUER DIDN'T KNOW WHAT SHE WAS TALKING about.

Sylvie turned onto Main Street and slowed the car. SUVs and trucks filled every single parking spot in front of the Christmas Café. She couldn't see any open spaces across the street or down the block either. She paused at the stoplight—one of only three in town—and exhaled the worry that had lodged itself tightly into her chest. All was well.

The Christmas Café had been a staple in Silver Bells for well over fifty years, and that wouldn't change now. She admired the red brick façade and the large storefront windows that were sandwiched in between the stately bank on one side and the quaint antique shop on the other. The town wouldn't be the same without the café's red-and-white-striped awnings stretching over the paver sidewalks or the ornate marquee sign blinking above the revolving door.

Colorful twinkling Christmas lights lined the windows all year, but during the holiday season, Sylvie adorned them with the silver tinsel Grams had always used on her Christmas tree.

The stoplight turned green, and Sylvie rolled past the café, a smile blooming. Even though it wouldn't be open for ten more minutes, a small crowd waited outside the doors.

Marion simply liked to stir up rumors, that was all. Like the time the woman had told the entire town that Gramps and Grams were headed for a divorce because she'd seen Grams pack up her Jeep and peel out of the driveway one evening. For an entire week after, poor Gramps had dealt with a new over-sixty bachelorette showing up on his doorstep with a casserole every day before he finally figured out Marion had started a rumor. Sylvie grinned, remembering how he'd put a notice in the town newspaper to inform everyone that, no, he and Grams were not getting divorced. She'd simply gone to be with her sister in Montana who'd had a heart attack.

That's all this Christmas Café business was. A rumor. Sylvie hummed along to "Deck the Halls" and turned onto the alleyway behind the café. Abe! Oh, shoot. His truck was parked outside the kitchen door. She'd completely forgotten she was supposed to meet him early for the delivery this morning.

After squeezing around his pickup truck, Sylvie pulled into her parking spot behind the dumpster and gathered up her purse and the dog treats. It looked like one of the waitresses had already opened up the place. "I'm sorry!" she called when she stepped inside the kitchen. Her kitchen. Grams's kitchen. Their kitchen. This was where Sylvie had grown up. Her happy place. It didn't matter what was going on in her life—or how many humiliating moments she'd already endured that day—when she stepped through this door, her whole world righted itself.

Even though none of the customers could see into this

space, the Christmas Café's kitchen continued the holiday theme with old-fashioned bubble lights lining the shelves, and festive wreaths and evergreen boughs hanging on the walls. Grams had worked part-time at the café for years, and had taken the liberty of decorating the space the same way she did her own home. Sylvie glanced at the wooden signs Grams had painted over the years with sayings like *Christmas calories don't count* and *We whisk you a merry Christmas*. Those homey touches toned down the pristine but bleak stainless-steel counters and appliances.

She could still hear the echoes of her grandmother's voice singing along to her favorite Christmas songs while Sylvie worked on her homework at the desk in the opposite corner. Of course, she'd never gotten much homework done. She'd always ended up as Grams's sous chef while they sang and danced their way around the kitchen.

But she would have to lose herself in the memories later.

"I didn't mean to make you wait," she said to Abe, scurrying past him.

Casually dressed in jeans and a flannel shirt, he leaned against one of the counters, nursing a cup of coffee. "No worries."

Sylvie'd never been good at reading facial expressions, but his jaw seemed tighter than normal. Not that the man ever looked particularly happy. Instead of jovial, she'd describe Abe's overall appearance as rough around the edges—unkempt dark hair with a slight wave, a trimmed beard that shrouded his mouth. His eyes were a contemplative sort of brown, wise and dark and deep—his best feature, she'd say.

She'd known Abe a long time. The two had gone through school in the same class every year, but he'd already lived a lifetime more than her as an Army Ranger before moving back to Silver Bells to take over his parents' goat farm after his dad was diagnosed with Parkinson's a few months ago. She'd asked him about his experiences overseas once. He said he could tell her all about his missions but then he'd have to kill her. He'd been joking, of course. Probably. But sometimes it was hard to tell with Abe.

Case in point, he simply stood there, staring at her while she shed her coat and unpacked the gourmet doggie treats. She selected one of her favorite aprons from the snowman coatrack in the corner—a red number with plaid ruffled edging and the words *Baking Christmas Cheer* embroidered across the front with gold thread. Another Grams classic. "Whew, I've had a morning." No response from Abe. "Crumpet escaped the house and almost got hit by a car . . ."

As usual, the man's silence induced a serious case of the babbles, and she brewed her own special pot of coffee—with a hearty helping of cinnamon in the grounds—while she gave him a play-by-play of the scenes that had already made this the longest day of her year. "And then Marion had the nerve to tell me that it's a good thing there's a movie filming here because the café is in trouble. Can you believe that?" Sylvie refilled Abe's coffee mug for him. He tipped his head in gratitude, but stayed silent. "I mean, seriously. This place already had a line outside the door. It's always packed. There's no problem here."

Saying the words out loud helped to chase away her doubts. The truth was, Silver Bells was a tourist town with two busy seasons, Christmas and summer. In that financial climate, no business could be completely safe. Sylvie almost lamented that fact, but . . . had Abe even managed to get in a word edgewise? She set the coffee carafe back on the warmer and waited in case he had something to say. She'd take any verbal acknowledgment right now. A grunt. A half-hearted *mmm-hmm . . .*

"Forget Marion," Abe finally muttered and then sipped from his mug. "I wasn't going to have another cup, but your coffee is the best. In fact, everything you make is the best. What would this town do without you? I don't even want to imagine."

The compliment rekindled her inner glow. Wow. It turned out that if you gave him a little space to talk, he had a lot to say. "Thanks, Abe." Yes, exactly. What would this town do without the Christmas Café? It was the center, the heart. And she got to be part of that.

"She's right, I guess. The movie'll probably be good for business." He set down his mug and pushed a box of eggs, butter, cheese, and milk down the counter toward Sylvie. "It's all anyone's talking about. I had to wait five minutes at the crosswalk for half the women in Silver Bells to cross. When I asked them what was up, one of them yelled that Royce Elliot was in town."

"Royce Elliot?" Sylvie started to pull the packages of butter out of the box. "Isn't he an actor?"

When Abe didn't answer, she looked up to see him giving her a deadpan stare.

"Come on. Every woman in America knows who Royce Elliot is."

"Sure. I've heard of him." She carefully withdrew the glass pints of goat's milk and brought them to her refrigerator. "But I don't think I've seen any of his movies."

"You've never seen a movie on the Holiday Channel?" Well,

at least Sylvie could read one expression on the man's face. His narrowed eyes shouted his skepticism.

"No, I haven't," she replied stubbornly. "I don't have much time to watch television, and when I do, I prefer my movies in black and white."

"Somehow that doesn't surprise me." The right side of Abe's mouth lifted into an amused grin, the curve of his lips changing underneath his beard. "You're different. Always have been."

Heat rose to her cheeks and she wasn't sure where it had come from. Embarrassment? Anger? She focused on examining the eggs from Abe's free-range chickens. They were gorgeous, in different shades of brown and white. "Right. I'm just weird, thirty-two-year-old spinster Sylvie who talks to my oven more than I talk to people." She knew what everyone in town thought of her. But it wasn't her fault that her oven happened to be way less judgmental than the lot of them.

Abe set down his coffee mug. "I was giving you a compliment," he muttered. "You're real. Which is more than I can say for Royce Elliot with his million-dollar hair and freakishly white teeth."

"No one can accuse me of having freakishly white teeth." Not with all the coffee she drank. Sylvie crossed the kitchen and found the checkbook in the desk. She scrawled out Abe's weekly amount.

"I mean, look at the guy." Abe held out his phone to show her a picture when she walked back to the counter.

The guy. *That* guy. She studied the screen. Blinked. Studied the screen some more. "*That's* Royce Elliot?" It couldn't be him. The man who had been holding her favorite Christmas bra in his hands earlier this morning. A movie star.

I'm jet-lagged so I woke up early.

Because Royce Elliot had probably jetted in from some exotic location where he'd been shooting his last movie. "I can't believe this. I can't believe—" She'd made a fool out of herself in front of a movie star. Sudden panic squeezed her heart, and she stared at Abe. "I told him to come here," she blurted.

"What?" Abe stuffed his phone in his pocket and took the check from her hand. "You talked to Royce Elliot?"

"This morning!" Sylvie silently replayed their conversation. "He's the one who stopped and helped me when Crumpet got out, and I told him to come to the Christmas Café for breakfast!"

"Don't tell me you're going to get all hysterical over him like the rest of this town." Abe neatly folded the check and stuck it into the pocket of his flannel shirt.

"No. It's just . . ." There had been some flutterings when she'd chatted with Royce. What could she say? The man had a certain vintage charm. Minus the overly white teeth—Abe happened to be right about that. "I humiliated myself in front of him." Needing to busy her hands, Sylvie rushed to the refrigerator to stash the eggs. "I mean, he pulled my bra out of my dog's mouth." God, Royce Elliot knew her bra size . . .

"Your bra?" Abe raised an eyebrow warily.

"Long story." She'd left out that part earlier, but there was no forgetting it now. "It's fine. I'll hide out back here like I usually do." She'd ask one of the waitresses to refill the baked goods case at the front of the house. No problem. "Hopefully, he won't even—"

"Sylvie!" Her sister, Claire, flew into the kitchen from the dining room. Based on the way she barged in, one would think she owned the place, or at least worked there, but nope. Being the mayor simply made Claire behave like she owned every establishment in town. "You're never going to believe who's out there."

"Royce Elliot?" Abe asked casually.

"Yes!" Her sister squealed. "This is huge! Royce Elliot is *famous.* And he's staying in Silver Bells through Christmas!"

"So I've heard." Sylvie knelt to remove her mixing bowls from the lower shelf of the island. She had to bake. Measuring out ingredients, beating butter and sugar and eggs was the only way to release the nervous energy churning through her stomach.

"He was raving about the cranberry orange scones." Claire stole the mixing bowls from her hands and set them aside. "So I asked him if he'd like to meet the chef."

"Oh, no." Sylvie backed away, her arms raised in the air. "Nope. I don't have time to meet him. I don't *want* to meet him."

Abe crossed his arms and watched her but he didn't give up her secret.

"Don't be so antisocial." Her sister linked their arms together and prodded her to the door. "We want Royce to feel welcome here, so he'll post all his happy thoughts about our town on his social media pages. Think of all the publicity we'll get! Just give him a quick hello. For the sake of the town."

Sylvie cast a desperate glance over her shoulder as Claire pulled her through the swinging door into the restaurant, but Abe shrugged as though he didn't know how to rescue her. It was useless. Claire always got what she wanted.

"Royce!" Her sister dragged her to the front counter, where glass cases showed off a vast array of baked goods. "I'd like you to meet the Christmas Café's chef, my wonderful sister, Syl—"

The man's head turned and, as anticipated, his jaw dropped. "Sylvie?"

Dear God, take me now. She gave a little wave and made her best attempt at a smile. At least she wasn't wearing her pajamas this time.

Claire halted mid step. "You two *know* each other?"

"Not exactly. Crumpet got out this morning, and . . . Mr., uh, Elliot helped me catch him." Instead of looking at the man who was no longer a mystery, she focused on her sister. Abe had followed them too. He probably needed a good laugh this morning, and she was giving them out for free today.

"When you recommended it, you didn't mention you worked at the Christmas Café." When Royce's blue eyes focused on her, everyone else seemed to fade from her peripheral vision.

"Well, you didn't mention you were a movie star." The words came out more clipped than she'd intended, but she wasn't great with people under the best of circumstances, let alone under pressure.

"Of course he's a movie star." Claire's uncomfortable laugh reminded Sylvie to watch her manners. "I can't believe you didn't recognize him, silly. He's an *incredible* actor." Her sister went on to mention the man's best movies while Sylvie stood silently by her side. Claire had been smoothing over her awkward social skills since Sylvie was three and her older sister was five going on twenty.

Standing side by side, she and Claire were quite the contrast. For all anyone knew, her sister could've just walked out of a building on Wall Street, with her expensive pants suits and sleek, freshly blown-out balayaged blond hair. Sylvie, on the other hand, had never quite managed to wrangle her curls after the whole Crumpet debacle. Instead of trying to tame her red kinks, she'd simply tied on a folded red bandana to keep the tangles out of her eyes. And if she wasn't wearing her jeggings on any given day, she had on her trusty yoga pants.

Their appearances weren't the only differences between them, either. Her sister had checked off most of the items on her life's to-do list: get a degree in business—check. Get a master's degree in business—check. Get married—check. Claire had reconnected with Manuel, her high school sweetheart who happened to be from one of the most prominent ranching families in the area, shortly after graduating from her master's program. And her most recent check mark was becoming the mayor of Silver Bells.

Meanwhile, Sylvie only had one item on her life's to-do list: find the kind of happiness Gramps and Grams had all those years together. Needless to say, that item wasn't so easy to check off.

"I was telling your sister how much I love these scones," Royce said, when Claire had finished paying homage to his cinematic accomplishments. "You were right. The Christmas Café certainly didn't disappoint." He didn't wink at her but he might as well have, the way he said the words, playfully . . . almost flirting.

"Oh. Uh. Yeah. Good." Her pulse revved up and made the words sputter. "Goat butter."

Royce narrowed his eyes, crinkling them in the corners. "I'm sorry?"

Ai yi yi. Why couldn't her mouth ever seem to connect with her brain? "I use goat's butter to make them. And goat's milk. It gives the scones better texture." Sylvie didn't even need to look at her sister's expression to cringe. This man didn't care about goat butter! "Abe. This is Abe." She pulled him to stand next to her so she wouldn't be center stage anymore. "He's the goat farmer. We were getting busy in the kitchen." *Wait. Oh dear.* That came out so very wrong. "I mean we were busy getting work done in the kitchen. A delivery."

"Hey," Abe said quickly, as though he didn't want to give her a chance to speak again. "Royce, was it?"

"Royce *Elliot*," Claire corrected. "And if you think the cranberry orange scones are good, you should try the chocolate pecan pie muffins. In fact . . ." Her sister shuffled Royce to the other side of the baked goods case, likely to get him far away from Sylvie. "Why don't you take some for the cast and crew? I'll help you deliver them. On the house."

Sylvie gasped a protest, but Abe tapped her shoulder. "We should get back to that business in the kitchen." There went that amused sideways grin again.

Why she kept blushing, Sylvie didn't know. "Yes. Back to business." Her voice had gone robotic. "Please take some muffins for the rest of your people."

"Thanks." Royce beamed his gracious smile. "Nice to see you again, Sylvie."

"You too." Leaving it at that, she whirled and followed Abe into the safety of her refuge. "Did I really say we were getting busy in the kitchen?" She covered her face with her hands as soon as the door closed behind her. "Did that come out of my mouth? What is wrong with me?"

"It wasn't so bad." Abe pulled on the plaid trapper's hat he'd left on the counter. "Why do you care what that guy thinks, anyway?"

"I don't care what he thinks." Okay, maybe she cared . . . but only a pinch. Sylvie snatched her mixing bowls off the counter and brought them to her work station. "I'd simply like to not be the butt of the joke someday, that's all." Clearly everyone in the café had heard her exchange with Royce. Marion had probably been lurking around somewhere in the shadows taking notes so she could report on Sylvie's latest gaffes during tomorrow's power walk.

Ugh. She didn't want to think about this anymore. She withdrew the bulk flour from the pantry and measured out eight cups. Time to change the subject. "Anyway. How's your dad doing?" she asked Abe. Over the last few months, Sylvie had made it a point to deliver any goodies left over at the end of the day to Jed and Loretta DeWitt at the farm a few times a week. They seemed to be struggling with the changes his diagnosis required, and she couldn't really help, but she could offer pie.

"He's okay."

Sylvie also knew how it felt to be okay. Not good. Not even bad. Just sort of . . . numb. "Well, tell them I'll be by with a batch of something sweet later on today."

"You don't have to do that." A quieter tone smoothed out his voice's usual rough edges. "I know how busy you are right now."

"I'm never too busy to deliver Christmas cheer." Lifting people's spirits is what made the Christmas Café so much more than a restaurant. She retrieved the baking powder from the pantry.

"I know they appreciate your visits. And so do I." His gaze raised to hers and she recognized a familiar sadness. This poor man. At least she'd had Brando and Claire and Gramps and her parents when Grams had been sick. They'd gotten through it together. Abe and his mom were on their own.

"How are *you* doing?"

Abe's head tilted up as though the question had surprised him. "I'm good." His eyes wouldn't meet hers.

"It's okay if you're not." She added four and a half teaspoons of baking powder to the flour. "You've been through a lot these last few months, and sometimes you have to—"

"I said I'm fine, Sylvie." Abe slipped on his denim trucker

jacket. "I gotta go." He bolted out the door, leaving Sylvie to stare after him.

Once again, she should've kept her mouth shut. She should've read his tone and backed off. Of course Abe didn't want to spill his guts to her. Why would he?

Sylvie trudged to the refrigerator to grab the eggs, carrying the weight of yet another awkward moment along behind her. She didn't like not being able to understand people or to be understood herself. *You're an introvert*, her mom had always told her. But, in a family of extroverts, that hadn't ever felt like a good thing.

It wasn't that she'd ever felt unloved or unwanted. Her parents had always been honest about adopting her as an infant. They'd *chosen* her, they said. She'd completed her family and they'd never treated her any different than her older sister or her younger brother, when he'd come along five years later. That didn't stop her from *feeling* different, though.

Sylvie had gone through a phase from ages eight through twelve trying to be exactly like Claire. She'd dressed like her sister, she'd tried to talk like her sister. Claire would even hold "trainings," teaching Sylvie how to walk in their dress-up high heels and how to smile and speak clearly when she had to give a book report in front of the class. None of the coaching stuck, though, and by the end of middle school she'd given up on becoming a mini-Claire.

That's for the best, Grams had told her. *One Claire is enough for this town.* Then her grandmother had gathered her in for one of her life-affirming hugs. *You need to learn to be the best Sylvie you can be.*

"I'm trying, Grams." Sylvie cracked an egg and dumped it into another mixer. Only eleven more to go.

She settled into her routine, working through the entire carton and then beating the eggs into frothy bliss. She was about to add vanilla when the kitchen's back door swung open. Jerry—the café's longtime owner and her boss—sauntered in, bundled from head to toe in wool.

"Hi there." Sylvie rushed to the sink to wash up and wiped her hands with a towel. "I didn't know you were coming by today." Jerry normally took Fridays off. "I wanted to talk to you, actually."

"Oh?" Jerry cleaned the fog from his glasses with one of her freshly washed hand towels.

"Yes. I ran into Marion this morning and she mentioned that the café is having some financial issues." No matter how much time Claire had spent coaching her, Sylvie'd never quite mastered the art of beating around the bush. "I told her she was wrong, of course. Everything's fine here."

She waited for Jerry to agree with her but instead he frowned, the handlebars of his white mustache twitching.

"Well . . ." He drew out the word long enough to make her stomach drop. "Here's the thing, Sylvie . . ."

With her jaw locked, she waited not so patiently while he removed his hat and then his scarf and then his coat and hung them up on the rack next to her desk.

Finally he faced her directly. "I was going to talk to you about this after the holidays."

No, no. Stop. She wanted him to stop talking right now. She couldn't lose this place. Not her happy place. Not the one place she felt like herself. Her knees started to buckle so she pulled out a stool and sat at the counter.

"You know how much food prices are up these days." Jerry patted down his white hair, slicking it to his head. "We've always done okay, but it's only getting harder. A buyer approached me, and I've decided to sell. While I can. The missus and I are moving to Texas to be closer to the grands." The words were apologetic but firm too. Unyielding.

This didn't make sense. None of this made sense. "But . . . but there are no mountains in Texas," Sylvie protested. "You've always said how much you love the mountains."

The man shrugged. "I love my family more."

Yes, she could understand that. Of course she could. She loved her family too, even with all of their quirks. But if Jerry sold this place and left, where would she go? What would she do?

"Who's the buyer?" Maybe it was someone she knew, someone who would keep her on—

"It's a burger chain looking to expand into Wyoming." At least Jerry had the decency to wince. "But I can't pass up this kind of offer. Surely you understand. Surely—"

"What if you could move and still make money off the Christmas Café?" Sylvie interrupted, hopping off the stool. She simply could not let this happen. She couldn't lose this place. "You could still have an income, and I could manage the whole café for you instead of only the kitchen."

"You want to manage this place?" His head shook slowly back and forth. "You're great in the kitchen. Really. I've never known a more talented baker, but to do everything I do . . ." He grimaced. "That takes a lot of . . . polished professionalism."

"I can do polished professionalism." She could learn. She *would* learn. "Hear me out." Sylvie started to pace. "You move to Texas, enjoy the retired life while still making a monthly income. I'll stay here and grow the business. I'll increase profit margins." She would find a way to draw people to the Christmas Café.

"Come on, Jerry." She stopped in front of him. "This place is iconic. There is no other restaurant like it in the entire region. Heck, probably in the entire country. We simply have to do more marketing. More social media." Her old-fashioned heart would fully embrace the façade of social media if it helped the Christmas Café stay open.

"I don't think—"

"Consider the possibility," she interrupted. "That's all I'm asking. Give me a few weeks to show you this can work." She stuck out her hand in Jerry's direction. "Do we have a deal?"

"I guess." His voice was as anemic as his handshake but she'd take it.

Hopefully a few weeks would be enough to pull off a Christmas miracle.

Three

ACCORDING TO HER GRAMS, THERE WASN'T MUCH THAT A fat slice of marshmallow-topped hot chocolate cheesecake couldn't fix, but even after eight decadent bites, Sylvie still hadn't come up with an idea for how to remedy things at the café before the end of the year.

Maybe nine bites would do the trick. Sylvie savored the flavors and textures of her grandmother's favorite treat—the richness of the milk chocolate and the creaminess of the marshmallow fluff and the sharp bite of the cinnamon that somehow brought the dessert together.

Grams had first created this recipe after Sylvie had worked up the courage to ask Vincent Compolo to the Sadie Hawkins dance by decorating his locker her sophomore year. Big shocker, he'd said no. The kid had been polite about it, but the rejection had still stung, so the night of the dance Sylvie had stayed at Grams and Gramps's house. They'd baked this new concoction and then had eaten most of cake while they'd watched *An American in Paris*. *You'll find your Gene Kelly someday*, Grams had insisted. *And he'll be so much more charming and handsome than Vincent Compolo.*

Well, she hadn't found her Gene Kelly yet, but this cheesecake—and many of Grams's other delectable confectionary remedies—had gotten her by so far.

"All right. What's wrong?" Jen, her head line cook, paused from punching the mound of cinnamon roll dough she was currently beating up on the counter across the room. With all of the leather and chains her friend wore, one might make the mistake of thinking Jen would be better at beating up people in an MMA ring, but the woman had a special way with dough.

Sylvie gazed at her, eyes wide, mouth too full of creamy marshmallow to speak. When Jen had come in—an hour late, true to form—she'd decided not to mention the news about Jerry's impending decision. No use getting everyone else worried yet.

"Come on." Jen gave the dough mound another good punch, her muscular arms tensed. "If you're digging into the marshmallow hot chocolate cheesecake at ten o'clock in the morning, you must have a real problem." She shot Sylvie a laser stare from behind her green-rimmed cat-eye glasses, which somehow perfectly complemented her purple-spiked hairdo. "You have a string of marshmallow hanging off your chin, by the way."

"There's no problem." Sylvie quickly swiped her chin with a napkin and took another bite. "I've just got a lot on my plate—preparing for the ChristmasFest and the Parade of Lights . . ." The possibility of being unemployed, of having to tell her staff they had no work. Though Jen likely wouldn't be worried. Her friend didn't seem to worry about anything. In addition to her job as the line cook, Jen also played in a country metal band and taught Jazzercise classes at the rec center. She, at least, had a diverse portfolio of skills.

What would Sylvie do if Jerry sold the café? Despite Jen's best efforts, she wasn't coordinated enough to do Jazzercise and the only instrument she was could play was the air guitar. Worry crowded her stomach and she pushed her plate away.

"You might as well spill it, sister." Jen folded the huge pile of dough over and started to knead. "Don't make me drag it out of you. I could, you know."

"Oh, I know." Back in college, Jen had competed in weight lifting competitions. Sylvie stood, her legs staggering underneath the panic. Everyone would find out soon enough anyway. "Okay. Fine. Jerry is considering retiring after the holidays. He might sell the café."

"Well, that's no surprise. The man is ancient." Her friend smacked the dough flat and then wielded a rolling pin. "So you're worried about losing your job?"

"Aren't you?" she squeaked.

"Nah." Her friend focused on rolling the dough into a perfectly symmetrical rectangle. "You know any restaurant in town would be happy to have us. We're the best there is, Syl. You don't need to worry."

"I guess you're right." But every restaurant in town wasn't the Christmas Café. No other restaurant in town held such a treasure trove of memories. Jen wasn't exactly sentimental, but Sylvie was. "I'm still going to try to stop him, to make this place so popular and so successful that he *can't* sell."

"And how're you gonna do that?" Jen deposited the rolling pin into the sink basin with a loud thunk.

"I'm not sure yet." What would Grams say about her current predicament? Lord knew Sylvie couldn't rely on her own personal connections to draw more people in. Nope. Yesterday, she'd posted a picture of her cheesecake on the café's social media page and so far she had exactly one like from her mother and one comment from her father. *Sure do miss your cheesecakes, sweetie!* She'd have to remember to send a package of goodies down to her parents in their Florida retirement community next week.

Right now she needed more. Something bigger—something newsworthy. She needed to go viral, darn it. And she had no idea how.

"Hey, Sylvie." Her favorite waitress, Teagan, traipsed into the kitchen, her blond braid swinging behind her. "Your grandpa is out there. I told him to sit at his favorite table by the window."

"Okay, thanks." She followed Teagan in the direction of the dining room. "Wait." Sylvie caught her shoulder before they separated. "Do you know much about social media?"

"Totally." The girl shot her a braces-laced grin. "I mean, I'm on pretty much every site." She started to name them off in rapid-fire succession, but Sylvie had never even heard of most of them.

"I may need a tutorial sometime." She'd stooped to asking a sixteen-year-old for advice. "What's the best way to go viral?"

The girl laughed. "The best way to go viral? Do something really out there. Or you could humiliate yourself, I guess. Either one."

"I can think of a few ways to humiliate you," Jen chimed in. "Just come back to a Jazzercise class, and this time we'll film you."

Sylvie shot a pointed glare over her shoulder but couldn't hold back her laughter. "Maybe we can come up with something less painful." After her feet had tangled on a particularly technical jazzy move, she'd fallen and had a bruise on her tailbone for weeks. She let the kitchen door close behind her so Jen couldn't offer any more suggestions.

"I can hook you up with some ideas," Tegan offered.

Feeling more hopeful, Sylvie meandered in the direction of Gramps's table.

"Can we get some coffee refills over here?"

That voice had been a thorn in her side since the second grade. Sylvie turned to see Beth Wyman sitting to her left, along with the woman's BBFs, Vicky and Alicia. Back in school, they'd dubbed themselves the Starlet Sisters since they were always starring in the school's theater productions or leading the cheer team or winning the votes required to take over student council. Once upon a time, Sylvie would've given anything to be a Starlet Sister, but they'd pretty much only talked to her when they needed something.

Old habits died hard.

"Sylvie?" Beth frantically waved her to their table. "Our coffee is cold. Would you mind hooking us up with a refill?" The extra wrinkles in her nose robbed her smile of any authenticity.

"Sure." Their coffee was likely cold because they'd been sitting there for two hours discussing the musical selections for the annual Christmas Ball. The Starlet Sisters were still running the show in Silver Bells, this year as the planning committee for the town's capstone holiday event.

She signaled to Gramps to give her a moment and rushed to get the coffee carafe off the warmer.

"Oh, you're a lifesaver," Vicky said when she approached the table. "We've been working so hard my brain is starting to hurt."

"There are just so many last-minute details," Alicia added.

"Mmm-hmm." These three had a different definition of working than she did. While Beth did own the—wait for it— Starlet Boutique, she certainly didn't have to work much, either . . . she was married to the president of the local bank. Vicky had married the only lawyer their age in town, and Alicia's husband had become the only accountant in Silver Bells after his uncle retired. So basically they had a lot of time to sit and drink coffee and listen to playlists.

"I think we should have the band set up in this corner." Alicia pointed to a spot on the blueprint of the famous Wingate Mansion while Sylvie carefully refilled her mug. "That way the music won't be too overpowering."

"But wouldn't you rather put the dance floor in front of the fireplace?" Sylvie found herself saying. The fireplace at the Wingate Mansion was the stuff fairy tales were made of— three stories of beautiful stacked stones accented with log beams. "Talk about a romantic ambiance."

Beth traded amused glances with the other two. "Are you coming to the ball this year, Syl?" The slight smirk she wore indicated she already knew the answer.

"I might," she lied. "You never know." Going without Grams would be too hard, but Sylvie refused to give them the satisfaction of slinking away with her head down. She refilled Beth's mug and then Vicky's. "Anything else I can do for you ladies today?" she asked brightly.

Beth dismissed Sylvie with a shake of her head and then the three of them proceeded to discuss why the area in front of the fireplace wouldn't work as a dance floor. What did they know? She carted the carafe back to the warmer, picturing that fireplace all lit up while she danced in the glow with Cary Grant. Definitely romantic.

She sat down across from her grandfather. "Glad you made it. I assume Prince Crumpet is in his playpen?" She hadn't had the heart to put the puppy in a kennel so she'd purchased a toddler playpen for when they were both out.

"Yep." Gramps stared out the window with a melancholy dullness in his eyes. She recognized the look: sorrow and longing, joy in memories but hollowness in the current moment. It didn't matter that two years had passed. During the holidays it might as well have been only one month.

Christmas had been Grams's absolute favorite. She'd start humming carols in early October when the leaves were changing. The decorating commenced on November 1, come hell or high water. Then there had been the planning and the cooking and the baking and the parties. Her grandmother had been at the center of their family's holidays.

But nowadays Gramps dreaded Christmas because the most special part of it would be forever missing.

"I thought you were going to ask Dean and Chuck to join you." She hated to see her grandpa so lonely. If she could take off the whole month of December just to keep him company and make him smile every hour on the hour, she would.

"Dean had to take Karen to her knitting class, and Chuck was taking Yolanda to lunch." He sipped his coffee, but she could still see the sadness that pulled at his mouth. Yes, both of Gramps's best friends still had their wives.

"Well, lucky for you, I finished my baking early." Thanks to plenty of nervous energy brought on by the morning's events. "Teagan," she called as the waitress passed by. "We'll take a round of the spiced eggnog scones, please."

"Coming right up." The waitress scurried to the baked goods case.

"I added extra glaze the way you like." Sylvie might not know how to take away the ache in Gramps's heart, but she did know how to soothe the pain with treats.

"You're the best." Her grandfather's smile put some of the light back in his eyes. "I don't mean to be such an old grinch. I've just been thinking about your Grams is all."

"I've been thinking about her too." Before losing Grams, she hadn't realized how memories could hurt and comfort at the same time. "Maybe I'll cook her pot roast recipe for dinner tonight." Pulling out one of her grandmother's hand-written recipe cards never failed to make Grams feel closer.

"I think that's a good idea." Gramps stirred some sugar into his coffee while Teagan delivered their scones and then rushed off to refill the drinks at another table.

"That's a lot of glaze." Her grandfather bit into a scone. "I don't know how you do it, sweet pea. It's like heaven in a bite."

"Between you and Grams, I had good teachers." Her grandparents had loved to cook and bake together. They used to dance their way around each other in the kitchen, stealing a smooch here and there as they passed dishes and spoons back and forth. Sylvie took a bite of the scone. *Mmm.* The touch of salt nicely balanced the earthy nutmeg and sweetness of the glaze. "Do you remember that time—"

"Gramps! Sylvie!" The sound of Claire's voice brought on a wince. Gramps seemed to share the sentiment. He quickly glanced around, but Sylvie already knew it was too late to hide. They'd been spotted. Lately, her older sister had been on a campaign to help their grandpa "snap out of his funk." Last week, she actually told him he needed to start dating again.

"I'm glad to see you out and about." Claire slipped off her coat and sat in the chair next to Gramps.

"Couldn't pass up an offer of spiced eggnog scones." The words were polite, but Sylvie could see him bracing himself.

"Yummy." Claire reached for one too. "By the way, Syl, I smoothed things over with Royce after the goat butter debacle this morning."

Gramps raised his woolly eyebrows at her, but she shook her head.

"Don't ask. But it sounds like the whole cast loved the muffins he brought to the set." Claire put the scone on a napkin and brushed the crumbs off her hands. "I just came from the park. They're actually filming there as we speak. How cool is that?"

"The last thing this town needs is a bunch of hoity-toity celebrities running around," Gramps muttered over his coffee mug.

"Don't be such a grump," Claire scolded. "This movie is going to do amazing things for this town. It's going to put us on the map. We really need to get you out of this mood you've been in lately." She shook her head impatiently.

Sylvie's posture went rigid. "Come on, Claire. Lay off." This line of conversation never ended well.

"What?" As usual, her sister pressed on. Sylvie was pretty sure Claire had to-do lists for both Gramps and her hidden away on her smartphone somewhere, and her sister was determined to help them start checking off the boxes. "I saw Joanie Wheeler at the park just now. I told her you'd love to take her out sometime."

"You what?" Gramps clunked his mug down to the table, his gaze sharpening.

Uh-oh. Sylvie scooted the mug to her side just in case he made any wild hand gestures.

Claire squeezed their grandfather's shoulder. "I'm trying to help. You're not happy. I only want you to be happy."

As if life were that simple. In Claire's estimation, things were simple—emotions and feelings could be resolved by "moving forward." But she didn't know. She hadn't had the same connection to Grams that Gramps had. She hadn't even had the same connection to Grams that Sylvie had.

Grams had always made Sylvie feel special. She had singled Sylvie out. Maybe because she knew the deep insecurities that had rooted themselves inside of her. Somehow Grams knew she needed to be the special one in someone's eyes. Grams had shielded her and protected her and had taken her for girls' days out, just the two of them. She'd taught Sylvie that she didn't need to be like Claire or like her younger brother, Brando. (Grams had shortened Brandon to Brando, in homage to her favorite movie star.) Grams had made her want to believe she was enough exactly as she was. Most days, she was still working on that belief. And if Grams meant that much to Sylvie, she could only imagine the void Gramps felt in his life.

"I am *not* going to take Joanie Wheeler out," Gramps bellowed, drawing stares from the nearby tables. He stood abruptly and shuffled away from the table. "Excuse me. I need to go to the restroom."

"I don't know why he's so stubborn." Claire used her knife to cut her scone into neat squares. "Joanie is perfectly lovely."

"He lost his wife," Sylvie reminded her.

"I just want him to be happy again." Her sister had never been exactly comfortable with emotions. Sylvie would never forget the time the sixth grade bully had made fun of Claire on the bus. He'd picked on her the whole way home, calling her names loud enough that everyone could hear. Two minutes into the torment, Sylvie had broken down in tears. But her sister had sat straight and tall, keeping her gaze focused forward.

Maybe Claire never let herself be sad, but Sylvie had no problem crying. In fact, her eyes teared right up. "I want Gramps to be happy too. But sometimes you have to be sad for a while before you remember what happiness is." Gramps was seeing glimpses of joy again—sometimes he asked Sylvie to make one of Grams's recipes. And when one of Grams's favorite songs came on the radio now, he'd smile and hum along. "These things take time." And patience. Claire had many gifts, but patience wasn't among them.

Her sister gave off a stubborn harrumph. "I just think—"

"You ready for our walk?" Gramps trudged back to the table already wearing his wool cap.

"Our walk?" Seeing his eyes widen, Sylvie scooted her chair back. "Right!" She glanced apologetically at Claire. "We'd planned to take a walk to the park." Her sister wouldn't be able to follow them in those stilettos. Sylvie had no doubt she'd driven her Cadillac SUV the three blocks from the park to the café.

"It's a good day for a walk," her grandfather grumbled, buttoning up his fleece coat.

Sylvie rushed to the kitchen to tell Jen she'd be back soon and throw on her winter gear then hurried back to Claire and her grandfather before one of them ended up in a headlock.

". . . I don't need you making plans for me," Gramps was saying.

"Ready?" Sylvie swooped in between them and prodded her grandfather toward the door. "I'll be back in an hour," she called to Teagan. Hopefully, that would give Gramps enough time to cool off.

The waitress gave her a thumbs up.

"I don't know why you get so mad." Claire followed them outside. "I'm only doing what's best for you."

"Nobody's mad. We're all great. Why don't you come by for happy hour sometime next week?" Sylvie asked Claire, purposely steering Gramps in the opposite direction of her sister's car. "I'll make your favorite mulled wine." While she didn't like being Claire's project any more than Gramps did, she loved her sister. When she wasn't trying to fix everyone's lives, Claire was hilarious and helpful. Plus, she was such a good auntie to Crumpet, always bringing him treats and loving on him.

"I will come by, thanks. Maybe on Wednesday." She clicked the unlock button on her key fob. "I have something important to discuss with you anyway."

Uh-oh. Every muscle in Sylvie's neck tensed, but before she could ask what her sister wanted to talk about, Claire had climbed into her SUV and revved the engine.

"Looks like I'll be making plans for Wednesday." Gramps started off down the sidewalk, hunching against the icy wind. "She'll probably bring Joanie along and ambush me."

"She means well." She watched her sister's car disappear around the corner. Yes, Claire always had an agenda but maybe that wasn't necessarily a bad thing. "She has a point."

Gramps stopped shuffling and gaped at her.

"Hear me out." Sylvie nudged his shoulder to get him walking again. She would get hypothermia out here if they didn't keep moving. They'd only made it halfway down the block, and her toes were starting to freeze to the inside of her boots. "She's right. Both of us can be a little reclusive some-times."

Her grandfather grunted out a stubborn harrumph. "Just because I don't want to date doesn't mean I'm reclusive."

"I'm not only talking about dating." Sylvie readjusted her scarf against the icy breeze. "But when's the last time either of us went out to dinner with friends?" Most nights she and her grandfather cooked whatever they had a hankering for and then parked themselves in front of the television while they worked their way through the flicks on Turner Classic Mov-ies. "Neither one of us are great at putting ourselves out there and trying something new." And now she didn't have a choice. If she didn't turn over a new leaf ASAP, she could lose her job. The café could be gone.

They reached the end of the block, and Gramps turned to face her. "So what are you saying?"

"I'm saying maybe we need to make a pact." She waved him into the crosswalk, and they slogged through the slush to get to the other side of the street. "Maybe this Christmas we both need to find a way to put ourselves out there." Sylvie guided Gramps around the large silver bells sculpture at the entrance to Town Center Park and they walked underneath the candy cane archway.

Up ahead, a crowd had gathered near the towering blue spruce that the Silver Bells decorating committee had selected for this year's Christmas tree. Claire had been right—the Hol-iday Channel crew was filming a scene. Or, at least, getting ready to film. They had gated off an area around the tree and set up cameras and lights and chairs. Sylvie couldn't stop her-self from looking for Royce. Ah yes. There he was, standing with another man and flipping through some papers. She didn't know how she'd missed him. Even from the distance, his eyes and smile smoldered.

"I'm not sure I want to put myself out there." Gramps delivered the words with a simple honesty.

"I know. It's hard." Especially when she felt all she did was humiliate herself, like she had this morning. "But maybe there is more for us. And maybe Grams has a special gift in store for us this Christmas." They might miss something wonderful if they stayed holed up at home. "Think about it. And if you see an opportunity to put yourself out there, take it."

"I suppose being more open couldn't hurt." Gramps eyed the crowd in front of them, likely making sure Joanie was nowhere to be seen. "But no dating."

She laughed. "It's not like that'll be a problem for me. Besides I have more important things on my mind." Still watching the crew milling around, she told Gramps all about the café mess. "I need to make something big happen, or Jerry is going to sell."

Gramps gave a sad shake of his head. "It'll be tough to see that place go. It was one of your grandmother's favorites."

"I know." Sylvie watched another group of people enter the park and head directly for the film scene. Half the town had to be out here now, trying to get a glimpse at the stars. She glanced around, squinting, trying to make out the faces beneath the beanies. *Wait a minute.* These weren't only people from town. She didn't recognize most of them. Which meant they had to be tourists . . . maybe word about the film had reached the closest of the ski towns.

"Look at this confounded crowd." Gramps's mouth folded into disapproval. "Can't even take a nice walk without that movie messing everything up."

"The movie's not messing anything up." Sylvie's heart had started to beat faster. "I can't believe I'm saying this, but Claire is right. This movie is the best thing that could've happened in Silver Bells right now."

Gramps studied her face like he didn't recognize her.

Yes, on a normal day she didn't like crowds any more than he did, but today was a new day. "Look at all these people." She clutched his arm. "They're here to watch them film a scene. That means word about Silver Bells is getting out." And she needed to tap into the excitement and use this to her advantage. Sylvie stared at Royce again. He'd been kind to her despite her clumsy attempt at a conversation with him. He'd even said he hoped he'd see her again. Maybe he'd be willing to help her with some publicity for the café.

Put yourself out there. The whisper in her heart almost certainly came from Grams. "We have to go." Sylvie dragged Gramps away from the spectacle. She clapped her gloves together. "I have the best idea."

Gramps lumbered alongside her, dodging tourists. "What're you gonna do?"

She was going to take Teagan's advice. "I'm going to do something really big." She was going to find out where Royce Elliot was staying so she could drop off dinner on his doorstep tomorrow.

Four

"DO YOU WANT TO TAKE SOME OF THESE SPICED GINGER-bread doggies home?" Sylvie wrapped the last of the adorable Crumpet-shaped cookies she'd made earlier into a to-go box.

Jen eyed the cookies, her mouth twisting into a frown of indecision. "You know I can't. If I take them home, I'll eat them all and my brand-new leather leggings are already getting tight. I've gotta pace myself this season."

See? That's exactly why Sylvie went with cotton leggings. They were much more expandable. "How about you only take two then?" And she'd bring the rest to the DeWitts' farm. Mr. and Mrs. DeWitt loved her gingerbread.

"One for dinner and one for lunch." Jen nodded. "I like it."

"Perfect." Sylvie wrapped up the cookies and handed them to Jen as her friend made her way to the door. "Good luck at your gig tonight."

"Thanks." She stuffed the cookies into the pocket of her leather jacket. "You'll have to come to one of our concerts again soon. It's been a while."

"Tell me about it." She hadn't enjoyed a night out in forever. But that was typical for her around this time of year, and this Christmas she had even more on her plate than usual. "Maybe after the holidays."

"Sounds good. I'll text you our January schedule." Jen pulled on her hat and then slipped out the door. "Don't stay too late, Syl."

"I'm on my way out too." She needed to get Gramps and Crumpie their dinners before those two got hangry. A glance at the Twelve Days of Christmas clock above the refrigerator filled her with a sense of urgency. How was it already after four o'clock?

After bundling on two more layers, she stepped out into the alleyway. Snow fell lightly, the flakes sparkling like glitter in the glow of the lampposts. It happened to be one of those perfect winter nights—no wind, everything so still that you could almost hear the flakes floating around you. Sylvie used her gloves to brush the fluffy layer of snow from her windshield and then slid into the driver's seat humming "Winter Wonderland."

While she wasn't a fan of the lack of daylight in the winter, the darkness is what brought the holiday magic. Colorful light strands decorated all of the trees in the park, and not just the traditional red and green, either; pinks and blues and yellows and purples made the whole area into a fairyland. And then there were the houses. She slowed to admire the displays lining the streets on the way to the farm—the snowman-themed house and the yard filled with blow-ups of all kinds. Some opted for more traditional looks—white lights outlining the angles or colorful bulbs spiraling around bare tree branches. All of them were festive.

Sylvie slowed the car around the bend and turned onto the DeWitts' driveway.

"Whoa. Whoa!" Goats wandered everywhere—in the middle of the driveway ahead of her, along the front of the massive red barn to her right, and . . . "Abe!" He sprinted in front of her car.

Sylvie slammed on the brakes and shoved open her door. "What's going on?"

"They got out," Abe grunted, trotting past her hot on the trail of a funny-looking black-and-white goat with a goatee. "I have no idea how, but the whole lot of them broke out of the barn."

"I can help you catch them." Sylvie cut the engine and wrestled out of her seatbelt. Oh! There went one darting to the other side of her car. "Come here, goat!" She hurried after it, cornering the small little sweetie near the trunk.

"Just pick her up," Abe instructed, snatching a goat under each of his arms. "We'll have to put them back one by one."

"Sure. No problem." Sylvie eased toward the goat, who had started to bleat incessantly. "It's okay," she soothed. "I won't hurt you. I promise." She held out her arms and, while the goat cowered, it didn't run away. "There. See?" Sylvie managed to get both arms around her. "I'll just give you a lift and everything'll be fine." Holding the goat, she followed Abe through a gate and then a door that led into the barn's massive open space.

"In here." He directed her to a network of fenced-off pens.

"That's good." Sylvie's arms were starting to cramp. "She's heavier than she looks."

Abe deposited his two goats into the fenced area and then came back to get the one Sylvie held. "This is Sunny. She's expecting a kid any day now."

"Aww." Sylvie followed him to the pen so she could give

Sunny a little pat on the head. "She's so pretty." Sunny had bright eyes and soft brown and white hair . . . fur?

Abe gazed at her, his mouth quirked. "Goats aren't pretty."

"Sure they are." Sylvie knelt down to Sunny's height. "You're pretty, aren't you? Yes, you are."

"We should get the rest of them." He stalked back into the night without waiting for her.

Well, fine then. "I still think you're pretty," she informed Sunny before heading back out.

Abe worked fast, hauling in two goats at a time while Sylvie was lucky to corral a few of the smaller animals one by one. She finally caught up to the last escapee near the highway. "You're going to get hit by a car," she scolded, scooping up the bleating animal. "No squirming now. This is for your own good." She hugged it against her.

Abe was waiting for her outside the barn. "I think that's it. They're all accounted for."

"That's good because I'm starting to break a sweat." She set down the last delinquent in the pen. "How'd they get out, do you think?"

"Who knows?" Abe locked the gate and then wandered to a nearby shelf, where he found a chain and padlock. "One of them must've figured out the latch. They're always pulling stuff like this." He wrapped the chain around the gate and a fence post and clicked the lock into place. "What're you doing here, anyway?"

"Oh." She'd almost forgotten that she hadn't come only for the goat roundup. "I brought cookies."

"You didn't have to. I told you that earlier."

Every time he wore that tight expression, she took it as a challenge to make him smile. "And I told you I wanted to bring cookies." She narrowed her eyes in mock outrage. "Are you saying you don't *want* one of my soft and chewy and sweet and spicy and absolutely delicious gingerbread doggies?"

"I didn't say that." The corners of his mouth twitched.

Of course not, because saying that would've required more adjectives than Abe seemed capable of speaking. He tended to use words without frills. "How about we go get them out of my car? I'll give you one bite then you can tell me how you really feel."

His full grin broke through and she couldn't look away. She'd looked at Abe so many times but now something in her heart shifted. Maybe it was the intensity of his eyes or maybe just the fact that he'd smiled for her. *Because* of her . . .

"Lead the way." He moved to open the door around her but at the same time Sylvie turned to catch her breath and they ended up standing toe-to-toe.

Abe's gaze fixated on her lips. Or was she imagining things? She had to be imagining things. So much for catching her breath. "Oops." Sylvie tried to laugh but it came out more like a gasp. "Sorry. I got in the way."

"You're not in the way." His tone seemed lower than it had been before. Or her hearing could be off too.

"We'd better get those cookies before they freeze." She quickly stepped out of the way so he could open the door.

When they walked outside, the cold air brought clarity back to her body. This was Abe! He wasn't looking at her lips or talking to her in a low, sexy vibrato. She'd been watching too many romantic Christmas classics lately.

"I owe you a thanks. For helping me get them all back into the pen." Abe walked alongside her, seemingly oblivious to her inner chaos.

"You don't owe me anything." She peeked at him but detected no trace of attraction in his gaze. She'd definitely been imagining things. "I never thought about how much work it must be to take care of so many goats."

"I swear they're worse than toddlers sometimes." Abe latched the door behind them and double-checked the lock. "I grew up here so I should've known what I was getting myself into coming back. But you forget a lot being away so long."

The statement made Sylvie pause. She'd almost forgotten that Abe had practically lived a lifetime somewhere else. His mom had kept everyone in town up-to-date when he was stationed in Italy or on missions in the Middle East. Loretta De-Witt constantly talked about her son, about the medals he'd earned, about the men and women he'd saved. How strange it must be for him now. To be back where he started after so long away. "Would you have come home if your dad hadn't gotten sick?"

Abe kept on walking without her. "'Would have' doesn't matter. They needed me, so I came home."

Sylvie caught up to him again. What had he left behind? What had he given up to become a goat farmer? "But it must be hard to—"

"It would be harder knowing I was far away when my parents needed me." He still didn't stop, but he slowed down at least, allowing her to fall in step with him.

"Well, did you *want* to be a goat farmer?" Sylvie asked. "Or did you—?"

"You ask a lot of questions." His tone was teasing. But he clearly didn't like *answering* a lot of questions.

"What can I say? I've always been curious about people." Sylvie stopped at her car and reached for the to-go container on her back seat. "Didn't you plan to come back and eventually take over your parents' farm?" she asked when they started toward the larger of the two houses on the property. A few years back, Mr. and Mrs. DeWitt had built themselves a new house, leaving the older original home for Abe to move into. Or at least that's what Gramps had told her.

"I didn't make many plans. The military made most of my plans for me." They approached the front porch and he took her hand. "Watch this step here. It's loose."

"Oh." A breath whooshed out and she teetered, but Abe kept a good grip on her. She couldn't seem to keep a grip on her heart, though.

What had he said again? Something about plans. The military. Right. He probably hadn't had a lot of choices once he'd enlisted. She had so many more questions, but before she could ask any, the front door swung open.

"I thought I heard voices out here." Loretta DeWitt ushered them inside. Abe looked like his mom. Sylvie had never noticed it before but now, glancing at his mother's dark wavy hair and those deep wise eyes, the resemblance hit her immediately.

"Sylvie! What a wonderful surprise!" Loretta glanced over her shoulder. "Jed, look who's here to see us!"

"Hiya, Sylvie." Abe's father sat in his overstuffed chair next to a crackling fire in the living room.

Sylvie quickly stepped out of her boots, leaving them on the rug by the door, and rushed to him so he didn't try to get up. She'd heard he'd been having balance issues as a result of the Parkinson's. "Hello, Mr. DeWitt. I brought you some spiced gingerbread cookies." She held out the to-go container.

"The ones that are shaped like Crumpet?" Hope raised his sparse eyebrows.

"Of course." She opened the lid so he could see inside, and he snuck one with a wry grin.

"I love these!" Loretta took the box from Sylvie's hands and brought it into the open-concept kitchen on the other side of the room. "They're almost too cute to eat. *Almost.*" She admired the cookies again before selecting one. "Why don't you stay for dinner, sweetie?"

Dinner! She'd almost forgotten that Gramps and Crumpet were likely both pacing in front of the door at her house waiting for dinner. "Oh, I really shouldn't." Her gaze landed on the oven clock. "I need to get home to Gramps."

"Well, at least stay for some hot cocoa to warm up, won't you?" Without waiting for an answer, Mrs. DeWitt scurried to the teakettle sitting on the stove and filled it in the sink. "Abe would love it if you stayed. Wouldn't you, son?"

"Sure." His jaw seemed a tad stiff to Sylvie, but he dutifully went to a kitchen cupboard and withdrew four mugs.

"You two can catch up." Mrs. DeWitt started to rifle through the pantry. "I'll bet it's been *years* since you chatted."

"Mmm-hmm," Sylvie murmured, pulling off her gloves and hat and shedding her coat so she could hang them up on the coatrack. She and Abe had never really *chatted*. She had chatted. He mostly grunted.

"Sylvie, do you remember that year Abe drew your name for Secret Santa?" Loretta dumped a few healthy scoops of chocolate powder into each mug.

"He what now?" She couldn't have heard right. Abe had never drawn her name for the school Secret Santa. She would've remembered that.

"It was in sixth grade, I think." Mrs. DeWitt glanced at her son, who was now facing away from Sylvie. "Wasn't it?"

"No. I don't know." Abe started to rinse dishes in the sink and stash them in the dishwasher. "Why would I remember?"

"Well, you agonized over what to get her for a full month!" His mom shook her head and chuckled. "He was so worried."

Sylvie stared at Abe's back, her mind jogging. Sixth grade . . . sixth grade . . . what had she gotten from her Secret Santa in sixth grade? Her heart caught. "It was that handmade embossed solid wood rolling pin!" It was so thoughtful, she'd suspected Grams had bought that for her and *pretended* it was a Secret Santa gift.

"You remember!" Loretta set a steaming mug of cocoa on the counter in front of her.

"Of course I remember." Sylvie picked up the mug, warming her hands. "It's seriously one of the best gifts I've ever gotten."

"See?" Mrs. DeWitt nudged Abe away from the sink and handed him a mug too. "And you were so worried."

"Was I?" Abe sidestepped Sylvie and headed for the door. "I guess I've forgotten all about it."

"You forgot?" Sylvie followed him. "I still use it, you know. The rolling pin. At the café . . ." That rolling pin was beautiful! A work of art! "But how'd you come up with the idea? Where'd you get it?"

His gaze kept shifting. And had his face flushed too? "Don't know." He opened the door and stepped outside, the cold air swirling around her. "Like I said, I don't remember. I've gotta go check the barn again. I'll see ya."

"See y—" The door slammed shut before she could finish. Sylvie walked back into the living room, where Loretta now sat on the couch near Jed. They were both sipping their hot cocoa. "I hope I didn't offend him." She couldn't seem to make it through a full conversation without sending Abe running in the opposite direction.

"Oh, he's not offended. Trust me." Loretta patted the spot next to her on the couch. "I'm afraid I might've embarrassed him by bringing up that rolling pin. He had such a crush on you back then."

"Boy was smitten," Jed added.

Sylvie set her mug on an end table. "No, he wasn't." He'd hardly talked to her when they were in school!

"He was." Loretta waved a hand as if sweeping the past away. "But that was a long time ago, wasn't it, dear?"

"Right. A long time ago." And yet that rolling pin still meant as much to her now as it had then.

Five

"TASTE THIS." SYLVIE HELD OUT A SPOONFUL OF THE GAR-
lic sage brown butter sauce to Gramps while he tossed the
watercress salad next to her. "I think it needs something more."

"Hmm. Mmm-hmm." Her grandfather nodded thoughtfully. "Sage. Only a pinch more and then it'll be perfect."

"A pinch of sage." Sylvie added the ingredient to the bub-
bling liquid in the pan and gave the sauce a slow stir. "How's
that salad coming?" She peeked at her grandfather's handiwork.

"It's green," he commented with an unimpressed smirk.
"Probably good if you like that sort of thing."

Sylvie laughed. "I'll bet I could get even you to like watercress with that dressing I whipped up." The right amount of
olive oil, orange zest, and lemon juice coupled with a dash of
cane sugar and salt could change anyone's opinion about anything. "There are more take-out containers on the table. You
can go ahead and pack up." Everything else was ready—the
braised chicken packaged in a thermal container and resting,
the tender risotto staying warm in the insulated cooler, and

the miniature chocolate yule log she'd spent all afternoon decorating.

"You sure this Royce Elliot fellow is worth all the trouble?" Gramps added the container of watercress salad to the crate she'd set out.

"I'm not doing this for Royce Elliot," she reminded him. "I'm doing this for the café." The man was famous. If he couldn't drum up some publicity for them, no one could. Sylvie poured the sauce into another take-out container and secured the lid.

"Well, you'd best be careful," Gramps warned. "That sauce is every bit as good as the Bolognese your Grams won me over with back in the day. You know what they say—true love is forged in the taste buds."

"Ha. No one says that." Except she did have a pretty passionate relationship with dark chocolate. "I don't have to worry about someone like Mr. Elliot falling for someone like me." Especially not after their first two meetings. He likely didn't pursue awkward babbling bakers who wore Christmas-themed bras.

She lifted the crate of food and set it by the front door so she could bundle up.

"Now what is that supposed to mean?" Gramps wrapped a scarf around his neck. "That man would be lucky to have you. Who cares if he's some big movie star? You're kindhearted, and pretty as a lark to boot."

"And you are a sweet man." She knelt down to put on Crumpet's warmest sweater. She couldn't deny Royce's charm or smoldering looks. She couldn't pretend being in his presence hadn't nudged a few fantasies into her thoughts today, but when she was with him in her head she spoke eloquently, had a few less freckles and better hair, and wore knee-length

A-line dresses with puffed sleeves like Donna Reed in *It's a Wonderful Life*. Obviously those little daydreams were not her reality.

"Come on." She patted Crumpet's head before standing. "We need to get going before Royce orders his own dinner and my gourmet meal goes to waste." Earlier that afternoon, Sylvie had taken a batch of scotcharoos over to Marion's place and had found out that Royce had rented a vacation home only a few blocks away, which meant this should be an easy operation.

"Remember, we're going to drop off the food with my note and then I'll get in the car and we can drive away before he opens the door." That way Royce wouldn't have to endure another clumsy conversation with her.

She pulled on her gloves and lifted the crate before Gramps could get to it. "Can you carry Crumpet, please? He doesn't squirm as much for you." She didn't want Gramps to try to take the box from her on the icy sidewalk. Lately she'd noticed her grandfather wasn't as stable on his feet as he used to be.

"Come here, you little ankle biter." Gramps lifted the dog into his arms, and they walked out the door. "Take it easy on the stairs. That sun this afternoon melted everything just enough to ice it over."

"Got it." Sylvie shuffled gingerly down the steps, balancing the crate in her arms. She loved her little bungalow, but this might be the year she actually bought herself a house with an *attached* garage. As long as she didn't lose her job after Christmas, that is.

Side by side, she and her grandfather plodded to her car while snowflakes gently fell around them. The vivid scent of sage wafted up and reminded her they hadn't eaten their own dinner yet. "I kept some chicken and sauce in the refrigerator so we can heat up a quick meal when we get home." She loaded the crate into the back seat on the driver's side while her grandfather settled in behind the wheel.

"Or maybe we should all go to the door and have our supper with Royce," Gramps suggested playfully. "He might like some company for dinner. You never know."

"He might like *some* company." Sylvie climbed into the passenger's seat and pulled Crumpet onto her lap. "But probably not my company."

"Now you need to stop that." His wiry gray eyebrows furrowed while he started up the engine. "You're the only one I ever hear taking shots at Sylvie West, and I don't like it one bit."

"I don't mean to take shots at myself." She clicked in her seatbelt. "But you've seen me stumble over my words. You've seen me get so flustered that I drop dishes."

"I've also seen you bring meals to anyone in town who's sick or hurt or who had a baby or anything. Doesn't matter who they are or even if they've been nice to you or not. You still take care of them." Gramps paused at the stop sign and turned to her. "I've seen how you drop off the day-old baked goods to folks who live on a fixed income. I've seen you take in a grumpy old man who's lonely for his wife."

"You're not grumpy, Gramps." Sylvie squeezed his mottled hand. "And I didn't take you in. I was lonely after Grams passed too. We needed each other." She still needed him.

Her grandfather continued to stare at her and then brought his palm to her cheek. "I just wish you could see yourself the way I see you, Syl. That beautiful heart of yours shines through in all you do." His piece said, he put his hands back on the wheel and turned his attention to the road.

She wished she could see herself the way he saw her too—focusing only on the good and ignoring the other stuff. "I promise I will try to stop poking fun at myself so much."

"I'm going to hold you to it," Gramps said sternly.

"Take a left up here. We're going to go two blocks and then another left." It hadn't been a surprise that Marion had known right where Royce was staying while he was in town, though it had taken some coaxing to get the woman to give up the address. Marion had relaxed when Sylvie said she was simply dropping a meal off on the doorstep.

The whole dinner drop idea had seemed solid at the time, but now that they were getting closer to the house, her stomach started to flutter. What if he saw her walking up to the porch? What if he opened the door while she was out there? "Maybe he's not home," she said almost hopefully.

"Then all that good food would go to waste." Gramps turned the car onto Starlight Lane.

There! The house Royce had rented was on the corner. Oh, God. The outside lights were on, and his rental car sat in the driveway. He was definitely home. "Pull over here." Her voice got all wispy and high. She handed Crumpet back to Gramps. "Remember the plan. When you see me come down those porch steps, drive past that tree right there, I'll jump in the car, and then we're out of here."

"I still don't see why we have to skedaddle like a couple of criminals," her grandfather grumbled. "If he opens the door, just explain that you're dropping off dinner as a representative for the café and you'd like to invite him and all the movie people to breakfast. Talking to him might be better than a note anyway."

"But the note says everything exactly how I want to say it." There was no guarantee what would come out of her mouth if

Royce opened the door and she had to face him. "Things will be better this way. Trust me."

Sylvie scanned the block. At the moment, the street was deserted. It was now or never. She quickly undid her seatbelt and scrambled out of the car, her heart clamoring the way it had when she'd walk-jogged the annual Turkey Trot 5k fun run at Thanksgiving.

"Take it easy," she reminded herself, lifting the crate out of the back seat. At least the drapes in the living room window were closed. Sylvie tucked her chin in toward her chest and made her way up the icy sidewalk with the crate. So far so good. She could do this. No problem. She made food drops around town all the time.

One by one, she took the steps slowly, pausing on the last one when the wood creaked beneath her boot. She held her breath, but the front door didn't open. *Whew.*

Sylvie crept closer and lowered the crate to the porch, positioning it to the left of the door. She glanced back at the car. Gramps had already started to pull forward, almost directly in front of the house. Now she simply had to ring the doorbell and make a fast getaway. Reaching out her finger to the doorbell, she inched as close to the steps as she could get and then pressed the button before whirling to escape. But her feet slipped out from under her on the bottom step and sent her tumbling not-so-gracefully into the snow.

She couldn't be sure but she may have squealed before landing on her back in a poof of powder. "Ow."

A car door opened and shut. "Sylvie!" Gramps sounded panicked. "Are you—"

Royce's front door flew open and the actor himself appeared, backlit by the cozy glow coming from inside the home. "What in the . . . Sylvie?" He stepped outside onto the porch.

"Yeah. Hi." She gave him a little wave, still wincing from the impact. She'd be sporting a few more bruises later.

"Are you okay?" Royce rushed down the steps. "Did you fall?"

"It would appear so." She pushed up onto her elbows—which thankfully still seemed to work—so she could sit up.

"Syl. Oh, Syl." Gramps reached her, kneeling by her side with Crumpet folded into his arms. "Don't move. I'll call for an ambulance. I'll—"

"No, no." She pasted a smile on her face when all she really wanted to do was cry. "I'm fine, Gramps. Really. Nothing hurts." Now that the burn of humiliation had consumed everything, she couldn't feel much anyway. She struggled to stand, her feet skidding.

Royce steadied her arm. "You're sure? I'm so sorry. The owner left salt for me to put down, but I forgot."

Sylvie made the mistake of looking into his eyes. His ice blue eyes that were somehow also warm enough to melt the snow in her hair. Her heart dropped about two levels lower in her chest. "I, um. Well. You see, I wanted to, uh. I brought you dinner." She pointed to the crate behind them. "I mean, it's from the café, actually. Not really from me, per say. It's courtesy of the café, since you're a visitor in town. There's a whole note explaining everything. You should probably read that . . ."

"It's braised chicken with brown butter sage sauce," Gramps offered helpfully. "I'm Walt, by the way."

"Yes, this is my grandpa." Sylvie smiled too big. "He helped me make the dinner. From the café. Not from me . . ." *Ugggh.*

"Nice to meet you, Walt." Royce shook her grandfather's hand and then walked up the porch steps and peered into the crate. "Wow. That's a lot of food. I won't even make a dent in that myself. Why don't you three come in and have dinner with me?"

"Now that's the best idea I've heard all day, son." Gramps cruised on past her and headed up the steps, making the decision for them. "We'd love to. Right, Sylvie?"

"Um. Well . . ." Dear God. Why did her heart have to flop around in her chest when she locked eyes with Royce? "Sure. Yeah. That's fine, I guess." She had to pull herself together and convince Royce to help her put the café on the map. Who cared if she had to endure more humiliation? Only one mission mattered right now. With that in mind, she marched up the steps behind her grandfather and held the door open for Royce while he brought the crate inside.

"This smells delicious." Royce skirted past her, getting close enough that she noticed he smelled delicious too—some cologne that was neither too strong nor too weak but exactly the perfect amount of sexy.

"Yip!"

When she stepped inside the living room, Crumpet stood on his hindlegs and scratched at her thighs until she pulled him into her arms. "Hush, now," she whispered. "You have to be a good boy. This is a nice place." She didn't want Royce to lose his damage deposit on account of her dog.

"This sure is a nice place." Gramps made himself at home and shed his winter gear, hanging everything up on hooks behind the door. Sylvie followed suit, trying to maneuver out of her coat with one arm while holding her puppy with the other.

"It's working out okay." Royce had moved into the open-concept kitchen in the opposite corner, where he started to unpack the box of food. "I like to rent houses as opposed to

staying in hotels when I travel. Then I can have my own space."
The man flashed her what could only be described as a pulse-
altering grin—all white teeth and charm. "I usually pick up
takeout, but this looks truly incredible. Restaurant quality."

"That's my Sylvie." Gramps marched into the kitchen and
snatched a plate off the stack Royce had removed from a cabinet. "She's the best chef in Silver Bells. Probably in all of Wyoming, if you want the truth."

"I'd believe it." Royce admired the chocolate yule log. "This
looks like the best dessert I'll ever have the pleasure of eating."
He fired up that darn smile again, rendering Sylvie speechless.

Wait a minute . . . was he *flirting* with her? "If this tastes as
good as it looks, I'll be having some sweet dreams tonight."
Yes. Yes, he was.

Heat swamped her cheeks first and then shot through the
rest of her. How should she respond? She didn't know how to
flirt! "I dream about chocolate almost every night," flew out of
her mouth. "One time I had this dream where all of the running water in my house turned to chocolate. So I had to
shower in chocolate and wash the dishes in chocolate and
drink chocolate. There was even chocolate in the toilet." Ack!
Spinning quickly away, Sylvie turned to the fireplace in the
living room, staring into the gas-powered flames.

Behind her, Royce simply laughed, as though he assumed
she'd been joking. "Can I interest either of you in a glass of
wine?"

"Sure." But it might take more than a glass to get her
through this.

"As long as it's red," her grandfather said.

"I have a nice cab I've been waiting to open." Royce told
Gramps about the vineyard while Sylvie rubbed her hands

together by the fire. Maybe she could stay here the whole evening—with her back to him . . .

A cork popped. "Here you are, Walt," Royce said. "And Sylvie . . ." The actor appeared by her side and handed her a stemless glass, his hand brushing hers. "This one is velvety smooth."

A lot like his voice.

Crumpet tried to wriggle out from under her arm to get closer to Royce while she sipped. "Mmmm." Honestly all cabs tasted the same to her. She didn't exactly have a sophisticated palate, but "It's really good, thank you," seemed like the right thing to say.

"How about some music?" He picked up a remote off a shelf next to the fireplace. "Any requests?"

"Uh . . ." Between her heart hammering and her head lightening she couldn't think of one song she liked right now. Was she really drinking wine in front of the fireplace with Royce Elliot?

"Something festive," her grandfather suggested.

"Festive it is." He pushed a few buttons, and then a jazzy version of "Santa Claus Is Coming to Town" started to play through the speakers.

"We'd better eat." Royce touched her lower back to gently prod her toward the kitchen. "We don't want your delicious food to get cold."

"Okay," she gasp-whispered. Heat radiated from where he'd touched her.

"The chef deserves to eat first for once." He held out a plate in her direction.

Right. She should stop staring at him like a deer mesmerized by headlights and move her body, even with the tension crowding her muscles. She'd been standing too tall and too stiffly for too long, but she had no idea how to act in front of a celebrity.

Gramps smiled encouragingly—and a little worriedly—as she set Crumpet down. She took the plate from Royce without making eye contact and helped herself to small portions of the chicken and salad without uttering another word.

"Does the café deliver food to all the visitors in town?" Royce didn't seem to realize she'd apparently taken a vow of silence. He hung back by the refrigerator while Gramps loaded his plate with chicken.

"Oh. Um. Well. No." She couldn't lie to the man. Sylvie set her plate on a placemat at the table and turned back to him. This was it—her chance to launch into the spiel she'd written in her note. One simple sentence, that was all she had to say. "I—we—actually wanted to extend an invitation to you and the producers and director to have a special breakfast at the café tomorrow morning." Pausing to assess herself, she detected nothing embarrassing or awkward in her speech. She'd managed to communicate effectively, a Christmas miracle!

"I think they're having food delivered to the set tomorrow. Thanks for the offer, though." Royce helped himself to a large portion of salad and chicken, drenching it with sauce. "I heard they called in an order to some fancy restaurant in Jackson." He walked to the table and set his plate across from hers but didn't take his seat.

Sylvie didn't take her seat either. Disappointment crumbled her. According to Marion, Royce was the executive producer of the film. She needed them to come to the café. She needed *him* to come, to plaster pictures of her charming café all over his social media pages. Forget eloquence and restraint.

She was desperate here. "The truth is, the café is in trouble," she blurted. "And I—we—thought maybe having you all hang out there would help us get some publicity. I mean, maybe you could even film a scene there or something. I'm not going to lie, we'll have to close the doors after Christmas if something doesn't change."

Gramps gave his nod of approval and wink before sitting down at the table with his dinner.

Royce stared at her, his wide eyes emulating concern. "I had no idea." He gestured for her to sit and then took his seat. "Sorry to hear that. I've never seen another place quite like it."

"I know." She grasped at hope. If she could make him see how important that café was, maybe he'd help. "The place is totally unique. If fact, I bet the movie could use the café for publicity too. Think of the articles this could generate—*movie crew films at local relic*. That kind of publicity could be mutually beneficial."

Royce stared at her across the table, a slow smile making magic in his eyes. "It's something to consider. I'll convince the other producers and the director to join me there for breakfast tomorrow morning." He sipped his wine thoughtfully. "It'll have to be bright and early. I can't make any promises about filming there, but maybe we can come up with something."

"Really?" Sylvie held her breath.

"Sure." His gaze held hers. "Your food is too enticing. I've never been good at resisting temptation."

"Thank you!" She launched out of her chair and threw her arms around him. Oh wow! She was hugging Royce Elliot! "Sorry," Sylvie mumbled, the smell of that delicious cologne clouding her thoughts. She rebounded back into her chair.

"Don't apologize. I'm happy to help." Royce picked up his wine, peering at her over the glass with an old Hollywood twinkle in his eyes. "Especially if it means I'll get to see you again."

"No!" she automatically blurted, her sudden panic flooding out. "I, um, have to stay in the kitchen." Or else she'd get all flustered and red-faced like she was now, and who knew what kind of humiliating scene she'd create then?

"So I won't get to see you at all?" The man somehow managed to make the same expression Crumpet made when she grabbed her car keys. Except sexy. He *was* flirting with her. Heat flashed across her face. Had anyone ever flirted with her before?

"Course you can see her," Gramps cut in, giving her arm a supportive squeeze. "Sylvie'd be happy to show you around her kitchen. Wouldn't ya, darlin'?"

After a few awkward seconds, Gramps's foot tapped hers, reminding her she had to speak.

"Yes." The more she tried to smile naturally, the more strained her face felt. "You're welcome to stop into the kitchen." Though if her racing pulse was any indication, inviting him back there could be dangerous. "Maybe when breakfast is over."

That way she wouldn't have the chance to embarrass herself until *after* she'd saved the café.

Six

SYLVIE PLACED A LACE DOILY ON THE CHOCOLATE CAKE'S surface and used her dusting wand to scatter powdered sugar over the top.

This is what set good food apart—the details, the artistry, the presentation. She carefully peeled the stencil away, leaving a perfect replica of the intricate pattern in a white contrast against the cake's dark glaze. "Perfecto." If she did say so herself. She'd been saying it all morning—when she'd slid the Christmas quiche into the oven earlier, when she'd stirred her poppyseed magic into the festive fruit salad she'd whipped up . . . so far everything had been *perfecto*.

Not that she could take the credit. Most of the recipes she used were Grams's originals. Though she knew them by heart, she'd gone into her file box and pulled out the cards her grandmother had handwritten in her intricate, loopy penmanship. Studying the words and seeing the smudges of chocolate and cinnamon and butter never failed to bring the woman back to life. She could still hear her grandma's voice working out the details of a recipe during one of their many taste tests. They would both take a bite of whatever Grams had concocted at the same time, and though Sylvie always thought everything tasted delicious, her grandmother would inevitably start nodding and mmm-hmming, and then she'd exclaim, "Needs more butter," or "We'll have to add a dash more sugar," and then she'd start scribbling on her recipe card.

Add a smidgen of nutmeg for a little extra zing! Grams had written on the chocolate cake recipe card. *Or spice it up with a sprinkle of cayenne!*

Naturally, Sylvie had done both. She needed all the zing and spice she could get right now.

Grams had always said that an infusion of love and flavor could win over every heart. She hoped the movie execs would agree.

Humming along to the country Christmas album blaring from her speaker, Sylvie carted the cake to the serving counter. Some people might say you didn't need dessert after breakfast, but she'd never been one of those people. Chocolate happened to be the perfect finisher for every meal—especially when you were trying to leave an impression.

Take last night for example. Royce had raved about her chocolate yule log when he'd tried a few bites. That decadence must have been why he'd walked her out to the porch, where he'd said he couldn't wait to see her in the morning. It had to be the chocolate's magical powers.

Sylvie hurried to the refrigerator and opened the door, sticking her head in to cool the sudden heat prickling her cheeks. It wouldn't do to sweat off all of her makeup before the party arrived. She had to refocus, stop thinking about how the man's eyes had kept finding hers last night. She had to stop thinking about how he'd winked at her, more than once . . .

This line of thinking was not helping to calm her nerves

before the most important breakfast of her life. She shut the refrigerator door and straightened her apron. Sheesh. She had no business getting gooey over a man who could have any woman he wanted—a man who likely *did* have every woman he wanted.

Sylvie hurried out into the dining room and looked over the table setting once more. At least Teagan would be here to do the serving. Jen wouldn't arrive for work for another hour, but Teagan could steal the show with her chipper enthusiasm. After a quick introduction, Sylvie could do what she did best—hide in the kitchen and plate the food.

She meticulously rearranged the pine cones around the centerpiece she'd fashioned with sprigs of juniper surrounding red candles in the middle of the table and then rushed back into the kitchen to check the quiche. *Perfecto.* The fluffy eggs were setting up nicely, and the cheese on the top layer had almost turned a golden brown. The dish should be ready precisely when Royce and his colleagues arrived. She glanced at the clock. In ten minutes.

Her phone buzzed from inside her apron pocket, and Sylvie closed the oven hastily to answer.

"Hey, Sylvie." Teagan's voice croaked through the line. "I'm not feeling so hot. There's no way I can come in today."

"What?" An icy panic slid down her throat. "No. You have to come in! Some very important customers are about to show up, and I can't plate and serve . . ." She couldn't charm them and serve them *and* keep the kitchen running. Sylvie couldn't do this alone . . .

"My throat is killing me," the girl croaked. "My mom's pretty sure it's strep."

Sylvie's gaze shot to the clock. Seven minutes. Royce and the producer and director were going to walk into the café in seven minutes. "You didn't call Evelyn, did you?" Desperation edged into her tone. Unfortunately the retired school teacher only liked to work two days a week. "Or what about Roman?" The part-time college student always seemed to be looking for more hours . . .

"They're both busy today." Teagan cleared her throat. "I'm so sorry. Maybe you should call Jerry—"

"Nope!" She couldn't call her boss for help if she wanted to show him she was capable of management. "I'll be fine. It's no big deal. Don't worry about me. You focus on getting better." Never mind the sudden spike in her blood pressure. If she was going to be in charge, she had to at least act like she could handle the pressure.

"Thanks! I knew you'd understand." Teagan said goodbye, and Sylvie hung up right as the jingle bells above the door in the front of the house rang.

"Okay." She exhaled her worries and glanced in the mirror that hung above her desk. *Yikes.* Her unruly hair had already started to escape from its messy bun, but she had no time to fix herself up. This was it. Her moment.

Putting on her brightest smile, she paraded out of the kitchen and met Royce and two women who stood just inside the door. "Good morning, and welcome to the Christmas Café." Somehow her tone struck the perfect blend of friendly and professional even though her heartbeat drummed at the sight of Royce in a deep green fisherman's sweater with dark jeans. He looked like he'd just stepped out of one of his movies. Maybe he had.

She simply couldn't look at him if she wanted to think straight.

"Sylvie, I'd like you to meet our producer, Jun Sano." He gestured to the woman on his left, who had sleek black hair and a flawless complexion accented with only a light touch of makeup. "And this is our director, Brenda Bosworth." The other woman was every bit as polished, with a stylish cropped haircut and expensive pants suit.

And here Sylvie stood in her velvety yoga pants and a long-sleeved T-shirt that said *Party Elf* under her apron. She quickly shook both of their hands, putting extra oomph into her smile to keep their attention off her attire. "Nice to meet you. Welcome to the Christmas Café." Had she already said that?

"Thank you." Jun's voice was poised. "We don't have a lot of time, I'm afraid. But Royce said we absolutely couldn't miss a chance to eat here."

"You have a very charming place," Brenda added.

"Thanks." She could only hope the place was charming enough to survive. Sylvie gestured to the table. "Everything's ready for you. You can get yourselves settled, and I'll have the coffee right out."

"Can't wait." Royce gave her upper arm a squeeze as he walked past her, weakening her knees to the point that she had to stagger back into the kitchen. *Okay.* She braced her hands against the counter and resorted to deep cleansing breaths. She could do this. She could go out there and serve these people breakfast. She would have to avoid Royce's flirtatious, lingering glances, that was all. Sylvie slung a towel over her shoulder, picked up the carafe, and then pushed through the doors, remembering to paste on her smile at the last second. "Coffee for everyone?" she murmured, calm and cool.

"We'd all love some." Royce moved his mug closer to his plate.

She filled his first, slowly and carefully. It had been years—before she'd become the chef—since she'd filled mugs in this place. And back then, she hadn't been very good at accuracy.

"So how long has the Christmas Café been here?" Royce's deliberate tone prompted.

Right. She paused from pouring so she could think. "Um, well, let's see . . ." She knew the answer, darn it. "Jerry—that's the owner—he opened this place thirty-two years ago." What else had she wanted Teagan to say again? She'd sent the girl a lengthy text last night with the messaging but now she couldn't remember. "As far as we know it's the only Christmas-themed café open year-round in the Rocky Mountain region." At least according to Google. "The Christmas Café is a favorite of locals and visitors alike." Okay, that may have sounded a little scripted.

Sylvie went to pour coffee into Jun's mug, but the carafe nearly slipped in her hand. She caught the handle again, but not before the steaming liquid sloshed all over the woman's plate and the tablecloth. "Oh, no. I'm so sorry." Perspiration prickled on her brow line. "Let me wipe that up and get you a new plate." She set down the carafe but bumped it over when she went to grab the woman's plate. Coffee spilled across the entire table, even soaking the juniper around the centerpiece. "Shoot. Oh my God. I'm so, so sorry." She scurried around trying to stanch the flow of coffee while Jun and Brenda scooted their chairs away from the table.

"It's no problem," Royce said as smoothly, as if this were all part of his script. "We'll move to that table." He stood and pointed to a booth in the corner.

"Yes, good idea." Sylvie hung her head, still mopping fruitlessly at the table with the soaked towel that had been over her shoulder. "I'll grab some new dishes." She collected what she could carry and dashed back into the kitchen, nearly running straight into Abe.

"Whoa." Abe's big hands caught her arms and steadied her. "What's all this? What's going on?"

Molten tears built in her eyes. "It's a disaster, that's what it is." She stacked the coffee-stained dishes in the sink while the tears escaped.

"Sylvie?" Abe came alongside her and studied her face. "What's wrong?"

She blubbered that she was trying to prove herself to Jerry so she wouldn't lose her job and she'd just spilled coffee all over two movie executives. "I can't go back out there. I'll probably end up dumping the quiche in their laps."

"Hey." The man looked into her eyes, his mouth softening underneath that wiry beard. "You make the best food I've ever tasted, Syl. So you spilled a little coffee on the table. No big deal."

"It's a huge deal." She used her apron to wipe her tears. "My food won't be enough to keep the doors open. I really thought maybe this movie would help. I thought this was our chance to get some publicity, but now I've ruined everything."

"Nothing's ruined." Abe left his plaid trapper's hat on her desk and walked to the coatrack near the back door and pulled a Christmas Café apron over his head. "You'll see."

He moved around the kitchen, gathering a tray, new place settings, the coffee carafe, and a selection of scones.

"You don't have to do that." He'd only come to deliver the extra butter she'd texted him about yesterday . . .

"I know." He stacked everything neatly onto the tray and then lifted it as though carting around dishes and coffee and baked goods required zero effort. "Relax. Get the food ready and I'll serve it."

Before she could steady her voice enough to thank him, he'd disappeared through the doors.

Wiping away a fresh round of tears, she crept over and peeked through the small window to eavesdrop.

"Sylvie is putting the finishing touches on her delicious quiche," Abe was saying.

He'd used an adjective!

"But in the meantime, she wanted to offer you a selection of the café's most popular scones." He set the tray on a nearby table and pointed out each flavor. "Here we have the classic pumpkin spice. This one is the spiced eggnog—one of my favorites. We also have a maple glazed gingerbread scone and a white chocolate peppermint right here."

Jun, Brenda, and Royce seemed to admire the confections before finally deciding to cut them into pieces so they could sample each one.

While he filled their mugs with coffee—not spilling one drop—Abe entertained them by telling them about the time Santa drove his sleigh down Main Street in the Christmas parade and made a stop at the café for a glazed gingerbread scone. Every kid that had been out on that street watching the parade had come in to take a turn sitting at Santa's table.

Wow. She'd never heard Abe so chatty. Those were exactly the kinds of stories Sylvie loved about the café—the memories that really gave this place its character. Sylvie found herself smiling as she retreated from the doors, put on her oven mitts, and took the quiche out, setting the dish on the counter to rest before she cut it.

The doors opened again and Abe sailed through, his tray now empty. "They love the scones," he informed her. "The coffee incident is ancient history."

"Thank you." Sylvie faced him. She'd known this man

since they were kids and, though he'd always been quiet and reserved and at times very hard to read, she'd forgotten how genuinely kind he was. "I owe you one."

"I'm happy to take payment in baked goods." He stole one of the white chocolate peppermint scones from the case at her baking station and bit into it, closing his eyes. "So. Good. This town won't survive without the Christmas Café."

She wanted to believe him, but Jerry had seemed adamant about unloading the restaurant. "That's why I have to prove this place can be profitable. I can't afford to buy it, but I'm hoping Jerry will let me continue running it." Though if earlier was any indication, she might not have what it takes to be promoted to management.

"Remember the bake sale you organized in eighth grade?" Abe dusted the crumbs off his hands, grinning.

The memory brought a smile back to her face. "I'd forgotten all about that." The animal shelter had been down on donations that year, so she'd decided to start baking homemade donuts to sell before school, donating every dollar that didn't go to ingredients to the shelter. When the principal found out what she was doing, she encouraged her to put together a larger-scale bake sale. "That was the only time in my life that I acted like Claire."

"I wouldn't go that far." Abe's grimace made it seem like he appreciated the fact she was nothing like her sister. "But I do remember you wouldn't take no for an answer, and we ended up raising over three thousand dollars."

Bringing that check to the shelter had been one of the best moments of Sylvie's life. She couldn't believe she'd forgotten all about it.

"You've got this, Syl." Abe washed his hands in the sink. "Don't let anyone stop you from getting what you want."

Sylvie met his eye, a strange, sunny energy humming through her.

"I'll get the quiche out there." Abe's eyes darted away from hers, and she realized she'd been awkwardly staring at him.

"Right." Sylvie spun to the counter, found a knife, and cut the quiche, arranging each piece on a plate and topping them with a sprinkling of fresh herbs. She added a hearty scoop of the fruit salad, bringing even more color to the arrangement. "Tell them I also made a chocolate torte for dessert, so they have to save room."

"Got it." Abe loaded up his tray and disappeared again. She was tempted to spy once more, but instead Sylvie retrieved the heavy cream from the refrigerator and brought it to her mixer so she could make a batch of homemade whipped cream to serve with the torte. The whir of one of her favorite kitchen appliances stilled her inner chaos. This was going to be okay. Abe had saved her from a complete disaster, and she knew the food was good.

This could work. This could actually work!

By the time Abe had made it back into the kitchen, she'd already plated the chocolate cake with a side of whipped cream and a mint sprig.

"Sorry that took so long." Abe set his tray on the counter and poured himself a mug of coffee. "They asked about the restaurant's hours and about the decorations in the dining room. Sounds like they're talking about filming here."

"Are you serious?" Sylvie slapped a hand over her mouth so Royce and his colleagues wouldn't hear her squeal and then started to dance around. "Yes! They're going to film a scene here! This will change everything. And I never would've convinced them without your help." She threw her arms around him in a victorious embrace, completely forgetting he was holding his coffee mug. "Oops." She snatched a towel off the counter and wiped the splashes off his cheek. "Sorry about that."

Abe's flecked brown eyes met hers for a split second before darting away. "I should get the cake out there."

"Right," she said weakly. "And sorry. Again."

He grunted and then hurriedly arranged the plates on the tray and flew out of the kitchen.

Okay. That was it. Next time he came back, she'd keep her distance, give him the space he liked. Sylvie started tidying up, washing the dishes and then sponging off the counter, humming "Rockin' Around the Christmas Tree." After tossing her rag into the sink, she headed for the doors ready to eavesdrop again, but they flew open and sent her stumbling backward with her feet tangling underneath her. "Whoa!" Her arms flailed but Abe caught her around the waist before she fell.

"Easy," he murmured, and now he was most definitely eyeing her lips. She eyed his lips too. They were curved and smooth and close enough to kiss—

"Sylvie?" Royce poked his head inside. "There you are." He stepped through the doors and Abe abruptly released her.

"This meal was impeccable," the actor said. "You really are an incredible chef."

"I . . . um . . . well . . . thank you." She glanced at Abe, seeing what appeared to be a flush on his neck and a twinkle in his eye.

Royce moved closer, catching her eye from where it lingered on Abe. "We're talking about rethinking an important scene in the film—and maybe changing the location to the Christmas Café."

"That would be amazing." This was the lucky break she

needed to save the café. She could get Teagan to help her set up a whole social media campaign around the news . . .

"But I think you and I should talk through things before we commit," he went on. "Are you available tomorrow night? I could pick you up at your place."

Pick her up? Like a date? "Oh. Um. Uh. Hmm." Her voice faltered. There was no way Royce Elliot was asking her out. She shook her head to scatter the thought. This was business. "I think I'm open. I mean, I'm definitely open. Yes. Tomorrow night works."

"Wonderful. It's a date." He handed her a card. "Here's my number. Text me your address and I'll be at your place at six. And thanks for helping out, Gabe."

The man's jaw visibly tightened. "It's Abe, actually."

"Right. Abe." He flashed a smile. "Anyway, Sylvie, you should come out to the dining room, so Jun and Brenda can chat with you."

"Okay. Sure." She peered at Abe. "You should come too." He was the one who'd sold the value of this place, who'd charmed them and talked up the café. If it hadn't been for Abe showing up, she doubted she'd have this chance.

"Nah, I should get going." He turned away from her.

"But I haven't paid you for the extra butter."

"Add it into next week's payment. See you around, Sylvie, and good job today," he said, already halfway out the door, his coat in hand.

Royce tugged on her sleeve. "Ready?"

"Um. Sure." Her gaze drifted to the window but Abe was already driving away. Running from her again.

But maybe it wasn't because she annoyed him after all.

Seven

꙳ ꙳

"IT'S NOT A DATE." SYLVIE SURVEYED THE ASSORTMENT OF sweaters and jeans she'd tossed onto her bed when she was digging through her drawers in a desperate attempt to find the perfect not-a-date outfit.

"Yip!" Crumpet poked out his head from where he'd taken cover under her pillow when the clothes had started flying.

"Tonight is no big deal," she told him firmly. "Technically this is a business meeting. A discussion between two professionals, if you will." No matter what kind of images her imagination was trying to conjure up of her and Royce getting cozy in front of the beautiful fireplace in his rental. "Strictly professional."

She held up a navy cashmere sweater—a gift from Claire that she'd only worn once, to her sister's post-election party. "What do you think, pups? Does this say 'professional business meeting'?"

The dog growled and lunged for the sweater, clamping his teeth onto the hem and inching backward for a game of tug-of-war.

"Okay. Sheesh." Sylvie let him win. "That's a no on the cashmere then." She sat heavily on the mountain of clothes, glancing down at the fleece-lined black joggers and the *I'll be gnome for Christmas* sweatshirt she currently wore. "How alluring do you think Royce finds novelty athleisure wear?"

Crumpet left the sweater in a heap and trotted to her, jumping up so that he had one paw on each of her shoulders. He looked intently into her eyes, wagging his tail and licking her cheek repeatedly, a move she interpreted as *I love you! You're perfect! You're the most beautiful girl in the whole wide world!*

"You're right. It doesn't matter what I wear." She selected one of her old faithful cardigans, a simple V-neck T-shirt, and jeggings, dressing quickly. "Tonight is about the café."

A knock sounded on her door, and Gramps poked his head in. "How's it going?"

"Great!" The word came on a little strong. "I'm only slightly terrified." This night was it—her chance to save the café. And somehow she had to maintain her cool with a movie star. No pressure.

"Just be yourself," Gramps advised. "That's what your Grams would say. Speaking of . . . wanted to give you something." He reached into the pocket of his worn flannel shirt and pulled out the art nouveau silver filigree bracelet she'd seen her grandmother wear on more than one special occasion. "Grams always wanted you to have this."

Sylvie gasped as he clipped the bracelet to her wrist. "Are you sure?" Her grandfather had had a hard time giving up Grams's things when he moved out of their home and in with Sylvie. Half the garage behind the house had been filled with boxes he hadn't been able to go through yet. "I mean, I love it, but if you want to hold on to it for a while longer—"

"I can't keep holding on to everything." His gruff throat clearing didn't disguise the emotion he clearly felt. "She would've wanted you to know how much she believes in you. She would've loved what you're doing. Fighting for the café. She was always so proud of you."

"Thank you. She'd be proud of both of us." Sylvie hugged her grandfather, holding on while tears slipped down her cheeks. She pulled away and studied the delicate bracelet. "This Christmas is going to be different. I can feel it. I mean, who would've believed that a movie would be filming in Silver Bells right when we needed it the most?" Somehow it seemed Grams was sprinkling her holiday magic on both of them.

Gramps's smile managed to blend tenderness with snark. "Your Grams always did know how to pull strings. Remember that ti—?"

The doorbell chimed.

"Bwooof!" Crumpet leapt off the bed and dashed down the hallway, unleashing his stranger-danger bark.

Sylvie's stomach lurched as she glared at the alarm clock on her bedside table. "Royce is twelve minutes early!" Who showed up for a non-date twelve whole minutes before they were supposed to?

"He must be looking forward to seeing you," Gramps teased. "Don't worry about a thing. I'll distract him. I can show him some of the flies I tied last week."

"Perfect." Her jaw unclenched. Gramps could talk about fly-fishing for hours.

Exactly eight minutes later, Sylvie stepped into her favorite pair of soft, Sherpa-lined boots and crept out of her room, hearing the sound of laughter coming from the kitchen. At the end of the hallway, she paused and peeked around the corner.

Gramps and Royce sat at the kitchen table, their heads bent together while they examined her grandfather's most recent fly-tying accomplishment. Crumpet had claimed a place of honor, curled up contentedly on the actor's lap.

"Now this one here's a conehead woolly bugger," Gramps was saying, glancing at Royce over the bifocals perched on the end of his nose. He pointed to what looked like a ball of fuzz in his tackle box.

"So that's for trout fishing, then?" Either Royce was a very skilled actor or he was truly interested in fly-fishing. Knowing his profession, Sylvie would bet on the former.

"Exactly." Gramps nodded encouragingly. "Rainbow, brown, brook, steelhead. This one'll never let you down."

"I'll keep that in mind." Royce petted Crumpet behind the ears. Her dog stretched, turning over so the man could scratch his belly, and Sylvie's heart turned into a pile of warm, melty wax. So much for keeping her thoughts strictly on business tonight.

As if sensing her presence, Crumpet suddenly sat up straight in Royce's lap, his gaze fixed on the hallway and his tail wagging.

No more hiding. Sylvie stepped into the room with a serious case of jitters. "I'm ready." Her voice sounded too tight so she tried to soften it with a smile. "Sorry to keep you waiting."

"Don't apologize." Royce gently set Crumpet on the floor and hurried to meet her, looking all dapper in his dark jeans and a twilight-colored crewneck sweater. "I brought you some flowers. I saw them at the gift shop in town and they were so festive and lovely . . . they made me think of you." He gestured to a bouquet of white lilies and red roses along with sprigs of pine branches that had already been set in a vase.

"Mmm-hmm." Sylvie's throat seemed to have melted too.

This wasn't supposed to be a date. Or was it? Royce had a way of making her feel like she'd stepped into some romantic movie, and she had no idea how to play the role.

Behind Royce, Gramps gestured with his hands, prompting her to speak.

Right. *Mmm-hmm* wasn't exactly the best response when someone brought you flowers. "Thank you. Um. We should probably get going."

"Yes," Royce agreed. He crossed the room and quickly pulled on his coat along with a wool beanie and thick gloves. "You'll need to bundle up." A mysterious glow lit his eyes as he helped her into her winter jacket.

Crumpet whined and then jumped up, snatching the leg of his tiny winter snowsuit in his teeth.

"Sorry, sweetie." Sylvie knelt and gave him kisses. "You'll have to stay home—"

"He can come." Royce lowered to a knee beside her. "I mean, it's okay with me if it's okay with you."

She nodded silently, mesmerized by how much care the man used to dress her dog in the snowsuit.

"You're sure you don't mind?" She lifted Crumpet into her arms.

"Absolutely." He guided her to the front door and pulled it open, gesturing outside to a horse-drawn sleigh waiting on the street in front of her house. "I brought plenty of blankets so hopefully we'll all be nice and warm."

"Wow," she breathed, stepping out onto the porch. She really had walked right into a Christmas fairy tale. Fleecy snowflakes floated down, illuminated by the glow of the colorful lights she had hung—at Gramps's direction—in October. Two stately white horses stood tall and alert in front of a red wooden sleigh adorned with gold runners and trim.

The driver—who was dressed like a cowboy version of Santa Claus—climbed down from the driver's seat. He tipped his red, tinsel-rimmed hat in her direction. "Evening, ma'am."

"I thought it would be fun to go look at Christmas lights." Royce stepped alongside of her and offered his hand. "I've never seen so many displays in one town in my life."

"There is no place like Silver Bells during the holidays." Snuggling Crumpet in with one arm, Sylvie took his hand and floated down the stairs. "Everyone decorates here. And neighbors pitch in for those who aren't able to put up lights on their own." Not everyone celebrated Christmas here, but the whole town did their part to light up the long, dark nights during the winter.

Royce led her carefully down the shoveled sidewalk. "I knew this town was full of magic."

This night was full of magic. Sylvie could feel the bracelet snug around her wrist, embracing her the way she was sure Grams wanted her to embrace this moment. "I've never been on a sleigh ride." She paused a few steps away, trying to decide if this was really happening. Maybe she'd fallen asleep on the couch in front of *White Christmas* . . .

"I've never been on a sleigh ride either." Royce urged her forward and then helped her climb up into the sleigh.

Sylvie sat on the red velvet bench with Crumpet nestled in her lap.

Royce settled in beside her and pulled two Sherpa blankets over them. "I met Gerald here on set a few days ago, and I figured this would be a fun way to see all of the lights in town."

The older Santa cowboy—Gerald, presumably—had climbed back up into his driving seat. "You two relax and enjoy. I'll take you to all the best spots," he promised. Then he clicked his tongue and jiggled the reins, and the two horses started to clomp down the street.

The cold night air chilled Sylvie's cheeks, but her inner glow only strengthened.

"Are you warm enough?" Royce sat close enough that his deep voice resonated through her.

"Nice and toasty." All afternoon she'd tried to come up with ideas for a scene the movie people could film at the café. That was supposed to be the focus of their discussion tonight, after all. But right now she couldn't remember a single thought she'd had. In fact, she didn't want to think at all. She wanted to be fully present in this dream, watching the dazzling lights as they passed by, hearing the clip-clop of hooves and the gentle swoosh of the runners over the snow. "My favorite house is coming up." The Wingate Mansion.

A sorrowful and joyful sort of anticipation simmered within her. The whimsical Victorian mansion had been Grams's favorite spectacle every year too. It wasn't only the amazing light display. Each year, the Wingate family also hosted one of the town's greatest traditions: the Silver Bells Christmas Ball. She and Gramps and Grams used to dress in their Christmas finest, bundle up, and walk down here, taking pictures and noting each new addition to the display. That's why she'd made it a point to avoid driving past the Wingates' every year from October to March since Grams had died. And she hadn't gone to the ball either. Too many memories.

"Is it that one?" Royce pointed ahead of them to the crown jewel of the town's Christmas light displays.

Sylvie couldn't answer. She could only gaze at the grandeur, bracing herself for the waves of grief. Only this time they didn't come. Instead, she found herself smiling, picturing

Grams all bundled up, the joy on her face sparkling every bit as much as the sequins on her beloved red hat and scarf as she pointed out her favorite details. Those memories—the happy, shiny ones—had started to overpower the sad ones.

"It looks exactly like a gingerbread house," Royce murmured, his eyes widening like a kid's as they drew closer.

"I know." She admired the lighted gumdrops dressing up the trim, and the candy cane columns holding up the front porch, and the spinning peppermint swirls covering the windows, and the life-sized gingerbread people waving from the yard. Memories crowded in but instead of breaking her heart the way they typically did, those thoughts filled her with joy. With magic. "I used to come here with my Grams," she said wistfully. "We lost her a few years back. She brought out the best in everyone. Including me."

Royce turned to her, watching, waiting, listening.

Sylvie felt the bracelet encircling her wrist again, the cool of the metal against her skin. A genuine smile bloomed from all the way inside of her. "I've missed Grams so much, but she's still spreading her magic around even though she's gone."

Royce let the words have a few seconds of space before he spoke. "I think when you love someone deeply, their magic becomes a part of you." The man's eyes caught the lights as they focused intently on hers. "And when they're gone, that magic lives on through you. So maybe you're the one spreading the magic now, Sylvie. Maybe it's all you." He took her hand in his again.

"I never thought of it like that." She tipped her head back, her eyes finding the stars and then the round moon.

She'd forgotten the wonder of the stars on a clear, cold December night. But now, as the sleigh rails swooshed gently through the powdery snow, she gazed upward at the tiny lights flickering in their own festive display above.

"I've never seen so many stars in my entire life. You don't get these in L.A." Royce rested his head back too, the resonance of his voice scattering goosebumps down her neck.

"You can see them more clearly in the winter." Sylvie let the fullness of the black sky fill her vision. "The air is thinner and more transparent." At least that was what Grams had explained to her one night when they'd gone for a walk and had witnessed fourteen shooting stars in thirty minutes.

"Everything seems brighter this time of year." Royce turned his face to hers, firing up that spellbinding smile again.

Oh lordy. Did he want to kiss her? "Mmm-hmm." Sylvie sat up straighter again, her heart doing the Cowboy Cha-Cha. What was she doing out here? With a movie star who seemed to always know the perfect thing to say while she found her tongue all tied up in knots? Sylvie hadn't kissed a man since a disastrous night two years ago when Grams had set her up with a friend's grandson.

"The moon seems brighter too." His voice had lowered to a hum.

"What do you want?" Sylvie quoted out of habit. "You want the moon? Just say the word, and I'll throw a lasso around it and pull it down."

Royce's forehead furrowed. "What's that from?"

"What's that from?" She openly gaped at him. "It's only a line from the best Christmas movie ever."

"And that would be . . . ?"

He was serious! "You've never seen *It's a Wonderful Life?*" And he called himself an actor? "It's a classic. The best. My all-time favorite."

"I've heard about it but I've never taken the time to watch it." At least his confession had an apologetic tone.

"It's a love story at its best." She turned to face him. "But it's also about loyalty and commitment and sacrifice for the greater good. You have to see it. I mean, you *have* to."

"I will," he promised, gazing deeply into her eyes. "The first chance I get."

Now was he going to kiss her? Nerves took over again, and Sylvie looked around them. "So . . . um . . . where are we going now?" They'd almost made it all the way down Holly Lane . . .

"I heard there's a pretty great display at some goat farm outside of town. So I thought we'd end our Parade of Lights there."

Abe's goat farm. They were going to Abe's place? "Oh, we don't have to go all the way out there." What would Abe think if he saw her tooling around in a sleigh with Royce? Probably that she was just another gold-star member of the Royce Elliot fan club.

"It'll be fun," Royce promised. He pulled a Thermos out of his backpack and poured her some hot chocolate.

Abe did indeed have one of the best displays in town. Each year his family outlined every line of their big red barn with colorful bulbs. And this year, the silo was adorned with red and white lights like a peppermint stick. She couldn't imagine where he'd found the cluster of light-up goats wearing red and green scarves, but they definitely completed the look.

"That's hilarious. Look at the goats." Royce snapped a picture on his phone. "Can you get closer?"

The driver turned onto Abe's driveway.

"We don't have to get closer." Sylvie's head swiveled side to side. Why had her heart suddenly started to pound harder?

The front door of Abe's house opened and a shadowy figure emerged. She'd recognize that plaid trapper's hat anywhere. "We should go. We should—"

"Sylvie?" Abe jogged toward the sleigh, slowing when he got close.

Busted. "Hi, there!" She waved . . . maybe a little too frantically. "How's it going? Royce and I were just having a little . . . business meeting." In a horse-drawn sleigh. "While we look at Christmas lights. Yours are the best! We love the goats."

"Thanks, I like them too. Sorry, I don't have time to talk now." He started to back away. "Sunny is in labor."

"Sunny?" Royce asked warily.

"She's in labor? Already?" Sylvie stood up. "I'd love to see the baby!"

"Someone's giving birth in your house?" Royce wore a horrified expression.

"Sunny's a goat," Sylvie told him. "I should stay and help."

Abe stopped abruptly and focused on her with a rare hopefulness brewing in his gaze. "I'd appreciate that."

She started to stand but Royce tugged on her coat. "We haven't even talked about the movie scene yet. We have a lot to discuss."

"Right." This whole evening was supposed to be about saving the café. She sat back down next to him. "I guess we have to go."

"See ya, then." Before she could read his expression, Abe turned and jogged to the barn, where he disappeared.

The sleigh lurched forward while she got Crumpet resettled on her lap underneath the blanket.

"So Gabe is a friend of yours, huh?" Royce picked up his travel mug.

"Abe," she corrected. "And yes. He's a friend." Someone

she'd casually interacted with almost every week since he'd taken over the farm. They'd chat when he dropped off her order, and he'd often tried some new concoction she was working on in the kitchen. He always gave her his honest opinion. But lately there'd been those moments. The glances and the protective way he'd touched her when he'd caught her. There'd been an energy purring between them. At least she'd thought so. And she hadn't realized until tonight, until right now, how much Abe's opinion mattered to her. But she couldn't sort any of those things out right now. "So what scene are you planning to film at the café?"

"We have it all figured out." Royce's eyes weren't smoldering anymore. "We'd originally planned to do a quick shoot at a coffee shop in Jackson. So we'll just swap out the location and move it to the café. The scene is short and simple. Jun and Barbara think it'd be great if you made a cameo as the waitress."

"Me?" Her body startled, and Crumpet poked his head out of the blanket as if he wanted to make sure she was okay. "Oh, no. That's so generous, but I . . . I think you misunderstood my request. I didn't want to put myself in the spotlight. Just the café."

"You won't have a huge part," he went on. "You'll only have to walk out and deliver some food to the table."

"I have to carry out food?" In front of a camera? With lights and action and all that? Royce clearly didn't know her at all.

"Yes, you'll have to carry food." He squeezed her mitten-clad hand. "You do it every day. I'll help you. I think you'll be great."

No amount of practice was going to help her walk and

balance a tray of food at the same time with all of the crew watching and the cameras pointed in her direction. "I can't do that." He might as well know now. Even just the thought generated a fair amount of perspiration underneath her winter layers. "But you know what? I'm sure my sister would love to take the job. She'd be perfect. She's used to being the center of attention. In fact she won a pageant in high—"

"We don't want your sister." Royce gazed at her intently, the lights from the houses they were passing casting a glow on his face. "We want *you*."

He didn't understand. She *wanted* to be someone who could stand up in front of anyone with confidence and eloquence. She wanted to bravely say yes even when fear gripped her by the throat. She wanted to be the one who people noticed for once. And with his help, maybe she could be. She forced a smile. "Maybe you're right. Okay."

"Okay." The actor turned up the voltage on his smile. "I'll let Jun and Brenda know you're in. And when I get back tonight, I can send you the script so you can see the scene."

"Good." She cleared her throat. "That's great." She could do this. She would do this. Then Jerry would have no choice but to keep the café open.

The rest of the way back to her house, Royce filled her in on the crew, but she didn't hear much. When the sleigh glided to a stop, her nerves took over again, bunching up in her stomach. He walked her to the door with his arm wrapped around hers while she held Crumpet snuggled into her coat.

"Thanks for the sleigh ride." She paused underneath her porch light.

"I'm glad you had a nice time." Royce's steady stare made

her heart throb with anticipation. But was he making an advance? Was he preparing to kiss her? Was he waiting for her to make a move? She didn't have enough experience to know.

Unable to languish in suspense, Sylvie raised her eyes to his. "I don't play games. Mostly because I have no idea how." She hadn't exactly had many opportunities to evaluate what a man's attentions meant. "So what is this? What do you want from me?"

"I just want to know you," he answered quickly. "I want to spend time with you. And maybe I can help you with the café in the process." The earnest sincerity in his expression disarmed her. "I'm not playing games. But I would like to kiss you if you're okay with that."

"I'm okay with that," she half whispered. The kiss seemed to happen in slow motion—just like in the movies—with his face drawing closer to hers, their eyes finding a connection point until hers closed and their lips touched in a breathless instant. His mouth was warm and chocolatey. It was a good kiss, she supposed. But there were no fireworks going off in her heart, no earthquaking tremors in her knees. Maybe those things were just legends. Or maybe they came later . . .

When Crumpet started to lick their chins, Royce pulled away and smiled. "I'd like to see you again. Maybe in a few days?"

"Maybe." Unless she woke up from this strange dream where a famous actor had kissed her.

"I'll call you." How did he make his eyes twinkle like that? "Or better yet, I'll stop in at the café and visit."

"Sure. Stop by anytime." Sylvie opened her front door. She'd have to start wearing her nice jeans to work. She stepped inside the cozy warmth of her bungalow and set Crumpet down before disrobing from her many winter layers.

"You were gone an awful long time," Gramps said from the couch. He paused the movie he was watching. "Did you have a good time?"

"We had a great time. He took me on a sleigh ride around town." For some reason she didn't feel like talking about Abe's farm or the kiss. So instead of elaborating, she joined him on the couch and grabbed the popcorn bowl. "What're you watching?"

"Some Royce Elliot movie. I thought I should see what all the fuss is about." Gramps started the film again. "He's no Jimmy Stewart, I'll tell you that. Every time he flashes that smile I'm tempted to put on my sunglasses, his teeth are so white."

"It can't be that bad." Sylvie settled back, more relaxed than she'd been all night. Crumpie jumped up and wedged himself between her and Gramps, uttering a loud, contented sigh. Her doggie obviously agreed.

"I think the movie's almost over, but I can start it at the beginning if you want." He clearly didn't want to start it over, judging from his slight wince.

"You don't have to start over. I can watch it another time." She likely wouldn't be awake much longer anyway.

Royce came onto the screen again with his larger-than-life personality and she marveled at how different he looked on TV, shiny and ethereal. He was walking through a snowy field with a woman whom Sylvie assumed was the female lead, a cute brunette with plumped lips and smooth skin and rosy cheeks, probably the type of woman he was used to spending time with. "Can you turn it up?"

Gramps obliged with a grunt, muttering something about movies these days.

"I just miss my mother so much," the woman was saying with sad eyes.

"I think when you love someone deeply, their magic becomes a part of you." Royce put his arm around her.

Wait a minute. Sylvie sat straighter, on high alert.

"And when they're gone that magic lives on through you," he went on.

She snatched the remote off the couch cushion and rewatched the clip.

"What're you doing?" Gramps grumbled. "Once was bad enough."

"I'm . . . it's just . . ." Had Royce used that same line on her? "I feel like he said something similar to me tonight. In the sleigh." But surely she was wrong. He wouldn't have used the exact same words he'd read off a script, right? He wouldn't. "I was talking about how much I miss Grams, and he said something a lot like what his character just said." She went back through the moment in her head but couldn't seem to recall the exact words he used. "It was definitely a very similar sentiment."

Her grandfather shrugged. "Maybe his movie lines get stuck in his head and he doesn't even realize it. Kind of like a song or something."

"Maybe . . ." Yes . . . she could see how that could happen. He probably had to rehearse those lines over and over.

Gramps paused the movie and turned to her. "Did he seem genuine when he said them?"

"I think so." But now she couldn't be sure. "How would I know?"

Her grandfather's mouth rumpled thoughtfully. "I guess you can't know for sure. You have to decide if he's worth the benefit of the doubt, I suppose."

"Well, he seemed thoughtful and kind." And not just any man would think up a sleigh ride to look at Christmas lights. "So I guess I can give him the benefit of the doubt."

For now.

Eight

"WHAT DO WE THINK, CRUMPIE?"

Sylvie inspected the table setting and rearranged the mini-poinsettias she'd picked up at the flower shop. Her kitchen table looked quite festive, if she did say so herself. Facing happy hour with her sister was easier if Sylvie focused on the presentation details rather than anticipating what Claire could possibly want to discuss with her.

Her sister never came to her unless she needed something—help on this committee or that committee, or someone to take care of their cats while she and Manuel were on vacation. But if Claire only needed her to help out with something, she would've put Sylvie on the spot rather than setting a special time to get together.

"Yip!" Crumpet sat taller on his booster seat, sniffing in the direction of the appetizers she'd set out. He was sure a handsome devil wearing his best Christmas sweater.

"Yes, I know you love my cranberry Brie bites." She'd let the dog sample one last night. "But maybe you'd like to try the sweet potato bites instead?" She'd used her kitchen torch to toast the marshmallows on top perfectly golden brown.

"Yip! Yip!"

"Sweet potato bite it is." Sylvie selected a particularly large one and set it on the dog's plate.

Crumpet happily licked at the marshmallow a few times and then shot her a huge grin before taking a bite.

"After you finish that one, you'll have to get down for a while." So she could hide Crumpet's booster seat. Claire didn't approve of her dog sitting at the table with them. And yes, maybe it was slightly overkill for Crumpie to have his own place at her table, but he was the best boy. Sure, once in a while he yipped politely, but he didn't beg or whine for food. Probably because he knew Sylvie would feed him plenty of scraps.

"Auntie Claire just doesn't understand us, does she?" Before this boy came into her life, she wouldn't have called herself a dog person. She'd always liked animals, but they'd never had them growing up. Too much work, her parents always said.

"You're one of the best things that's ever happened to me." Sylvie patted his head while the dog licked every last morsel off his plate. "But I'm afraid it's time to get down now." She pulled him into her arms, and he gave her cheek a sugary kiss.

"Are we having company?" Gramps lumbered into the kitchen, his wispy silver hair all askew from the nap he'd been having on the couch.

"Yes. Claire's coming over. Remember?" Sylvie set Crumpet down and hid his booster seat in a cabinet.

"That's right." Gramps patted down his hair and snuck a Brie bite from the platter. "And I also just remembered I have a lot of work to do in the garage."

"Oh no you don't." She handed him a glass of her white Christmas sangria, which she'd garnished with rosemary sprigs and cranberries, to sway him. "You're not leaving me alone with her. She's coming to see both of us."

"She's not coming to see me." Gramps set his glass on the counter, his signature stubbornness pulling at his mouth. "She's coming to harass me about Joanie. Or some other potential match. So I'll be out in the garage finishing up that rocking horse I promised for the toy drive." He made his way to the coatrack and started to bundle up.

"Fine then. Go ahead and abandon your sweetest granddaughter," Sylvie teased. "I'll send you out there with a plate full of yummy appetizers and a heart full of guilt."

Gramps chuckled while he wrapped the scarf Grams had knitted him around his neck and then came over to kiss her cheek. "You are the sweetest. That's for sure."

"Yeah, yeah, yeah." She found a paper plate and selected a few sweet potato bites, Brie bites, bacon-wrapped dates, spinach puffs, and parmesan-encrusted Brussels sprouts. She always went overboard when Claire came to visit.

Her grandfather took the plate. "I'll pop in to say hi soon," he promised before disappearing out the back door.

Sure he would. Sylvie had half a mind to take the party out there. But she didn't feel like huddling next to his space heater while he sawed and hammered. Instead, she cleared away Gramps's place setting so she didn't have to explain why he hadn't joined them.

"I guess it's just you and me—" She looked around for Crumpet, but he'd abandoned her too—already curled up in his cushy bed next to the fireplace across the room.

"A lot of help you two are," she mumbled as she got to work mixing up two fresh glasses of white Christmas sangria.

A few minutes later, her sister breezed in through the front door. "Sorry I'm late."

She was actually five minutes early.

"I've been working with the Miss Christmas committee all morning." Claire shed her coat and hung it up on the rack before lugging her leather purse/briefcase combo to Sylvie's table. "Hey, you should fill out the entrant's form for this year's title."

"Yeah, right." The Silver Bells Miss Christmas honor used to recognize the woman in town who displayed the most holiday spirit, who practiced the most generosity, and who had made the most contributions to making Silver Bells a Christmas wonderland each year.

Grams had won the title three times in her lifetime. But these days the whole spectacle was nothing more than a popularity contest. Hence the reason Claire had won it twice and Sylvie had never even entered. "Why don't you put yourself in the running?" she asked. Her sister could easily pull off a three-peat.

"I'm the committee *leader*. That would be a conflict of interest." Claire set her purse on the table, pushing two of the mini-poinsettias out of the way. "Besides, I've already won *twice*."

Drinks. It was time to get the drinks going. Sylvie picked up both glasses and handed one to her sister before sitting in the chair across from her. "We both know I would never get enough votes to be Miss Christmas." Gramps would vote for her for sure. And maybe Claire out of obligation and pity, but that was about it. "Besides, I have enough on my plate trying to convince Jerry to hold on to the café for a few more years." That mission had to be her singular focus for the duration of the holiday season.

"Yes, I heard about that." Her sister carefully inspected the appetizers on the platter before selecting one of each kind. "I think it's great you want to save the place, Syl. But I don't want you to be disappointed if he decides to sell."

That was Claire's *nice* way of saying she didn't believe Sylvia could pull off a miracle like this in a few weeks. And maybe the old Sylvie couldn't have. But she'd changed a lot in a few days. She'd gone on a date with a famous actor. She'd agreed to be in a movie scene! But she wouldn't breathe a word of those secrets to her sister. She was nervous enough without Claire pressuring her, too.

Speaking of pressure. "This might be a good time for you to evaluate what you really want to do with your life." Her sister withdrew a leather-bound notebook from her bag. "Surely you don't want to be a baker forever."

Sylvie sipped her drink. She should make up a drinking game whenever Claire came over for happy hour. Every time her sister fired off a veiled insult, she'd take a glug of white Christmas sangria. But she'd likely end up completely pie-eyed, and who knew what she'd say then. In situations like this, her best course of action was always to change the subject. "I'll think about it, but . . . uh . . . wasn't there something you wanted to talk to me about?"

"Yes, actually." Claire pulled a pen out of her purse without even having to dig around. "What are the pros and cons of being adopted, would you say?" Her sister gazed at her expectantly with the pen poised over her notebook paper.

"Excuse me?" Maybe she'd already had too much white Christmas sangria. Sylvie eyed her glass. Nope. Still three-fourths left. "I'm not sure I understand what you're asking."

"You know." Her sister made a move-it-along gesture, her hand rotating in an impatient circle. "What do you like about being adopted? And what do you dislike about being adopted?"

She moved the pen back over the page of her notebook, but all Sylvie could do was gape at her.

"Come on." Claire's left shoulder slumped the way it always did when something irritated her. "There have to be both positives and negatives. And I would like to know what they are."

"Why?" Sylvie blurted. What . . . did Claire think she kept her own notebook of pros and cons regarding something that had happened to her when she was a baby? Sylvie knew nothing about her birth parents. They had requested a closed adoption, and she supposed they had their reasons for that. Of course she'd wondered about them, but Grams and Gramps and Dad and Mom and Claire and her brother Brando were her family, plain and simple. Every family had their challenges. She wasn't sure going over all the pros and cons of their family with her sister would result in an uplifting or productive conversation.

Claire's audible sigh signaled waning patience. "Do you feel like an outcast in our family?"

Sylvie flinched at the interrogation. "I have always felt loved." Her parents and grandparents had given her everything, and her gratitude for them often brought tears to her eyes. A gust of courage prompted more. "But, yes. I guess there have been times when I've felt like an outsider." Wasn't that normal?

"But not because we made you feel that way, right?" Her sister's posture went rigid. "You must've felt that way because you knew you were adopted. I've never looked at you as anything other than my real sister, Syl." The words were firing out of Claire's mouth, not giving her any chance to respond. "I know we don't always see things the same way, but I love you."

Sylvie very nearly dropped her glass. *Love?* Had Claire just told her she *loved* her? It had been *years* since her sister had said those words.

"And I just need to know that you've been happy being a part of our family," her sister went on. "I need to know that you've felt valued and cared for and . . . happy. I just really need to know that you've been happy."

Sylvie took in her sister's anxious expression, the uncharacteristic tremor in her hands, and her heart dropped. "Oh my God. Are you dying?"

"No." Her sister's chin lifted as though she was trying very hard to shrug off an obvious weight burdening her shoulders. "I haven't been able to get pregnant. In almost two years of trying." A slight waver in her voice was the only indication of the sadness her sister had to be keeping trapped inside. "The test results say it would be difficult for me to carry a baby. So now it's time for Manuel and me to consider adoption."

Sylvie tried to swallow back her tears. She really tried, but . . . oh, she'd never been one for hiding her feelings. They came running out of her in the tears and the sniffles. "I'm sorry. I had no idea." She blotted at her cheeks with a napkin. "You've never said anything." All this time her sister had been walking through a struggle and here Sylvie'd thought Claire's life was perfect.

"Now you can understand why I'm asking."

Sylvie shook her head. How in the utter hell was her sister sitting there with her shoulders straight, eyes clear, expression all business? Sometimes she wanted to shake Claire's shoulders and yell, "It's okay to have feelings!"

Meanwhile, Sylvie let a few more tears slip out. "Um. Sure. Yeah. Well . . . I'm very grateful that I was adopted into our family." It helped that she fully believed her birth mother must've have loved her, going through all of the trouble to have her and then giving her to someone else. "Being different from you and Brando mostly doesn't bother me." At least not as much as it used to. "Listen, the bottom line is you and Manuel would be amazing parents. I know you would give a child a very happy and loving home like the one I've had." Regardless of the pros and cons.

A crack appeared in her sister's mask, a slight tensing of her jaw . . . as though she was straining against emotion. "Do you really believe that?"

"I really do." For all her sister's intensity, Claire was dedicated and loyal, always putting others' needs above her own. Wasn't that the very definition of a mother? "But I'm not sure an adoption process is something you can run like a business. I mean, from what I've heard you don't have a lot of control. You have to be open and flexible."

"Perfect. I'm very flexible." Her sister raised her glass with a bright smile and took a sip.

Sylvie struggled not to laugh. "It might help to talk to someone who's been through—"

The back door opened, sending in a whoosh of frigid wind. Gramps shuffled inside, rubbing his hands together as though warming them. "Hiya, Claire."

"Hey, Gramps." She checked her watch. "Yikes. I have to get going soon. The town council has a budget meeting this evening." After shoving her notebook back into her bag, she pulled out the chair next to her for their grandfather to sit. "Have you asked Joanie out on that date yet? Because if not, I was talking to Winifred and—"

"Yep," he interrupted. "Sure have."

Sylvie sent him a silent reprimand. *Liar.* He should know better. Claire would realize he'd fibbed within an hour of leaving the kitchen and she'd be right back on their doorstep.

"Good! You should take her to that new Italian restaurant in Jackson." Claire magically pulled her phone right out of her purse—again, no digging involved. "I have an in with the manager there. I could easily get you a reservation."

"Maybe." He sent Sylvie a panicked look. "We'll see."

And this was why it never paid to lie to Claire.

"How about Saturday night?" her sister pressed. "I can give my friend a call right now." She waved her phone around.

Gramps's cheeks turned ruddy. "Oh, I think Saturday's out. I have to be here for Crumpet while Sylvie goes on another date."

Sylvie kicked him as gently as she could under the table, but it was too late.

"*Date?*" Claire asked, wide-eyed. "You went on a *date?*"

"Did I say date?" The poor man started to sputter. "Heh, heh. I think that new blood pressure medication is messing with me again. I meant to say that I have to be here for Crumpet while Sylvie goes to *work*."

"Oh, come on. It's too late to backpedal now." Claire leaned halfway over the table, invading Sylvie's personal space. "You *have* to tell me who you went on a date with. Abe? It was Abe, wasn't it?"

"No." Damn it. She should've gotten pie-eyed while she could. "Why would you say that?"

"Abe's always liked you." Claire casually sipped on her drink. "Ever since, probably, third grade."

Heat flashed across Sylvie's forehead. "Maybe Abe had a crush on me once, but that was years ago. Trust me." Her hands fidgeted with a napkin. Sure, they'd shared a charged moment here and there, but he didn't have *feelings* for her. "That's ridiculous."

"I'm sorry, but he's still crushing. It's obvious to pretty much everyone except for you." Claire popped a Brie bite into her smirky mouth.

"Whatever." Her sister thought she knew everything. "I went on a date with Royce Elliot." Ha! What would Claire say to that?

"*You're* the mystery sleigh ride woman?" Claire slammed her glass down, but thankfully it didn't shatter.

Sylvie moved her sister's glass out of reach. There was no reason for Claire to take her shock out on the nice crystal. "How'd you know about the sleigh ride?"

"Everyone in town has been talking about how Royce took some woman on a sleigh ride last night." Her sister stared at her, blinking like she'd never seen Sylvie before. "But no one seemed to know who she was. We assumed it was a cast or crew member."

No one would ever assume Sylvie West had gone on a date with a movie star, that was for sure. "It was no big deal." But it kind of was. He'd kissed her and everything.

"You went out with Royce Elliot." Her sister's head was shaking. "*You.*"

"Why is that so hard to believe?" she asked, even though she knew the answer. Claire clearly couldn't believe that someone like Royce would be interested in someone like her.

"He's a lucky guy, if you ask me," Gramps interjected. "Personally, I think you're too good for him."

"It's not that it's hard to believe," Claire lied. "It's only that . . . well . . . he doesn't seem like your type, that's all."

Now who was the one backpedaling? "Well, for someone who isn't my type, he was certainly very attentive." She couldn't resist messing with her sister, given that utter disbelief parting her lips. "He made me hot chocolate and he kissed me good night." Just when she thought Claire's eyes couldn't get any wider.

"And he asked if she wanted to go out again," Gramps added.

"Wow. That's great, Syl. Really." The shock on her sister's face turned into something else . . . skepticism. "Just . . . you know . . . be careful. Okay? I mean, you don't know him very well. Right? I don't want you to get hurt."

Sylvie took a drink. Veiled insult number five? Six? "Yes, because clearly a man like him wouldn't really be interested in a woman like me," she said when she set down her glass.

"That's not what I meant, and you know it." Claire stood and gathered up her bag, quickly shoving it onto her shoulder. "I need to run. We can talk about this later."

"Sure." Sylvie stood too. They would not be talking about this later because all Claire would do was ruin the fun she was having with the man. Maybe Sylvie didn't want to be careful for once. Wasn't it time she went on a few dates? Even if they were with the wrong man?

After she closed the door behind her sister, she went back into the kitchen and sat across from Gramps.

"What did she want to talk to you about if not Royce?" He was working his way through the uneaten appetizers on her sister's plate.

"She wanted to know if I've been happy in this family. Being adopted." She didn't expand on why Claire had asked. The news wasn't hers to tell.

The question seemed to startle Gramps. He dropped the spinach puff back to the plate and dusted the crumbs from his hands. "What did you tell her?"

Sylvie reached her hand to his. "I told her that I love being a part of this family. Even with all its quirks." And they had their quirks. That was for sure. The biggest one being her sweet baby brother. "I feel very blessed."

"Me too." He patted her hand over his. "Sorry I spilled the beans about Royce. I thought for sure she'd heard from someone else and she was going to interrogate you."

"It's not your fault. She would've found out eventually." Sylvie hadn't wanted to tell her because she'd known exactly how Claire would react.

And what if her sister was right?

Nine

❧❧

"WE NEED SOMETHING BIG."

Sylvie sat at her desk in the café's kitchen with her head bent over Grams's handwritten recipe book, the dishwasher softly swooshing nearby while Crumpie napped in his bed at her feet. "We need something really incredible."

"Everything you make is incredible." Jen ran a rag over the prep counter. "And you've been sitting there obsessing for hours now."

Hours? Sylvie glanced at the clock. How was it almost closing time? After the early morning rush had died down, the restaurant had cleared out, minus people popping in for scones and muffins and coffee to go. She'd lost herself in these pages, flipping through her grandmother's notes, searching every entry for the magic holiday elixir that would help her save the café. "I can't seem to stop obsessing." The date on her open paper calendar had her stomach knotting up. Time was passing much too quickly. Yes, the film crew would be shooting a movie scene at the café, but not until December 23. In the meantime, she needed more momentum—something special to tease for the menu. Something new and exciting to draw in all of those crowds she'd promised Jerry. "If I come up with something good enough, we can feature it in the movie scene too." But it had to be a recipe that would make the Christmas Café famous.

"I still can't believe you're going to be in the movie."

"Neither can I." But she couldn't think about that right now. Sylvie flipped a few more pages in Grams's recipe Bible. *Peppermint Pie.*

"Ohhh. I have an idea." Sylvie paged back to the chocolate mocha cake she'd seen earlier. "What if we combined the peppermint pie and her famous chocolate mocha cake to come up with an epic new dessert?"

"You really think that would work?" Jen tossed the rag into the laundry pile.

"I don't know. But I have to try." She reached down to pat Crumpie's head, mulling over the possibilities. "We could put layers of the buttercream icing between the layers of chocolate mocha cake." Sylvie popped out of her chair. "We could pile on the peppermint mousse frosting like whipped cream!" If that didn't get people excited about the Christmas Café, nothing could. "We'll call it Grams's Peppermint Mocha Cake! It can be a play on everyone's favorite holiday coffee drink! We could even make the cake look like a mug . . ."

"I love it." Jen stepped out of her clogs and into her boots. "But I've gotta run. We're trying out a special Jazzercise lunch hour at the rec center."

"We can talk more about it tomorrow." Sylvie sat back down, already jotting a few notes. "Thanks for cleaning up." There still might be a few more orders coming in for the next half hour, but at least most of the work was done for the day.

"You bet." Her friend zipped up her coat and left.

Hmm. Sylvie stared at the pie recipe. She'd have to adapt the filling to be more like a frosting in order to give it that whipped cream look . . .

The back door to the alley creaked open and Sylvie turned around, expecting to see Abe, who was officially ten minutes late making his delivery, but instead her brother walked in.

"Surprise!" Brando held out his arms.

"Yip! Yip!" Crumpet shot out of his bed growling and barking in full security detail mode.

"Who's this little dude?" Her brother dropped to his knee and had the dog's leg twitching in bliss within three seconds.

"That's Crumpet. I adopted him." Sylvie almost couldn't believe her brother was standing there. But, then again, she shouldn't be surprised. He did like to pop in unannounced from time to time. "It's good to see you, Brando." She often still thought of him as a little boy—with tufts of dusty-blond curls and a smattering of freckles across his nose. It was almost a shock to remember how much he'd grown up—he was two heads taller than her and, though his hair was still a bit wild, his face had matured—tanned skin and squared jaw and no more freckles. There were still traces of the mischievous boy he'd been, though, evident in his expressive green eyes.

"Good dog." Her brother stood up and left Crumpie pawing at his leg for more.

"Wow." Sylvie hugged him "What're you doing here? I thought you were going to miss Christmas because of your assignment in Prague." At least that was the last text she'd gotten from him a month ago. As a traveling photographer, her brother had a habit of popping in and out of Silver Bells. She wasn't sure exactly how much money he made following his passion around the world, but he must've made enough to keep him traveling at least. It wasn't like he had to pay rent when he was constantly on the move.

"Nah. We cut the Prague gig short and finished up early." He closed his eyes and inhaled deeply, as if drawing in all of the sugary scents around them. "And I just couldn't miss another Christmas in Silver Bells with you and Gramps. And your food," he added with a wink.

"So you're staying through Christmas?" Sylvie quickly hid her wince under a smile. Her brother was great. She loved Brando. He'd always been funny and energetic and full of good ideas. But . . . he had a tendency to revert back to teen boy habits when he came to visit—crashing in her small den for weeks at a time, filling her sink with dirty dishes, leaving his stuff all over her house, hogging her television (he didn't appreciate classic film the way she and Gramps did, even given his namesake). And last time he'd stayed, Sylvie had even ended up doing his laundry for him after she got tired of seeing his dirty clothes basket sitting in front of the washing machine for nine days in a row. Nine days! Who could go nine days without doing their laundry?

To be fair, he hadn't visited her for a year and a half. Everything could be different now.

"Hey, I was hoping I could crash on your futon again while I'm here." Brando had been using that fun party-boy grin to get what he wanted ever since Grams had told him he smiled like James Dean. He'd inherited their father's expressive green eyes too, so basically it was nearly impossible to tell him no.

But maybe she could try. "Um . . ." Sylvie picked up Crumpet, who'd now started to scratch at her leg so he could get a better view of his new favorite uncle. "How long will you be staying?"

"Not sure yet." Brando walked to the coffeepot and helped

himself to a mug. "I'm waiting for a project that will really inspire me. Could be weeks. Could be months before I find the right opportunity."

That's what she'd been afraid of. She walked to the island a few feet away and pulled out stools for them to sit together. "Are you sure you don't want to stay with Claire? I'm sure she really misses you—"

"Are you kidding?" Her brother dumped a fair amount of sugar and goat's milk into his coffee. He might as well have been drinking hot chocolate. "All I hear from Claire is how it's time for me to get a real job and buy a house and become as uptight and boring as you two are." He sat next to her, wearing that impish grin again. "No offense. I'm an artist, Syl. Claire doesn't get that, but you do. You'd never try to push me away from who I really am."

"No, of course not." She only wanted him to be happy. "It's just that I've got a lot going on this year." She filled him in on the current situation at the café. "So, I have to devote all of my time to saving this place." And she wouldn't have extra hours to devote to waiting on an extended-stay houseguest.

"Then it's perfect timing for me to be here." Her brother scanned the kitchen as though searching for a perfect shot. "I can help, you know. I can take pictures for you. And then I can hit up some friends to post on social media. I can help you save the café."

"That'd be great." But she wasn't sure how he would be able to take pictures of people enjoying their breakfast and coffee at the café when he tended to sleep in until noon. Unless . . . maybe they could focus on her food. She was always seeing amazing shots of delectable desserts in magazines. "I *could* use help with food photography." And hopefully if they drew in more customers, he'd be able to pitch in at the restaurant too. "If things get busier like 1 hope they will, we might need extra help waiting tables. Or in the kitchen. Since you're not working right now—"

"Not sure about that kind of help." Her brother's easy smile had disappeared. "I find that working indoors really takes a toll on my creativity. I'm sure you get that."

"Um, sure, but—"

"Hey, Syl." Teagan poked her head in through the doorway of the main dining area. "We ran out of the maple glazed gingerbread scones."

"Again?" Sheesh. She'd only restocked the case an hour ago. "I'll bring out more." Though she was down to her last dozen in the refrigerator. She'd have to spend half the night baking to ramp up their supply.

"Can you keep an eye on Crumpet for a few?" she asked Brando, removing the scones from the refrigerator.

"Course." Her brother didn't look up from his phone, but she resisted the urge to scold him. She was not his mother.

"I'll be right back." Balancing the tray in her hands, she whirled through the swinging doors that led to the dining room. A few of the tables were still occupied, despite the late hour, and a small line had formed at the baked goods case. That was a good sign, right? Usually by one o'clock in the afternoon, business had died off. Maybe word about the Christmas Café was already getting out because of the movie.

"Everyone's loving the scones." Teagan took a break from manning the cash register to help her reload the baked goods case. "People have been taking them to go all day."

"Wait until they see the treat 1 have planned for next week." She spoke loud enough that everyone in line could hear. "It's a surprise. I can't reveal any details, but it will be heavenly, I can promise you that."

"Can't wait," a woman called from the back.

"It involves chocolate and peppermint," she whispered loudly. "But I can't say any more than that." Maybe the hint would get a buzz going.

"Sounds delish." Teagan went back to the cash register, and Sylvie headed for the kitchen before she got too excited and gave all of her secrets away. She'd have to figure out how to make the icing sturdy enough to maintain a shape, but she could experiment this weekend.

She was just about to push through the kitchen door when she heard a baby start to cry across the restaurant. Aww. Miranda Dunn was trying to wrangle her two toddlers while her newest little bundle of joy screamed. Sylvie rushed to the table. "Hi, there."

Miranda peered up at Sylvie from her knees, where she was trying to wrestle two-year-old Marley into his coat. Most of her curly black hair had escaped from her ponytail and the usual brightness in her lovely amber eyes had dimmed. "Hey," she said wearily.

"Can I hold Paisley? Please, please, please?" She had no problem begging when it came to babies.

"Sure." The young mother offered up a grateful smile. "I hope you remembered your ear plugs today, though."

"Oh, it's fine," Sylvie cooed, carefully lifting the four-month-old into her arms and nestling her in. "We're fine, aren't we, sweetheart? You're such a sweetheart, aren't you?" she murmured in a soothing tone.

Paisley's wail softened into a series of forlorn whimpers. "I know, honey." Sylvie swayed side to side. "Everything'll be all right." She wandered to the Christmas tree to show the baby the colorful lights. "Look. Aren't they pretty?"

"You're a natural." Miranda strapped Marley and Mabel into the Cadillac of all strollers and joined her. "She's been so fussy lately. I think her first two teeth are coming in. Needless to say, we're not getting much sleep."

"Well then, you must take a quiche home for dinner. On the house," Sylvie insisted. "I was going to put the leftovers in the freezer but they'd taste better fresh." Before Miranda could refuse, she called out to Teagan. "Can you wrap up the bacon quiche, please?"

"You don't have to do that."

"I know I don't have to." Sylvie carefully snuggled Paisley back into the car seat that was clipped into the stroller. "I would like to, though."

"Thanks." Miranda gave her hug. "You've really brightened my day."

"And you four have brightened mine." Sylvie walked to where Teagan was packaging up the quiche. "Add some of the Christmas tree cake pops too."

"You've got it." Teagan wrapped up the treats and then handed the package to Miranda.

When Sylvie traipsed back into the kitchen, Brando's gaze was still glued to his phone.

"Where's Crumpie?" Her heartbeat immediately picked up.

"I let him out to go to the bathroom." Her brother pocketed his phone.

"You let him *out? Alone?*" She was already running to the coatrack. "Like, out into the alley?"

"Well, yeah." He frowned. "The dog was scratching at the door and whining. I thought that meant he had to go out."

"Of course, he scratched and whined! He's an escape art-ist!" And Crumpet also knew a sucker when he saw one. Sylvie pulled on her wool beanie. "I asked you to watch him for five minutes." She shoved her hands into her gloves and opened the door. "Geez, Brando. He's not even wearing his sweater!"

"Your dog wears a *sweater*?"

When she shot him a murderous glare, his eyes repented. "I'm sorry. I'll help you look."

They stepped outside, and Sylvie gave his shoulder a shove in the opposite direction. "We have to split up. You go left, and I'll go right."

"Got it." Her brother ambled away cheerfully. "I'm sure he didn't get too far with those little legs."

Ha! He didn't know Crumpet. At the first taste of free-dom, that dog would be sprinting with his silly ears flopping in the wind. She only hoped he wouldn't run out into the street. Or run into a bigger, meaner dog. Or a kidnapper!

"Crumpet!" Adrenaline took over, pushing Sylvie through the snow along the alleyway, searching for paw prints. She should've known her brother would mess this up. The boy—*man*—couldn't even take care of himself! "Crumpet!" she half shouted, half screamed. "Here, boy! Come back to mama!" At the end of the alley, she saw no footprints, so she stepped out onto the main road. *Please please please don't let him get hit by a car.*

"Crumpet!" She stopped and listened for his bark, but the only sound was the car engine noise behind her.

"Sylvie?" Abe's voice called out.

She spun, nearly blind with tears and the cold.

He'd pulled his truck over to the side of the road a few feet back.

"You okay?" He quickly climbed out and rushed to her side.

"Crumpet got out." She turned in a slow circle searching the street. "I don't know where he went. And it's so cold . . ."

"I'll help you find him." Abe ushered her to his truck and opened the passenger's door for her. "How long has he been gone?"

"Probably not more than ten minutes." She did her best to hold back the tears. "But he's quick when he wants to be."

"All right, let's head left on Main Street." Abe got into the driver's seat, blasted the heat, and rolled down the windows. "I'm sure someone's already found him and is bringing him back to the café as we speak."

"Maybe." Pretty much everyone in town knew Crumpet. If someone had seen him on the loose, they could've easily lured him indoors with a treat. She dug her phone out of her pocket and glanced at the screen. "I don't have any messages or texts."

"We'll keep watching." He drove slowly, his gaze darting from the road to the sidewalks.

"Crumpet!" Sylvie yelled out the window. There weren't many people out today, likely thanks to the frigid temperatures. And based on the clouds swirling in the sky, they'd be getting more snow soon. "He's going to freeze." Why didn't her darling dog understand that he was much safer staying close to her?

"Crumpet is very resourceful." Something new hid in Abe's smile, a conspiratorial spirit like they shared a secret between them. And maybe they did share something . . . only Sylvie couldn't figure out what yet. The mystery of it all made her shaky.

"Wait a minute." He brought the truck to a stop by the curb. "Do you smell that?"

Sylvie inhaled deeply, breathing in the fire-scented cold air. But there was something else too. Something savory and aromatic. "Meat. Barbecue."

"Barbecue," Abe repeated, another slow smile spreading across his face. "You know who likes barbecue."

"Crumpet has never met a food he didn't like." But a smell like this one would surely lure him in.

"I'll bet it's coming from the YuleHouse." He eased the truck down the block and parked in front of the A-frame tavern. They both climbed out and raced in through the heavy wooden door.

"Crumpet!" Sylvie rushed to where her dog sat in the seat of honor at the head of a long table, working his way through a small plate of brisket.

"Told you he was resourceful." Abe was cracking up.

"Yip!"

Crumpet peered up at them with a scrap of brisket hanging from his chin and Sylvie cracked up too. "You rascal."

"Sylvie . . ." Carlos Navarro, the YuleHouse's owner, appeared in the doorway. "I'm so sorry. I just called the café to tell you that Crumpet was having a visit. I found him out back by my new smoker . . . sniffing around and shivering. So I brought him in and gave him a snack."

"Thank you, Carlos! I'm the one who's sorry. My brother accidentally let him out." She should text Brando, but maybe she'd give him a few more minutes of wandering around town fruitlessly searching in the below-zero temperatures first.

Carlos waved off the apology. "I probably shouldn't have fed him, but it's hard to say no to that face."

"You're telling me." She couldn't even stare her dog in the eyes when she was trying to discipline him. "Come on, Crumpet." She went to pick him up, but he hopped down to one of the chairs. "Hey now. It's time to go."

Her dog gazed up at her, eyes forlorn and a piece of brisket in his mouth.

"He's welcome to stay a few more minutes." Carlos started to wipe down the bar a few feet away.

"At least let me pay you." After saying it, she realized she didn't have her purse.

"That's cool." The man picked up a crate of glasses and headed for the back. "Consider it his Christmas present."

"We should have lunch with Crumpet." Abe pulled his wallet out of his back pocket. "How about two more plates of brisket and some of your cornbread, Carlos?"

"Coming right up." He disappeared into the kitchen.

Abe gestured to a chair to his left. "Have a seat."

Sylvie only stared at him. This from the man who didn't even want to drink a cup of hot cocoa in her presence the other night? "Really? You want to have lunch with me?"

"Sure." He sat in the chair next to Crumpet. "I'm a big fan of brisket, too."

Ah, that explained it. Sylvie removed her winter layers and sat across from him. "Thank you." If Abe hadn't stopped to help her, she'd likely still be wandering outside in search of her dog. "Crumpet thanks you too."

Her dog was too busy snarfing brisket to agree.

Abe shrugged. "You would've found him."

But she didn't have to search alone. And that had made the whole ordeal easier.

"Two plates of brisket and cornbread." Carlos brought out their order and set the plates in front of them before running the credit card Abe handed him.

"I guess it's a good thing I was late for the delivery," Abe said when Carlos walked away. "Sunny's new kid has had a rough start."

"I totally forgot! Did she have a girl? A boy? Do you have pictures? I wanted to stay but—" She stopped short.

"She had a boy." Abe held out his phone for her to see. "Bambino."

"Oh my." A little fluffier than the older goats, and he had the most unique black-and-white markings. "He's adorable."

"He hasn't been wanting to eat so I have to bottle-feed him." Abe pocketed his phone and then dug into the brisket.

"That sounds fun. Bottle-feeding a goat." Sylvie took a few bites too. Crumpet had finished his feast and hopped down from his chair to scratch at Abe's leg.

Of course. Whenever there happened to be a man around, Sylvie was chopped liver.

"Come here, you little stinker." Abe lifted the dog into his lap and Crumpie curled right up. "So, how was your sleigh ride the other night?"

"Oh. Um." Sylvie found herself unable to look into his eyes for too long. "It was . . . well . . . good. Very productive." She took a glug of the water Carlos had brought with their plates. Whew. Had Carlos cranked up the thermostat?

Abe said nothing.

"I mean, we had business to do . . . or talk about. The movie scene. They're going to film one at the café, so we were sort of discussing that and then . . ." Well, she wasn't about to say that she kissed Royce Elliot on her front porch and quite honestly it hadn't been the thrill she'd expected.

Why didn't she want to tell him? She didn't know. He was looking at her so intently—so patiently—and things were happening inside of her. Weird things. Her heart beat faster, for one. And her legs felt all tingly even though she was sitting. "Wow. It's getting late. I really need to get back to work." She shot up and out of the chair, hastily pulling on her coat. Crumpie jumped out of Abe's lap and whined at her. "We can walk, Crumpet and I." She picked up her pup. "You should stay and finish eating."

"You don't have to walk." Abe stood too, carting both of the half-eaten plates to the trash. "I wasn't that hungry." He bent to pick up the glove she hadn't even realized she'd dropped and handed it to her. "I'll drive you back. I have to leave the delivery anyway."

"Right. Sure," she tried to say casually. But her voice was high and weird too.

Abe waited for her to move first, so she walked in front of him, Crumpet tucked under her arm while she pulled on her gloves and stumbled her way to the front door.

"Easy." Abe rested a steadying hand on her back as they walked out the door.

Now her knees were loose and wobbling. Yes, something was definitely wrong with her.

"Yip!" Crumpet licked her chin. This was all one big adventure to him. Lucky duck. The only emotions he ever felt were pure love and hunger.

"Hop in." Abe opened the truck's creaky door for her.

"Yep. Got it. Thanks." Cradling Crumpet, she scooted into the passenger's seat.

The two-and-a-half minute drive back to the café was awfully quiet, but for once she didn't know how to fill the silence.

"Everything okay?" Abe pulled the truck into the alleyway but didn't cut the engine.

"Yep! Why?" The tingling in her legs had made it to her stomach.

"You're not talking."

He gazed at her again, and those eyes. Wow. How had she never noticed the amber tones in the depths of them?

"You usually talk."

"I have a lot on my mind." Namely what had shifted inside of her. Sylvie climbed out of the truck, and Abe followed her and Crumpet inside, carrying the small box of extra milk, butter, and eggs she'd requested.

"I'll get you a check." She set Crumpie down and turned to go to her desk but somehow Abe was there right in front of her. "Oops." She ran into the solid wall of his chest. She'd never noticed how muscular he was. Must be all that farming. "Sorry." She went to step around him at the same time he tried to step out of her way.

"My bad."

They both dodged in the same direction and collided again.

"Oh geez." A nervous laugh spilled out. "Sorry."

Another secretive Abe smile appeared, and he took her elbows in his hands, gently guiding her to step around him. "There. I'll stay out of *your* way."

"You're not in my way." Now warmth spiraled up through her chest. She had a clear path in front of her, but her head was still angled toward Abe. She couldn't seem to move. Not with his eyes locked on hers. What did she see in them? Intrigue? He leaned back against her desk, one ankle crossed over the other and continued to stare at her like he really saw her. But the real question was, did he *like* what he saw?

A sudden clamoring outside the door interrupted her train of thought.

Brando stepped into the kitchen. "You found him?" Her brother knelt to pet Crumpet. "You could've called, you know. I was worried."

"Right." Blushing furiously, Sylvie focused on scrawling out Abe's check. "Sorry. I was getting around to it. Here you go." She handed the check to Abe, but avoided his eyes so she didn't get lost again. "Thank you for the help."

"Hey, Abe." Brando left Crumpet on the floor flat on his back still begging for more belly rubs. "I heard you were back in town. How's it going?" Her brother clapped Abe's hand in a macho greeting.

"Can't complain."

"What's new?" Leave it to Brando to not know how to read the room.

While they continued chatting, Sylvie stripped off her coat and hat and carted the butter, eggs, and milk to the refrigerator.

Maybe the rush of cold air would put out whatever flames the last half hour with Abe had kindled.

Ten

SYLVIE TURNED UP HER BLUETOOTH SPEAKER AND THEN danced her way to the sink, flicking it on to rinse the red wine sauce off a plate before stashing it in the dishwasher. Royce would be here to pick her up any time now, but she had a strict policy against leaving dirty dishes in the sink. Currently Gramps was snoozing on the couch, and she didn't want him to have to trouble himself with cleaning up anyway. He'd helped her cook, so he'd earned the right to a good after-dinner nap.

Humming "And the Beat Goes On" to herself, Sylvie finished rinsing the plates and then washed the roaster, turning it upside down in the dish drainer.

"Sylvie . . ." Her brother appeared and turned down the music. "Crumpet is eating my shoe."

She spun to give him a look of disapproval but didn't stop dancing. "Are you seriously tattling on a tiny dog right now?"

Ah, that scowl was familiar. "Every time I try to get my shoe back, he runs away from me."

Did he really expect any sympathy from her? "I seem to

remember you doing the same thing to me that time you stole my diary." Sylvie did a spin-turn away from him to turn the music back up, humming again.

"That was different," he pestered. "I wasn't going to *eat* your diary. I was going to read it and blackmail you. Come on. What should I do?"

Sylvie reached into Crumpet's treat jar and selected a bacon biscuit and then handed it to her brother with an extra audible sigh. "For such a big international traveler, your problem-solving skills need work, Brando."

"Treat, Crumpet!" Brando bellowed.

Before he'd even finished saying it, her dog bolted into the kitchen, dropped the shoe at Brando's feet, and sat his little angel butt down, tail sweeping the wooden plank floor.

"I shouldn't even give you this treat after that stunt you pulled."

She could swear her brother's stern frown prompted an eye roll from Crumpet. You didn't see her chastising him for his life choices, now did you? At least not out loud. "Give him the treat or he will start chewing on your shoe again. Lectures don't go very far with a dog."

"Fine," Brando grumbled, tossing the biscuit to the floor before quickly swiping his shoe out of the dog's reach.

Holding the biscuit between his jaws, Crumpie trotted to his bed next to the fireplace and curled up to gnaw.

With that dispute settled, Sylvie turned her attention to more pressing matters. "You need to spend some quality time with Gramps while I'm gone tonight," she half whispered. Gramps could sleep through the vacuum cleaner just fine but the minute you mentioned his name from across the room he was wide awake.

"Sure. Can do." Brando pulled a can of his favorite pale ale out of the refrigerator. He'd taken the liberty of stocking up on beer, and Sylvie had been tempted to remind him that she also needed room in her refrigerator to store things like vegetables and goat cheese.

"It's so weird that you're going on a date." Her brother took a swig. "Did you go on *any* dates in high school?"

"Yes, I went on dates." Kind of. There'd been that one homecoming dance with Nathan Burgess, though he'd only asked her so she would help him with his math homework. "I didn't go on as many dates as you, but we can't all be as charming as the golden boy of Silver Bells, now can we?" She reached out and tweaked one of his curls.

Though he'd never admit it, having two older sisters had been the best thing that had ever happened to her brother. Not only did he spend a lot of time around their friends— well . . . Claire's friends—he also knew how to communicate with women, which had given him a major advantage in the dating game.

"High school," her brother uttered through a dreamy sigh. "I miss those days. Adulting sucks sometimes."

Adulting? Was that what he called his current lifestyle? On the other hand, maybe having two older sisters had been the worst thing that had ever happened to him. Had she helped turn him into a princeling? "Hey, would you mind unloading the dishwasher when it's done?"

"Uh, hmm . . ." Brando's face crinkled as innocently as her pup's. "I don't really know where all of the dishes go in your kitchen, so—"

"I believe in your ability to figure it out." She patted some encouragement into his shoulder. "Try opening a few cabinets."

"Maybe Gramps could help me."

"Help you what?" their grandfather called. She swore his hearing aids had a setting for selective listening.

"Unload the dishwasher," her brother said louder.

"If you need help unloading the dishwasher, you got some serious problems, kid," the man grouched.

Sylvie snickered at her brother for old time's sake.

"I just meant maybe you could show me where things go," Brando replied cheerfully. "Since we're going to be spending some quality time together tonight and everything."

Gramps laboriously pushed himself up to a standing position. "Who says we are?"

Her brother tipped his beer can at her. "Sylvie says."

"You two are babysitting Crumpet for me tonight. Remember? So I was telling Brando it would be the perfect opportunity to enjoy some quality time together." At her grandfather's scowl, she smiled brightly. "You could play checkers. You two loved playing checkers together."

"He's probably afraid I'll beat him the way I used to."

"I let you win when you were a kid. But that ain't gonna happen anymore." Gramps opened the old china cabinet that held their card and game stash and found the checker board. "It's high time I kicked your ass, man to man."

"You're on." Brando sat at the kitchen table with a wink at Sylvie. That was the thing about her brother. He might have struggled with cleaning up after himself, but he got away with it because he was so charming. He could talk to anyone anytime about anything. She envied that.

"Do I get to meet the big movie star you're going out with tonight?" Brando asked.

"Nope." She knew better. Her dear brother had always

managed to embarrass her in front of her crushes at school. One time he'd even told his friend Sylvie thought he was hot right in front of her. "You don't *need* to meet the movie star I'm going out with." Times hadn't changed all that much. Brando would still relish the chance to embarrass her. In fact, if the temperature outside wasn't hovering right around fifteen degrees, she would wait for her date on the porch. "I'll just watch out the win—"

The doorbell cut her off. Before she could step into her boots, her brother shot past her to open the door, aiming an evil grin at her the whole way.

"Come on in." Brando ushered Royce into her living room.

Why did the man always insist on being early? "Actually, we really should get going," Sylvie tried to say over Crumpet's overjoyed yelps, but no one seemed hear her. By the time she had her boots on, her dog was lying in Royce's arms like a baby and Brando was chatting him up.

"So what exactly do you have planned with my sister tonight?" Her brother's eyebrows raised in an expression so much like their father's she had to do a double take.

"I'm afraid I can't say." Royce's blue eyes held her gaze while his small smile simmered into a grin. "I don't want to ruin the surprise."

Sheesh. He was downright smoldering tonight. Not a hair out of place.

"What time will you have her home?"

Brando's tone snapped Sylvie out of a serious swoon. "I'll be home whenever the hell I want to come home." She grabbed Royce's hand and tugged him to the door.

"Just watching out for you," Brando muttered. "You never can be too careful these days."

"We won't be too late. I promise."

She yanked on her beanie and then hustled Royce out the door so they could be alone. "Sorry about that."

"Your brother seems like a nice guy." Royce held out his elbow to help her down the slick steps. "I get the questions. He's only watching out for you."

"I guess he's forgotten that I've been watching out for myself for quite a while." Sylvie held his arm all the way to his SUV, where he opened the door for her.

Swoon!

"So he's your older brother?" Royce asked when they were both settled in their seats.

"No, but thanks for that." He just kept racking up the points. "He's the youngest. I'm the middle child."

"Me too." He blasted the heat and pulled away from the curb. "Except I have two older brothers and one younger sister." He paused at a stop sign. "You and Brando don't look much alike."

"No, we don't." She put on a smile in anticipation of his reaction. "Because I'm adopted."

"Oh. I didn't realize."

She'd gotten used to seeing the look of bewildered sympathy when people found out she didn't live with her birth parents, but she truly didn't need any. "How could you have known? It's no big deal. My parents are the ones who brought me home from the hospital. I've always been theirs." As her mother often reminded her. "I don't know anything about my birth parents," she added before he could ask. "It was a closed adoption and I never really wanted to know."

"That's understandable." Royce seemed to have recovered from his surprise. He eased the car down the icy road and

turned onto Main Street. "It sounds like you have an incredible family."

"I really do." Even with her futon-surfing younger brother
and her high-efficiency older sister. She wouldn't trade any of
them for anything. Sylvie watched out the window as Royce
pulled the car up in front of the old second-run movie theater.
The building had always been one of her favorites in town,
with the original brick façade still intact and the oversized
lighted sign.

Now showing: *It's a Wonderful Life*.

Since when? Just yesterday that sign had said *The Sound of
Music* was playing.

"Surprise." Royce cut the engine. "After how much you
talked about those classic Christmas movies on our sleigh
ride, I thought I would rent out the theater so we could watch
It's a Wonderful Life."

She turned to properly gape at him. "You *rented out* the
theater?" Sylvie had to blink a few times. Any minute she
would wake up in her bed with a smile on her face, thinking
about that wonderful dream she was having.

"Yep. We'll have the place to ourselves." He got out of the
car and hurried around to open her door. "Now you can intro-
duce me to one of the best Christmas films of all time. Though
I might have to argue that *Saving Christmas Past* could be your
favorite, if you'd give it a chance."

Sylvie shot him an apologetic smirk. She had no idea what
he was talking about.

"That was last year's release. He offered her his arm again.
"It earned the network the highest ratings in December, I'll
have you know."

"I'm sure it's brilliant. But *It's a Wonderful Life* is timeless."
She hurriedly climbed out of the car and wrapped her arm

through his. "I still can't believe you haven't seen it, especially since you're a romantic leading man."

Royce laughed. "What can I say? My agent got me a part in one and then the rest is history."

They stepped into the lobby, stomping the snow and slush off their boots on the doormat before continuing onto the plush red carpet.

"The truth is, it's easy to get boxed into one thing," he continued. "Once people label you, it's hard to step away and do something different." He hung their winter gear on a coatrack inside the door.

"Yes, I understand something about that." On a much smaller scale, of course. But in school she'd been labeled shy and awkward and naïve—an oddball. Most people in town would likely describe her the same way now. "I couldn't do what you do. Deal with all of that constant attention. I would hate being in the spotlight."

"You get used to it." Royce waved her in the direction of the concession stand, where a bag of popcorn and two drinks already sat waiting for them. "And actually, the attention can be pretty fun. I was born to be in the spotlight, my mom always likes to say."

She could see that in him. His million-dollar grin might light up at any moment. Was it possible that someone could really be that charismatic all the time? Or did he have moments when he only wanted to hide behind the comforts of anonymity? Maybe she would find out when she got to know him better.

Sylvie took her drink and led the way into the dimly lit theater. "Don't you ever get tired of living like that—out in front of everyone?"

"Nope." He followed her into a row in the middle and they

sank down into the velvety folding seats. "Being in the spot-light gives me energy. I love the traveling and the cameras and the busy schedule. Acting is the best job in the world."

"I'll take your word for it."

The lights turned down, and Royce leaned toward her armrest, sitting close and offering her the popcorn. Music filled the theater and the bell tolled and tears immediately gathered in her eyes. She lost herself in the story the way she always did, alternating between smiles and tears during the moments playing out in the simplicity of black and white before them. A few times she couldn't help but point out certain themes to Royce, in case he'd missed them.

"So what did you think?" Sylvie asked on the drive home.

"I enjoyed it more than I thought I would." But his neutral expression indicated he hadn't loved it the way she did. "Movies from that era are a lot slower."

"That's because they focus on storytelling instead of only on the entertainment." Old movies mostly relied on the characters and plot rather than on special effects. "Maybe they're not efficient or flashy, but they get to the heart of emotion." And that was why she loved them. Those movies struck the chords of human emotion in a way some of the newer ones didn't seem to.

"You have a different perspective on life, Sylvie. I like it."

"My Grams always told me I was an old soul." And maybe she belonged in a different era. One that wasn't so rushed and hurried and constantly striving to find the next best thing. Maybe she belonged in that black-and-white film along with Jimmy Stewart and Donna Reed.

"I think you're a beautiful soul."

Her smile faltered. Had that line come from one of his movies too? She hated that she even had to wonder, but the words did have that scripted ring to them. Or maybe she was only being paranoid. She didn't know. And all of the analyzing was starting to get exhausting. "Thank you."

"I liked your commentary in the theater too." Royce parked the car along the curb in front of her house. "I don't usually analyze movies."

"Even the ones you're in?" she couldn't help but prod. What was the point of watching a movie if you couldn't find universal truth in it? Wasn't that the whole point of telling a story?

"Not really. I'm there to play a part, so that's what I focus on." He aimed his smile at her. "But I really like hearing you analyze movies. You're good at it."

"I've had a lot of practice."

Once again, Royce helped her out of the car and they carefully made their way up her icy sidewalk. He paused on her front porch, turning to face her, and the shiver coursing through her had more to do with nerves than with the cold.

"I like hanging out with you, Sylvie."

Was it just her, or did his voice sound deeper?

"I like hanging out with you too." A fluttering ruffled her heart. Surely he was going to kiss her again. Surely—

Yes . . . his face drew closer, and his eyes lowered to her lips. Did she want him to? Sylvie brought her hands to his chest, trying to focus on what was happening instead of what seemed to be missing, but her front door opened in a *whoosh*.

"I heard something out here. Thought you might have been another racoon." Brando stepped out to join them. "Kissing the movie dude. Way to go, Sis. Up top." He raised his hand for a high five.

"Get in the house." Her jaw strained to smile at Royce. "Um. I'm sorry. I should go in."

"No, no. You two carry on." Her brother slipped back inside.

"Don't let me interrupt anything," he said before closing the door.

It was too late for that. Talk about a mood killer.

As usual, Royce waved off the interruption good-naturedly. "You want to come and visit me on the set tomorrow? We're shooting in the park again."

"I have to bake extra goodies for the Silver Bells Christmas-Fest this weekend. But I'll try." Truthfully, nothing sounded better to her than holing up in her kitchen. If they were shooting in the park tomorrow, it'd draw a crowd. And she didn't need any big public appearances with Royce Elliot right now. "Good night. Thanks for the movie. It was really thoughtful." He was thoughtful. He was good-looking. He was funny and easygoing. So where were the fireworks?

"You're welcome," he said in that low, alluring voice. "Before I go, I have one more question. I've heard there's a big Christmas ball at that house with the gingerbread lights. Are you going?"

"Oh, uh, no, actually. I wasn't planning to go." How could she go to the Wingate Christmas Ball without Grams?

"Would you go with me?" He twinkled a half-smile at her, the perfect blend of humble confidence.

Sylvie didn't answer right away. He really wanted to be seen with *her* in front of the whole town? "You want to take me to the Wingate Christmas Ball?" Maybe she'd misunderstood.

"I would be honored." He accented the statement with something resembling a bow.

Sylvie quickly glanced around to make sure there were no cameras rolling. Was this man for real? Because sometimes she had to wonder if his entire life was an act.

"I'm a pretty good dancer. I can do a mean Electric Slide."

She laughed. "It's not really that kind of party." The Wingates preferred nostalgia over the latest dance crazes. So there was definitely dancing, just no Electric Sliding.

"Well . . ." Royce stepped closer, into her space. "Whatever kind of party it is, I would love to go with you."

She had to hand it to him . . . he knew how to play the part of the debonair leading man. "Okay. Sure. That sounds like fun." Maybe she was leading lady material. Maybe it *was* time for her to go to the ball again.

Besides, she kind of couldn't wait to see the looks on the Starlets' faces when she walked in with Royce Elliot.

Eleven

WELL, THAT DIDN'T WORK.

Sylvie studied the glob of whipped peppermint frosting that hadn't set up quite well enough to maintain any shape. The whole dessert had collapsed in the middle in a mess of gooey icing and soggy crumbs. Instead of calling this a peppermint mocha cake, she'd have to put it on the menu as "The Blob."

Ugggh. She picked up the platter and shook the unsightly pile into the trash can.

"Hey, I would've eaten that!" Jen slid a tray of peppermint mocha muffins into the oven and then walked to the garbage can, surveying the contents. "Seriously. You've wasted three perfectly good attempts."

"Nobody should eat that. Ever." After three blob-like failures, she might have to admit that she wasn't going to be able to create the most epic, unique dessert Wyoming had ever seen. The problem was, at Teagan's urging, she'd already posted about the new menu item on their social media page. A "teaser," the waitress had called it. Only eleven people had liked the post, but now those eleven people would be expecting something monumental. How could she let them down?

"So they didn't look fancy. I bet they tasted great." Jen moved to the sink and started to wash dishes.

"Maybe if I made the frosting thicker," she muttered, hurrying to scrawl some notes on the new recipe she'd been altering. "And add a thinner coating between the cake layers . . ."

"It's worth a try." Her friend shut off the water and started to dry the mixing bowls. "But you can't stay here all night. You know that, right?"

"Mmm-hmm." Sylvie was only half listening. She had to get this right. This was the recipe they would feature in the movie. It had to be perfect. *More pudding mix in the mousse*, she wrote. *Chill before frosting.* That way the icing wouldn't turn into ooze. Sylvie sipped on the salted caramel mocha Jen had made her after failed attempt number two. The coffee had long grown cold but it helped to give her a second wind . . . er, fourth wind.

"So do you have another hot date with Royce tonight?" Jen stacked the mixing bowls on the shelf.

"Not tonight." Sylvie set down her pen, allowing herself to be drawn out of the recipe conundrum. "But he did ask me to the Christmas Ball."

"The ball?" Jen's gasp sounded like shock and excitement. "You're going this year? With Royce?"

"It looks that way." And it would be fun. Really. Once she got there. But trying to think through what she would wear and how she would do her hair had proved overwhelming. She'd much rather obsess over a recipe.

"Now I wish I was going." Her friend moved around the kitchen tidying up, likely so she could leave. Three o'clock was already too late for Jen to stay when she had a gig.

"You could always cancel your concert," Sylvie suggested. If Jen went to the ball too, she'd at least have some moral support.

"Not this one." Jen started the dishwasher. "It's at that new club in Jackson. One of our biggest venues so far." She approached the desk, looking down at Sylvie, her eyes sharp and knowing behind her glasses. "So you like this Royce character, huh?"

"I do like him . . . and he's fun." And she couldn't deny that he'd been thoughtful when it came to the movie and the sleigh ride. "I'm just not sure he's genuine."

"How could he be? He plays make-believe for a living." Jen cruised to the door and pulled on her leather jacket. She retrieved her guitar case from behind the pantry door. She never liked to let it sit in her cold car. "But who cares? He's fun. And you, my dear, deserve some fun. Speaking of . . . you're not going to hole up here all night, are you?"

"No." She had too much to do at home. "I will only make one more epic dessert attempt and then I'm leaving too."

"I'm calling in an hour to hold you to that," her friend said sternly.

Sylvie grinned at her. "Thanks for handling the cleanup."

"That's why you pay me the big bucks," Jen grumbled playfully as she walked out the door.

With the kitchen quiet again, Sylvie bent her head back over the recipe book. Maybe she could reduce the sugar. If only she could figure out how to—

The door to the dining room creaked open, and Jerry stepped through but stopped abruptly when he saw her. "Oh. Sylvie. What're you still doing here?"

"Just catching up on some work." She scurried back to her mixer, so he wouldn't realize she'd wasted supplies on three failed desserts. "I had a lot to do for the ChristmasFest. And we're getting a lot more foot traffic through here too lately."

They'd been busier over the last week, she was sure of it. "What're you doing?"

A man cleared his throat loudly from behind Jerry. "I have another meeting in an hour."

"Oh. Yes. Of course." Jerry stepped out of the doorway and a suited man Sylvie had never met paraded into her kitchen.

"Sylvie . . ." Her boss hesitated, clearing his own throat. "This is Shawn McGovern. He's the owner of the restaurant that will be purchasing this space."

Flames shot up the sides of her neck. "*Will be* purchasing?" she squeaked. "But you and I had an agreement. You might not sell."

"What's this?" Shawn McGovern glared at Jerry. "My lawyers are drawing up the contract as we speak."

"Well, no one's signing any contract," she informed him. This man didn't belong in her kitchen in those shiny shoes. And what about his slicked hair? He and his *chain* restaurant didn't even fit in Silver Bells!

"Sylvie." A sharp edge cut through her boss's voice. "May I speak with you for a minute, please?" He pointed to the large walk-in pantry.

Oh, yes. They could speak. They'd had an agreement and Jerry would not back out of it now. She marched into the pantry behind him. "You told me I had until the New Year," she reminded him before he could get a word in edgewise. "That's almost three more weeks."

"Yes, but do you really think that's enough time to see much of a difference?" Her boss kneaded his forehead. "I'm not going to sign any contract until the first of the year, but I have to start making plans regardless. McGovern wants to see the space and get some measurements, so I need you to stay out of the way."

A chest-tightening anger boiled inside of her. Jerry didn't think she could do this. He had no confidence in her ability to right the ship. "We're filming a movie scene here. Did you know that?"

"No, but—"

"And I am making the most epic dessert the Christmas baking world has ever seen," she went on, not mentioning the three blobs in the trash can. "It's going to go viral, Jerry. Everyone will want to eat this dessert for Christmas." If she could perfect the recipe, that was.

The man's sigh ruffled the handlebars of his white mustache. "I hear you, Syl, but I need to see a significant bump in revenue. Epic dessert or not, you need to prove this place can be profitable after I retire or there'll be no reason for me to hold on to it."

"I will." The promise came out shaky at best. "During Christmas week, we are going to see a steady stream of new customers coming through here—all the way from Denver, I'll bet." Heck, maybe even all the way from California.

"We'll see." The man's firm frown didn't budge. "But for now I expect you to leave Shawn alone so he can go about his business measuring. Or you'll have to go home for the day."

"Understood." Sylvie smoothed her apron and attempted the yoga breathing Claire had tried to teach her that time they went to a rec center class together. It didn't work, but she put on a calm smile and stepped out of the pantry anyway. She would simply tune out the horrible man eyeing her space with his greedy eyes.

Across the room, Shawn had already started to examine the ovens. "It's a total gut job," he said into his phone. "You should see this place. Everything is completely outdated. These ovens are relics."

And what was wrong with a relic? Sylvie wanted to ask. But Jerry was watching her closely. So she dutifully moved to her mixer and started to set out ingredients for another batch of cookies for the ChristmasFest. If you asked her, older appliances were ten times better than the newfangled ones that were all computerized and broke down after a year.

"We'll need to increase the reno budget."

She tried to tune him out, she really did.

"You wouldn't believe this place, Tony," Shawn barked into the phone. "It's like walking into a *grandma's* kitchen."

Oh boy. Oh no. He had to go there, didn't he? He had to go and insult grandmothers. Sylvie's ire finally boiled over. "And what's so wrong with a grandma's kitchen, huh?" She stalked to where the man stood, spatula waving in her hand. "I will have you know, sir, that my grandma's kitchen was the happiest, coziest place in the world and she made everything with love. I'll bet your grandma did too, didn't she?"

Shawn simply blinked at her, the phone still attached to his ear.

"Sylvie," Jerry growled behind her.

"I know, I know. I'll see myself out for the day." She ripped off her apron and accidentally caught the hem of her sweatshirt in the process, pulling both up over her head. "Oh! Whoa. Oopsy-daisy. Sorry about that." She separated the apron from her shirt and pulled the hem back down to cover up the view of her red bra and her stomach, which wasn't quite held in by the waistband of her yoga pants. Both men had likely gotten a good view.

"Ahem." The righteous indignation heating her cheeks quickly deteriorated into a humiliated blush. Head down, she did a walk of shame past Shawn and quickly stashed the entire mixing bowl into the refrigerator. Then she put on her coat and grabbed her purse. "If you'll excuse me, gentlemen," she said meekly, as she slipped out the door. Once it closed behind her, she inhaled a lungful of the frosty air. Leave it to her to try and make an impassioned point and then flash them instead.

Despair edged in as Sylvie got into her car and drove down the alleyway. How would she make up the kind of money Shawn McGovern had likely offered for the café? She had to come up with more than a movie scene . . . more than a dessert. But she didn't know what else to do. Maybe Royce would have some ideas.

Instead of turning to go home, Sylvie followed Main Street all the way down to the park. When she pulled up alongside the curb near the gazebo, it was clear she wasn't the only one there to get a look at the movie crew. A large crowd milled around the fencing they'd put on the perimeter of the mass amounts of equipment—cameras and lights and huge reflective screens.

"Sylvie!" Claire snuck up out of nowhere and knocked on her window. Yeah, she should've gone straight home. But it was too late to escape now, not with her sister gesturing frantically for her to get out of the car.

"Hey." She begrudgingly joined Claire on the sidewalk.

"Did you come to watch them film? It's so amazing to see this happening right in our own town." Energy practically radiated out of her eyes. Claire pulled on her arm, leading her toward the spectacle in the park, and Sylvie regretted not wearing her snow boots today.

"So, how was your second date with Royce?" her sister asked, half dragging her to the crowd.

Sylvie put on the brakes. "How did you know I had another

date with Royce?" She had purposely withheld that information from her sister.

"I ran into Brando at the market." Her sister snapped a few pictures of the set on her phone.

"I should've known." Brando had always been such a tattletale. "The date was no big deal. We went to see a movie."

"Well, are you going out with him again?"

"Look, they're filming." Sylvie beelined across the snow-covered grass to the fencing, where the largest camera had started to pan across the scene—the same sleigh she'd sat in with Royce last week. Now, though, he sat with his lovely co-star, all snuggled in together beneath a blanket.

"Well, well, well. They look cozy," Claire commented dryly. "He seems to be very good at charming women."

And there it was. Another thinly veiled warning. "He's an actor. And they're filming a romantic comedy. It's his job to sell the scene." And the man was good at that. An expert. His facial expressions were perfectly on target. He stared at the woman sitting next to him with the perfect blend of longing and confidence. In fact, he'd looked at Sylvie like that once or twice.

"Cut!" Another woman approached the sleigh and started talking to the actors, using a lot of hand gestures. Oh, wait. Sylvie squinted. That was Brenda . . . the director she'd met.

"How are things going with Brando staying with you?" Claire asked while the movie crew appeared to make some adjustments. At least she'd dropped the Royce line of questioning.

"Things are fine." She didn't need to give her sister any extra ammunition.

"Okay, but don't you think he's taking advantage of you?

You really shouldn't coddle him." Claire pulled out her phone. "Let's schedule a night when we can all get together for dinner, and then you and I can help him—"

Claire's phone interrupted, breaking out in the "Hallelujah" chorus. *"Hallelujah," was right.*

"Oh—this is Marcy down at the paper." Her sister swiped the phone. "She wants an exclusive interview with the mayor about the film." Claire hurried away, already talking loudly.

When Sylvie turned her attention back to the set, she noticed the crew milling around chatting as though they were on break. Royce hopped out of the sleigh and walked toward her with the producer.

"Sylvie." The man hugged her across the fence, and she was aware of the audible whispers nearby. "I'm glad you came. You remember Jun." Royce gestured to the woman next to him.

"Yes. Hello." She couldn't very well vent to Royce in front of the producer. So instead she made polite small talk. "It looks like things are going well."

"It's been a long morning." Royce said the words too cheerfully to make them believable. "But we're almost there."

"Are you ready for your big movie debut?" Jun asked.

"Yep. Sure am," she lied. "Can't wait."

"Wonderful." The woman flipped through a manila folder she held. "Right now, it looks like we still have the scene at the café scheduled for December 23. Before we break for the holidays. But we'll let you know if the schedule changes at all."

"Sounds great." The manufactured smile made her lips twitch. That gave her a whole week to freak out over dropping the tray of food. Not to mention solving the puzzle of her peppermint mocha cake.

"We'd better get back before our good light starts to fade," Jun said to Royce.

"Right." He gave Sylvie a wave. "I'll see you soon."

"Mmm-hmm." She waved back, the stares of more than one woman boring into her.

"Did Royce Elliot just give you a hug?" Marion joined her at the fence, never content to stay on the outskirts and speculate.

"We're friends." She snuck a glance over her shoulder. People were definitely whispering now.

"Close friends it would seem," Marion prompted, her eyes scanning Sylvie's whole face for information.

"Just friends." It wasn't like she knew the man past his smiles and extravagant surprises. She glanced over Marion's shoulder and noticed a familiar face at the other edge of the crowd. "Excuse me." She sidestepped the woman and wandered to where a certain tall, lanky farmer stood. "Abe?"

"Hey." He shoved his hands into the pockets of his denim trucker jacket and glanced down at her, his cheeks ruddy from the cold.

She wasn't cold. In fact, warmth suddenly hummed through her. "You're the last person I would expect to be watching them film a scene for a Christmas romance."

"Why's that?" He eyed her with a hint of amusement peeking through his frown.

"You don't seem like a romantic." She scanned the scene again because for some reason that felt easier than gazing into Abe's eyes. The crew still hadn't started filming. The makeup people were working on Royce and his costar, and the man had them all laughing. No surprise there.

"And how would you know if I'm a romantic?" Abe leaned his forearms on the fence, lowering his upper body to her height.

Now she had no choice but to look at him. "Oh. Well. Um."

That fever she thought she had the other day might be coming back. "It's just that you . . . uh, I mean . . ." What did she mean? "You're not sentimental." Sylvie winced. That sounded judgmental. "I mean, you don't seem to show your feelings a lot." *Yikes.*

But Abe simply grinned at her. "You might be surprised."

She was surprised. By the way his eyes searched hers. By the softening of his mouth. By the way he seemed to speak to her with only his eyes. His whole face had changed.

"I've never thought real romance should be some kind of big show." He turned his gaze to the sleigh, where Royce and his costar were climbing back in. "To me, romance is in the small things. The everyday moments. Showing up when people need you, letting them see your true self. You know?"

Sylvie blinked at him, gripped by his conviction. That might be the most Abe had ever spoken at one time. And hadn't he just described exactly what she yearned for most? Something so simple and yet remarkably profound. "Yeah. I know," she half whispered.

Abe stood to his full height, his gruff expression taking over again. "I've gotta get back to the farm. I'll see ya."

"Right." Sylvie turned all the way around to watch him walk away. "See ya," she called before he got too far. She did see him. Even though he was walking away from her again, she saw him better than she ever had before.

Twelve

SYLVIE PLUGGED HER VINTAGE RECORD PLAYER INTO THE generator and set the needle on her favorite album—*White Christmas*. There was nothing like listening to Bing Crosby's rendition on an actual record while it skipped and scratched.

Already the music started to fill the park with the Christmas spirit while local business leaders worked on setting up their booths for the town's annual ChristmasFest. Though it always involved a ton of extra work, this might just be her favorite event of the entire holiday season. Crafts for purchase! Games! Ice skating on the frozen pond! In another hour, the live band would start up, and nearly everyone in town would show up to officially kick off the holiday season.

Replacing her gloves, Sylvie hummed along while she organized the individually wrapped sugar cookies she'd spent two days icing. She'd made the typical popular shapes, of course—red-and-white-striped candy canes and pudgy snowmen and green Christmas trees adorned with candy ornaments. She'd also frosted some snowflakes and dusted them with edible glitter. The Santa faces might have been her favorite, with their jolly rosy cheeks and the dollops of buttercream frosting accenting the white trim on their hats. And then there were the snow globes—her greatest work of art out on display. Those had taken her the longest—she'd been meticulous with the details. She'd even made miniature antique Ford pickup truck cookies, frosted them red, and then put them in the center of the snow globes for an added festive affect.

She couldn't wait to see everyone enjoying the cookies and the hot chocolate and coffee she and Brando had lugged along in heated carafes. "Don't you love the ChristmasFest?" she asked Brando, who was still working on finagling the lights she'd brought onto the top of the tent over their booth.

"Yeah, it's real great," her brother muttered. He'd never been a fan of Christmas lights. Too many memories of their father cursing and stewing and losing his temper fulfilling his obligation to Silver Bells. Looking back, it wasn't surprising that Dad and Mom had up and moved to Florida a few years back.

Her brother climbed down the ladder, and Sylvie stepped back to admire the colorful globes. "That looks perfect. Thanks for all of your help," she said sweetly.

"That's a lot of cookies." Her brother eyed the table and stole a snow globe. "You want me to take a few pictures for social media?"

"I don't know. Maybe just of the cookies." She hated taking pictures. Inevitably her eyes would be too squinty or the angle would make it look like she had a double chin.

"Come on. Let me take a few of you and the cookies." Brando finished his cookie and dusted the crumbs from his hands. "We won't post them if you hate them. I promise."

"All right. Fine." She adjusted her hat and lifted her chin just in case.

"You have to smile, Syl." Brando stood at an angle in front of their booth, clicking off what she hoped were test shots. "That's a fake smile. Smile for real." Her brother lowered the camera.

"I never know how to smile for pictures." Showing teeth seemed to be a little overkill, but a closed mouth smile always felt more like smirking.

"Think of Grams pulling one of her pies out of the oven on Christmas." Brando raised the camera back up and snapped. He lowered the camera and checked the screen. "Perfect." Her brother held out the camera so she could see.

"Wow." She looked . . . good. Natural and happy. "How's your photography going, anyway? You haven't said much since you've been home."

Her brother's gaze shot away from hers—a telltale sign that he was hiding something.

"Last time we talked, you said you'd landed this amazing contract with that huge hotel company," Sylvie pressed. He'd been so excited that he'd forgotten about the time difference and had called her in the middle of the night. "You went to Tahiti, right? And then you were supposed to go to Prague?"

"Uh, yeah." Brando came around the table and hunched on the stool next to her. "I got fired. Okay? The people running the Tahiti project hated every shot I took."

"What?" She turned to face him. "But you're so good."

"They didn't think so." Her brother removed the camera from around his neck and turned on the screen, scrolling through a series of pictures. "They said they wanted me to capture the resort and stuff to do in the area." He paused on the picture of a Tahitian woman sitting at a market, working on a beautiful woven basket. Her eyes were focused on the work and her lips were curved with the same sort of pride Sylvie had felt when she put the finishing touches on those snow globe cookies.

"That is a beautiful image." It told a story.

"I like taking pictures of people." Her brother swiped to another shot of a little boy carrying a basket of colorful homemade bracelets. "But that wasn't what the resort wanted, apparently."

"Can I see more?" She held out her hand to take the camera and swiped through picture after picture of faces—all animated and full of life and emotion. Pride swelled in her chest. "These are incredible, Brando. I can actually see the different personalities."

"Yeah. I guess." He took the camera back, shut it off, and looped the strap around his neck again. "But no one seems to want candid shots of real people. They want staged images of models."

Sylvie glanced to her left, where families had started to wander down the sidewalk underneath the canopy of lights at the west end of the park. "Maybe that's what your resort client wanted, but resorts aren't the only clients out there." She stood, preparing herself to hand out the cookies and cups of hot cocoa. "In fact, I think you should take pictures tonight instead of sitting here with me. You could set up a place to take family Christmas shots and offer to e-mail them to people."

"Nah. I said I'd help you and I will." Brando's gaze fixated on a family down the sidewalk.

"You're already picturing how to capture them, aren't you?" Sylvie asked.

He didn't hesitate. "I mean, the gazebo with the Christmas tree in the background would be the perfect shot."

"Go." She pushed his shoulder. "I'll manage."

"I don't know." Brando continued to hesitate, so Sylvie escorted him away from the booth.

"This is one of the best events of the year. You'll get a ton of really fun pictures. What do you have to lose?"

"I guess I could take a few shots. See what happens." He was already walking away. "But I'll be back to help you soon."

Sure he would. Sylvie simply waved, pride pulling at the seams of her heart. Brando was growing up. Maybe his life didn't look exactly like she or Claire thought it should, but he was out there learning lessons and finding himself. She was starting to think that finding yourself was a lifelong pursuit. It always seemed that just when she got comfortable, everything would shift and she'd find herself lost once again.

That's why she needed to hold on to the café. It made her the best version of herself.

"Hey, Syl!" Claire hurried to the table and helped herself to a cookie. "The crowds are here. Look alive!"

"I'm ready." Though her energy didn't hold a candle to her sister's.

For the next several minutes she was busy handing out cookies and filling hot cocoa cups for the early arrivers—the Knowles family with their sweet twin girls and the members of the high school band that tried to charm her out of extra cookies. She turned around from assessing her stock to see Abe walking down the sidewalk.

"Hey. You're busy over here."

"Yeah." She peered at the line starting to form. "Everyone came at once."

"I can help." He joined her behind the table and started to pour hot chocolate. "I got Mom and Dad all set up on the other side of the gazebo. They won't miss me for a while."

"Are you sure?" She handed cookies to a few kids from the choir. "Don't they need your help?"

"Nah. We have all the samples packaged, so people can grab them quick." He found another stack of cups under the table. "They told me to walk around and be social."

"This is a good place to be social." It seemed everyone had a hankering for a cookie and cocoa right now. She fell into a rhythm alongside of him, handing out cookies and napkins while Abe poured cup after cup of cocoa and coffee. He made the kids laugh and shook hands with their moms and dads and wished everyone that passed through a Merry Christmas.

He wasn't outgoing. He wasn't gregarious and overtly charismatic, but he connected with people. He listened more than he talked, that was all.

When the rush had died off, Sylvie collapsed into the chair.

Abe set a cup of cocoa in front of her and then poured one for himself before sitting beside her. "You must be nearly sold out."

"I think everyone comes hungry." Her feet were sore from standing, but it was the best kind of ache.

Abe sipped his hot cocoa and sighed deeply. "You put cinnamon in there, didn't you?"

"I did." Pure delight warmed her through. There was nothing better than seeing someone savor her creations. "Here's a cookie too." She reached to the side, where she'd set aside a snow globe and handed it to him. "You can get back to your parents anytime. I don't want to keep you." That statement wasn't entirely true. She liked sitting here with him, sipping cocoa and having some company while she waited for the next rush. And the more she sat with him the closer she got to uncovering the mystery that was Abe DeWitt.

"I told them to call me if they need me." He checked his phone. "Nothing yet." Abe unwrapped the cookie and seemed to admire the design. "This is a work of art. I don't know if I can eat it."

She laughed. "You have to eat it, or I'll be offended."

"We don't want that." He took a big bite out of the cookie. "*Delizioso.*" He pronounced it with an Italian accent and everything.

"Did you like living in Italy?" She'd always wanted to go. Grams had been there twice and told her the food was the best she'd ever eaten.

"I loved it." A smile reached for the corners of his eyes. "The people are different. Everyone's hospitable." Abe's eyes caught the glow of the lights flickering above them. "And the food. You would love it, Sylvie."

"I think I would." She was so transfixed by the light in his eyes, it took her a few minutes to realize a line had formed at the table again.

Together they handed out more goodies, wishing people a Merry Christmas as they went.

"Actually, your desserts remind me a lot of Italian *dolci,*" Abe said when they were alone again. "They're not overly sweet, just nuanced and flavorful."

"I do love a good lemon ricotta cake." That might be a fun new thing to add to the Christmas Café menu. If there was going to be a menu in the future, that was. She'd rather hear more about Italy than dwell on the thought. "What was the best thing you ate while you were there?"

"Every day I walked to this little hole-in-the-wall bakery and got a vanilla cream cornetto." Abe finished the cookie and sipped his hot chocolate again. "I would go back just for one of those."

"Hmm." She would have to remember that. She'd never attempted the Italian pastry but that didn't mean she couldn't try. "Did you get to travel around? Did you see the Colosseum and the Sistine Chapel and the Spanish Steps?"

"Yes." Abe picked up the carafe and refreshed both of their cocoas. "But I liked the countryside better. The green rolling hills stacked with vineyards and the small farms and the unassuming towns tucked into the valleys." Abe's face had changed again, his mouth curving into a fond half-smile and happiness crinkling the corners of his eyes.

"I can picture it." And she could see Abe there too, smiling the way he was now.

"Italy made me a romantic." His voice dropped lower, and her heart dropped too. "Italy made me believe—"

"Hey, Sylvie!" Royce waved at her from the other side of the gazebo.

It took a few seconds to reorient herself to the Silver Bells ChristmasFest. She'd been in Italy, wondering what the beautiful countryside had made Abe believe . . .

"Hey." Royce sauntered to the table looking ready for a romantic comedy casting call, dressed in a navy wool coat and a red scarf. "These cookies look amazing."

"Help yourself."

"I wish I could try one, but I try to stay away from sugar." The man patted his washboard abdominals. "Can't take the extra calories, you know."

In her opinion, a few extra calories wouldn't hurt him but she didn't say so. "Then no hot cocoa for you, I'm assuming?"

"Nope." How he could so easily dismiss melted chocolatey goodness was beyond her. "But I am hoping you're free to walk around with me. The rest of the cast really wants to meet you tonight."

"Oh . . . no." She looked at Abe and then back at Royce. "I have to stay—"

"Go ahead." Abe refilled her cup with hot cocoa and handed it to her but he wasn't smiling anymore. "Take this with you. I can handle things for a while. When will you get another chance to meet a whole movie cast?"

Sylvie opened her mouth to decline again, but Royce didn't give her the chance. "I won't keep you long. I promise. Just a quick meet and greet. We've got a trailer set up and everyone's hanging out."

"I'm not sure I'm up for a party." Honestly, she'd rather hear more about the vineyards and farms in Italy.

"It's really low-key. Trust me." Royce took her hand and started to lead her away. "Besides, Jun wanted to talk to you about the scene at the café. Just some last-minute details."

She cast one more glance at Abe.

"Really, I'm fine. You go ahead. I'll hold down the fort."

"I'll be right back," she promised. After Abe nodded, she turned and fell into step with Royce.

"This festival thing is pretty sweet." He paused to admire a lighted display of Santa and his reindeer perched on the hill overlooking the skating rink. "It's like a real-life scene from a movie."

"This is one of my favorite events of the year." Sylvie scanned all of the vendor booths lined up along the sidewalk— the homemade crafts and gifts for sale, the special face painting for the kids, and even the pony rides near the gazebo. Lighted displays were interspersed among the trees, giving the entire park a festive glow. It still seemed every bit as magical as it had been when she was a young girl riding on the back of one of those ponies.

"The party trailer is over here." Royce urged her toward a huge bus-like RV. Sylvie followed him up the steps, reeling when she saw how many people could fit inside one of those things. There had to be at least twenty members of the cast and crew milling around, some sitting on the many couches while others stood and mingled.

"Can I get you a drink?" Royce opened one of three refrigerators and took out a beer for himself.

"No, thanks." Who would rather get their calories from beer than chocolate? Besides, the cup Abe had given her was still warm.

"Let's find Jun." He led her past a table covered with store-bought cookies still in their packages. Before Sylvie could comment, Jun approached them, cradling a glass of wine in her hand. "Sylvie! Glad you could come."

"Me too." She quickly sipped her hot chocolate so no one would see through her flimsy smile. She didn't belong here.

"Hey, Royce!" someone called from the back of the bus. "Let's go! One round of blackjack."

"I'll be right back," he promised before rushing away, leaving her alone with Jun.

Sylvie cleared her throat. "So Royce said you wanted to talk about the scene at the café?"

The woman's face blanked for a second but then she nodded. "Yes, yes. I forgot to tell you the details. We need you to check in for makeup at seven a.m. Oh, and we need your measurements for your costume."

"Costume?"

"Right." The woman waved to someone behind her. "Our designer will find you the perfect waitressing outfit to wear."

Waitressing outfit? The hot chocolate curdled in her stomach.

"Just text your measurements to this number." She handed her a card.

"Um. Okay." Sure. She'd love to text her body inches to someone she'd never met. That wasn't weird at all. Sylvie stuffed the card into her coat pocket.

"Other than that, we should be all set," the woman continued. "I'm assuming you've looked over the script for that scene?"

"Yes." Not only did she have to carry the tray of food, she also had to individually serve the desserts without her hands shaking. And she would get to do that wearing God only knew what kind of waitressing costume? Visions of a short skirt and high heels closed in on her, making it difficult to breathe.

She had to get out of here. "Um, I have to run back to my booth," she said as calmly as she could. "Could you please tell Royce something came up, and I'll see him later?"

"Sure thing." Jun was already moving on to talk to someone else.

Without a proper goodbye, Sylvie bolted out of the RV, gasping in a lungful of fresh chilly air. She never should've agreed to this movie scene thing. What had she been thinking? Keeping her head down, she navigated the sidewalk, dodging people and booths. But when she got back to her station, everything had been torn down and was neatly stacked where the table had been.

Abe was coiling the string lights. "Hey. Everything's already cleaned up?" she asked.

"Yeah." He set the lights in their box. "We had another big rush and ran out of cookies and hot drinks, so I thought I'd tear things down and make it easier for you."

"Thanks. Brando can help me load it into my car later." She looked for his smile again but it was gone. "I guess I'll walk around for a while. Care to join me?"

The man hesitated and then sighed. "I probably shouldn't, Syl. You have a lot going on right now. And I . . ." He stopped abruptly. "Well, I should get back to my parents, anyway."

No. That wasn't what he wanted to say. She could tell. "I'm not busy tonight." Yes, she'd walked away with Royce earlier but she wanted to be *here*. With Abe. "What did Italy make you believe?" She hadn't stopped wondering.

"That love is simple." The quiet admission gave her heart a hard tug. "That love should be simple," he amended.

"Yes, I agree," she uttered, venturing a step closer to him.

"Sylvie!" Royce stole the moment. "Jun said you left and I wanted to make sure everything was okay."

"Uh. Yeah." Her lungs were fresh out of air.

"She was just going to walk around the festival." Abe had already started to walk away. "You two have fun. I'll see you later."

"See ya," Royce called cheerfully.

But Sylvie couldn't answer. She could only watch Abe retreat down the sidewalk, taking a piece of her heart with him.

Thirteen

"I CAN'T BELIEVE THERE'RE ONLY NINE DAYS UNTIL CHRIST-mas."

Teagan filled the water glasses on the café table Sylvie had set up for her brunch with Gramps and Claire and Brando.

"All I can think about right now is getting through this morning." Who had time to even start thinking about Christmas Day right now? Not her. She couldn't think too much about anything. Not about the café. Not about Royce. Not about Abe. Right now she had to focus on getting through this meal.

Claire had informed Gramps and Brando they'd better be at the café by ten o'clock sharp so they could enjoy some "quality family time."

Sylvie figured a family gathering would be better off here anyway. In public. Hopefully no one would get too loud with other customers nearby, and she'd also be able to escape to the kitchen if she needed a moment's reprieve.

If nothing else, maybe the chocolate fudge cake donuts she'd made would keep everyone on their best behavior. "This should be a good trial run for Christmas dinner at least," she decided. Brando had missed the last two years and who knew what throwing him back into the mix now would do to the family dynamics.

"At least you don't have two sets of grandparents who are at opposite ends of the political spectrum," Teagan muttered. "Talk about ruining Christmas."

"Thankfully our issues have nothing to do with politics."

"You could always do what I do." Teagan stole a chocolate donut from the platter. "Keep your earbuds in and turn on some music to tune people out. They seriously have no idea. Just make sure you nod once in a while."

Oh, to be sixteen years old again. Actually . . . scratch that. Sixteen hadn't been her favorite year, what with the braces and the unfortunate perm. Maybe eighteen. Yes, she could go back and do eighteen again. That was the year she discovered she could do what she loved for a living. Earning money to bake treats for people? It seemed like a dream! But then she'd won the Silver Bells Christmas Bake-Off with her boozy eggnog fruitcake (assisted by Grams, of course), and Jerry had offered her a job the next day.

"I'm afraid earbuds won't help me today," she told Teagan. Mostly because she couldn't let Brando and Gramps fend for themselves. She would have to claim her rightful place as the family referee. "Thanks for helping me set up. We should have a signal in case I need you to interrupt a heated discussion."

"I'm in." The girl shot her a conspiratorial smirk. "If things get dicey, move your water glass to the right side of your plate, and I'll refill glasses while I chat with everyone."

"Perfect." If any of them remained employed after the

New Year, Sylvie would have to talk to Jerry about giving the girl a raise.

"I'll be watching." Teagan whirled with a swing of her braid and went to check on a nearby table.

"Where are Gramps and Brando?" Claire asked, somehow directly behind Sylvie. "I have a meeting at eleven thirty."

Here we go. "I'm sure they're on their way." She waited until her sister chose a seat on one side and then she sat next to her. Unfortunately, she'd left her referee's whistle at home. "Hey, do you have any updates on the adoption process?"

"We've started the paperwork." Her sister was scrolling through her phone. "There's really a lot to do."

"I'll bet. Let me know if I can help at all. I'd be happy to."

Her sister froze, lifting her eyes away from her phone screen. "Really?"

"Of course." Why did she look so shocked? "I want to be part of the process. I can't wait to be an auntie."

Claire started to blink faster. Wait . . . were those tears glazing her eyes? "Sometimes I don't know if I can do this, Syl. I don't know if I'll be a good enough mo—"

"There're the two best sisters in the world," her brother's voice broke in, and the show of emotion on her sister's face disappeared as quickly as it had come.

But Sylvie didn't move on as easily. Claire didn't know if she would be a good mom? Was that what she'd almost said?

Before she could ask, her brother sat across from Claire while Gramps sat next to him, eyeing her sister warily. "What's a man got to do to get a cup of coffee in here?" her grandfather asked, already wearing a scowl.

Right on cue, Teagan appeared. "Morning, everyone!" She

walked around the table filling mugs from the steaming carafe she held. "How are we today?"

"I'm great." Brando yawned. No surprise there. Sylvie had noticed he'd been up past one o'clock in the morning watching TV. They were lucky he'd rolled out of bed to be here.

"And how about you, Gramps?" Teagan moved on to Sylvie's grandfather. "You're looking very dapper in that sweater vest, Mr. Walt."

"I can't complain." A smile crossing his lips, Gramps lifted his mug and inhaled deeply. "Especially when I've got a full cup of coffee poured by such a nice young lady."

"I'm just glad you two finally made it." Claire dumped creamer into her coffee. "I don't have much time. I have a meeting."

"You're the one who told us to be here at ten." Brando's shoulders took on a defensive stance.

"And it's 10:03," their sister informed him.

Sylvie shared a pained look with Teagan. This gathering was off to a great start. "Look." She pointed to the platter sitting in the center of the table. "I made chocolate fudge donuts." If there was one thing they could all agree on, it was the power of a donut.

"Looks awesome." Brando picked one up and crammed half of it into his mouth.

"Still eating like a barnyard animal, I see," Claire commented.

Teagan winced and skittered away. Sylvie wished she could follow the waitress back to the kitchen, but her mission was to keep this breakfast on track. "I thought we would do a big Christmas meal at my house," she said, trying to steer her siblings away from nitpicking each other to death. "Would four o'clock work for everyone?"

"Manuel and I will plan on it." Claire took a donut and proceeded to dissect it neatly with a fork. "Now Gramps, I talked to Joanie and she said you never asked her out."

"That's because I didn't." Gramps spoke firmly. "And you can't make me. If you like Joanie so much, you take her out on a date."

"No need to get all cranky." Her sister had resorted to her mayoral voice. "I was simply going to say, if you don't want to go out with Joanie, I have another idea. What about Gail McDonald? Sure, she's a few years younger but—"

"Brando . . ." Sylvie interrupted. "How did it go taking pictures of families at the ChristmasFest?"

"Awesome." Her brother dumped a couple of sugar packets into his coffee. "When people found out about it, almost everyone in town wanted pictures taken. It'll take me a while to get them all edited, but then I'll throw them up on a website so everyone can download."

"Why would it take you a while to get them edited?" Claire demanded. "You're literally doing nothing all day, every day. I mean, you have zero responsibilities, Brando."

Sylvie braced herself.

"Who wants some quiche?" Teagan appeared, a true hero bearing savory pastries. "Swiss, bacon, spinach today," she said cheerfully, handing out the plates.

But the distraction didn't last long enough. The second she stepped away, Claire went back to her agenda. "Maybe it's time to put down some roots instead of gallivanting around the world," she said to their brother.

Brando's face deepened from red to purple. "What, you want all of us to be like you? Stuck-up and judgmental and bossing this whole entire town around?"

"Try the quiche." Sylvie picked up her fork, hoping the

others would follow. "I delivered some to the movie set this morning and everyone loved it." Royce had been especially complimentary and mentioned how much he'd missed her when she'd decided to go home early.

One by one her family members obliged, but eating didn't keep them quiet.

"Speaking of the movie, I heard you were spotted walking around with Royce at the ChristmasFest." Claire arched an eyebrow. "What, exactly, is going on between you two, anyway?"

"I don't know. Who told you that?"

"Only pretty much everyone I've talked to mentioned it." Her sister poked at the quiche in front of her. "That's all I've heard about lately. About how Sylvie and Royce went on a sleigh ride. About how Royce rented out the movie theater for Sylvie."

She dropped her fork.

"You two have been spending a lot of time together, and I'm a little concerned," Claire continued.

Or jealous. She studied her sister's tight frown. "You're just mad because people aren't talking about you."

"That's not true at all." Now Claire adopted the overly controlled tone she used at city council meetings. "I don't think Royce is a good guy, that's all." She glanced at their brother as though looking for backup.

"Yeah, I don't like that guy either," Brando said around a mouthful of quiche.

"Are you kidding me right now?" Sylvie looked desperately at Gramps, but he raised his hands.

"Sorry, Syl," he said apologetically. "I can't get past Prince Charming's laugh. It doesn't sound real. No one laughs like that."

"What?" Now they were all turning on her? "You don't even know him. None of you do." Royce might not be perfect, but they hadn't exactly earned the right to judge him. "He's an actor, so yes, he's always the center of attention, but there's more to him."

"But how well do you know him really?" her sister shot back.

"Pretty well if you're kissing him on the front porch, I'd say," Brando offered.

Sylvie kicked him under the table.

"Ow." He leaned over to rub his shin.

"You actually *kissed* Royce Elliot again?" At least her sister whispered the name so the whole café didn't hear.

"I can kiss whoever I want." Her volume increased with each word. "I can go out with whoever I want. I can date whoever I want. My love life is none of your business."

A hush came over the dining room and Teagan practically galloped over with the water pitcher. "Anyone need a refill over here?"

They all stared at their full water glasses.

"Nope? All righty." Her smile didn't even waver. "Um, Syl . . . there's a problem in the kitchen. I'm gonna need you to come with me real quick."

"Right. Yes." She stood and followed Teagan, humiliation pinching at her cheeks.

"Wow, that was intense," Teagan said when they'd made it to the kitchen. "Did you really kiss Royce Elliot?"

"Wait. Say what?" Jen marched over from the stove. "You kissed that guy?"

"Kind of." And now the whole town knew. She squeezed her eyes shut. "Having this brunch in public was a bad idea."

"Forget about that. Tell me about the kiss." The teen's eyes got all starry. "Was it romantic? Was he a good kisser? God, he's so hot."

"He is pretty sexy," Jen agreed. "I loved him in that one movie . . . what was it?"

"*Kissing Santa Claus*?" Teagan asked.

"No." Jen tapped her forehead.

"*Christmas in the Country? Mistletoe Mischief?*" Teagan offered. "*The Holidaze Bake Shop?*"

Jen pointed her spatula at them. "That's the one!"

Sylvie gaped at her. "I didn't know you watched the Holiday Channel."

"Every Tuesday night." Her friend ran back to the stove and started to stir the caramel sauce. "It's not like I have a lot of time for real romance."

"So was he a good kisser?" Teagan asked again.

"I guess." There honestly wasn't much to say about kissing Royce. Either time. But maybe she'd been expecting too much. It wasn't like he'd been a bad kisser. But she didn't need to analyze this with Teagan and Jen. "Anyway, thanks for stopping me from making even more of a fool out of myself." She just couldn't believe that no one liked Royce. Not even Brando! Her brother liked everyone. She sighed. "I should probably go back out there."

"Fine. But I want details later," Teagan called as Sylvie pushed open the door to the dining room.

"Sylvie, hey." The actor himself stood by the baked goods case at the front of the restaurant.

Of course he would show up right now. She glanced at her family's table in the opposite corner, defensiveness still heating her veins. You know what? Who cared what they thought anyway? The bottom line was that Royce liked *her*. He genuinely liked her, and it didn't matter that Claire thought that was outside the realm of possibilities. She would show them. He'd made his interest pretty clear.

"Hey, Royce." Instead of going back to her seat, she walked up to him, smiling confidently. "What're you doing here?"

"Just stopped in to get a coffee refill."

She had no idea what Gramps was going on about . . . Royce had a nice smile and a good, totally normal laugh.

All eyes were on them—she could feel it. And for once that attention didn't make her want to shrink away. No. Instead, she wanted to turn to everyone and shout, "He likes me! So there!" But she didn't. She simply gazed at him as though they were the only two people in the room.

"I was also thinking how we could get more buzz going about the café." He tipped his to-go cup toward her. "You up for going live right now?"

"Live? Right now?" Sylvie blinked.

"Yeah. We could broadcast live on social media." He came alongside her and held up his phone. "Ready?"

"No." She stepped away, but Royce moved with her.

"Hey, y'all," he said to the camera on his phone. "What's up? I'm hanging out at the Christmas Café in Silver Bells, Wyoming, while we shoot scenes for *All About Christmas*." He panned the phone around the restaurant as Sylvie ducked out of the way. He was really live for the whole world to see right now? What was wrong with him?

"My friend Sylvie here is the baker at the café." He turned his phone directly on her this time, giving her no escape route. "Say hi, Sylvie."

She couldn't speak. She couldn't even swallow! She raised a hand to wave, her eyes frozen open.

But he didn't even seem to notice. "The Christmas Café

has the most creative holiday treats." Royce panned his phone across the baked goods case. "So if you're ever in the area, make sure you stop in. It's literally less than an hour from Jackson—good news for everyone hitting the slopes this weekend. Who knows? If you come soon, I might even be hanging around." He flashed his camera-ready smile and then lowered the phone.

"That was terrifying." She finally found her voice.

Royce laughed as though he assumed she was joking. "This place'll be crawling with people in no time. Trust me." He squeezed her hand, running his thumb over her knuckles in an affectionate gesture. "I've gotta go, but I'll see you soon."

"Bye," she said, her voice husky. He might not send volts of electricity through her when they kissed. But he liked her. And he was doing everything he could to help her save the café.

Whether Claire and Brando and Gramps liked him or not.

Fourteen

SYLVIE ADDED A PINCH OF SALT AND A DASH OF PEPPER TO Crumpet's scrambled eggs and set the plate in front of her pup at the table.

"Go easy," she reminded him. Yesterday Crumpie had nearly choked while he was snarfing up his eggs, and she thought she was going to have to do the Heimlich. After that, she'd spent a half hour watching online videos detailing how to perform the Heimlich maneuver on dogs and she still wasn't sure she'd be able to pull it off.

Somewhere down the hall, a door creaked open. A few seconds later, her brother staggered into the kitchen all bleary-eyed and wild-haired. A true picture of his six-year-old self.

"What're you doing up so early?" Sylvie filled him a mug of coffee before he keeled over or something.

"Proving I'm responsible." He paused in front of the refrigerator and did a double take at the kitchen table. "You make scrambled eggs for your dog?"

She disregarded the blatant objection in his tone. "You'll understand when you're a parent." She served him up a plate, too, adding a dash of hot sauce.

Her brother accepted the eggs with a repentant nod. "Hey, I never got to tell you how sorry I was for telling Claire that you kissed Royce again." He sat across from Crumpet. "I was trying to get her off my back but it wasn't fair to sic her on you."

"It's fine." Sylvie brought her coffee to the table and sat next to him. "Don't worry. I'm already working out ways to get my revenge. You know what Dad always said."

"Don't get mad, just get even," they recited in unison while sharing a good laugh.

Crumpie gave a yelp, letting her know he was all finished, and then the dog smiled at her with a morsel of egg hanging off his doggie chin.

"I wonder how we could enact some revenge on Claire," her brother mused. "For all the times she's insulted us without meaning to."

"Oh! Maybe we could leave an empty coffee cup in her car!" Sylvie had made the mistake of doing that once and now every time she got out of Claire's SUV, her sister did a full-scale inspection.

"Or we could secretly pick up her dry cleaning so she thinks her clothes are missing." Brando scraped the rest of his eggs into his mouth. "But then she'd only accuse me of being irresponsible again. Revenge would be no fun with Claire."

They both had another good-natured laugh—this time at their sister's expense.

She'd missed laughing with her brother. "You know you don't have to prove you're responsible to me, right?" Everyone should have someone to see the good in them, and she could do that for Brando while he was trying to find his way. "You're talented, and I'm actually really proud of you for staying true to your vision even though you lost a big client."

He finished his eggs and pushed the plate away. "As much as I hate to admit it, Claire is right. I need to figure out my life. So I'm going to start by editing all of those pictures I took at the ChristmasFest." He grinned at her. "After I do the breakfast dishes for you, of course."

Hands clasped over her heart, Sylvie shook her head slowly back and forth, adding in a few fake sniffles for good measure. "They grow up so fast."

Brando balled up his napkin and threw it at her.

"Hey, can you do me another favor today?" She carefully got up, maneuvering around her baby, and brought her mug to the sink.

"Sure. What d'you need?"

"Can you get Gramps out for a while?" Since their family brunch two days ago, he hadn't left the house at all. "I know this time of year is always hard for him without Grams, but this year seems to be especially difficult." With each passing day, Gramps seemed to grow quieter, more withdrawn.

"Yeah, I got you." Brando stepped in front of the sink. "I wanted to go to Jackson to do some holiday shopping anyway."

She raised her eyebrows in surprise.

"*What?*" he demanded as he started to load the dishwasher. "I'm not totally broke, you know. I want to get my sisters and my grandfather something special for Christmas."

She gave him a sideways hug. "Awww, thanks, Brando."

"You should wait to say that until you see what I get you for Christmas."

So true. Brando had a knack for finding the worst gag gifts. Over the years he'd gotten her a potty golf set, a pair of trout slippers, a toilet night light, and a mug that said *Being my sister is the only gift you'll ever need.* "Ha! But you're responsible now, so I'm expecting something sparkly and expensive." She went to slip her cellphone into her purse, but it buzzed with an incoming text from Abe.

Morning, Syl. Truck's not starting. Any chance you could stop by on your way in to pick up the delivery?

"Who's that?" Her brother tried to get a look at the screen. "You're smiling."

"I'm not smiling." But she was. Not a full smile maybe, but even seeing Abe's name had made her lips curve. Interesting.

Sure! she responded. *I'll be there in about ten minutes.* She added a few smiley face emojis but maybe that was overkill? She deleted two of them and left one.

Great. Just come on into the barn.

"I have to get going." She slipped her phone into her purse. "Abe needs me to pick up the eggs and butter and milk at the farm. He can't deliver them today."

"One day you're doing live videos with actors and the next you're rendezvousing with the goat guy." Her brother shook his head with mock concern. "I had no idea you were such a player. But I gotta say, I'm impressed."

Scoffing, she pulled on her coat and gloves. "A woman is allowed to have friends, you know." That seemed to be all Abe wanted from her anyway. He'd had the opportunity to spend more time with her after the ChristmasFest and he'd turned her down. She swept Crumpie up into her arms for a goodbye kiss.

"I know. I'm just giving you a hard time." Brando took the dog. "Don't worry about him. I've got this pooch's number. He's not gonna pull anything over on me today."

She walked out of the house laughing.

Above her head, pink swaths of clouds still filled the sky,

with the rising sun slowly waking up the surrounding peaks. It was the start of a perfect winter day. The night had left behind only a light film of snow—not even enough to need to brush off her car but just the right amount to make everything sparkle. She belted out "It's Beginning to Look a Lot Like Christmas" along with Michael Bublé all the way to Abe's farm.

She turned into his driveway, marveling again at all of the festive outdoor decorations. All she'd seen on the sleigh ride were the lights and goats, but now she admired the evergreen boughs dressing up the outdoor pens and the red velvet bows attached to the fence posts and the large globe ornaments dangling from the branches of the evergreen trees on the outskirts of the property. It must've taken him days to put all of this up.

She parked outside of the large red barn and entered through a side door. The cramped room clearly served as his office, but he wasn't sitting behind the beat-up desk. Sylvie stepped further into the square space, drawing closer to the display of photographs and ribbons and medals on the wall.

"Hey, Sylvie." Abe walked into the room from the hallway, the sleeves of his flannel shirt rolled up.

"Hi." She gave him a quick smile but couldn't take her attention away from the display on the wall. "Wow. I knew you served in the army but I didn't know you were such a decorated hero." She paused to study a picture of Abe standing by another man with some young boys gathered around them.

"That was my best friend, Chase." Abe came to stand next to her. "I lost him over there. We came up through the ranks together. Went on missions together."

"I can tell you two were close." They were dressed in their

army uniforms but they were laughing. Both of them. Care-free and unburdened.

"That was my favorite picture of him." Abe straightened the frame. "We were playing a game of soccer with those kids. They totally schooled us."

It was strange to see this part of him displayed on the wall . . . the part she'd never known anything about. Abe had experienced a whole other lifetime while he'd been away. He'd experienced pain and loss, fear and grief. Sylvie felt herself getting choked up. "I'm sorry about Chase."

"Me too." He stepped back to the desk. "Mom is actually the one who hung all this up. Said my office needed some de-cor." Obvious amusement set his lips askew. "She does love her decor."

"Did she collect all of those Christmas decorations out-side too?" Now she couldn't look away from Abe's face. Before last week, she'd never noticed how expressive his face was— the happy, the sad, the amused were all there, just more subtle than most. It was like getting to know him for the first time.

"Yes. Mom loves Christmas decorations." He walked to a large crate in the corner labeled *Sylvie's Order* and lifted it onto the desk. "She brings out a lawn chair and watches while I put everything up so she can tell me exactly where it goes. She loves this time of year."

It sounded like Mrs. DeWitt was the Grams of Abe's fam-ily. "What does your family do for Christmas every year?"

He shrugged and straightened some of the papers on his desk. "All of our extended family is in California, so it's pretty quiet. It's usually only the three of us for dinner."

"Well, you're coming to my house this year," she decided. With everything Mr. DeWitt had been through, they should have someone else do all of the cooking and the cleaning that day. "We're having a great big dinner—Gramps and Brando, Claire and Manuel, and Crumpet and me. And now you and your parents too. I won't take no for an answer, Abe."

That smile right there—the big bright one that made his eyes shine—made her heart stutter.

"All right, then. We'll be there." A timer dinged from his old-fashioned watch. "Oops. I need to go feed Bambino his bottle real quick. Can you wait a few before I load up your supplies?"

"Are you kidding?" A little squeal slipped out. "I get to see a newborn goat drink a bottle?" She couldn't imagine anything better happening to her today.

"You can help, if you want." Abe waved her down the hallway to where the barn opened up into a huge heated space, dissected by corral fencing, where goats of all colors milled around, munching, head-butting, and bleating. "In fact, you can feed Bambino."

Sylvie grabbed his arm. "Are you serious?"

"Sure." He led her to a small enclosure, where the little one was gnawing on the metal chain that held the gate closed.

"Yep. He's hungry." Abe hopped the fence and herded the little guy to the other side of the pen. "He hasn't been drinking well from mama, so I've been supplementing with bottles a few times a day." He pointed to a large bottle that sat on a table a few feet away from her. "I'll hold him while you come in. He always tries to escape."

Something Bambino and Crumpet had in common. "I get to feed a goat!" Sylvie hurried to pick up the bottle and then let herself into the pen through the gate.

Abe set Bambino down and Sylvie sank to her knees. Right away, the newborn goat toddled up to her.

"You. Are. Adorable," she informed him. Sunny came over too, curiously nosing around her shoulder.

"You can hold one arm around him and the bottle in the other hand." Abe demonstrated.

"Okay. Sure." That looked easy enough. She slipped her arm around Bambino and gathered him close, offering him the bottle. The goat latched on and nearly ripped the bottle out of her hand. Sylvie laughed. "He's stronger than he looks."

"Especially when he's hungry." Abe knelt and gave Sunny some attention, and the goat actually licked his hand like a dog.

"You're a good boy, Bambino," she murmured while the baby sucked down the bottle. When it was gone, the goat nestled himself into her arms and rested his head on her shoulder, snuggling her. "Awww." She petted Bambino's head.

"Watch out." Abe carried the empty bottle out of the pen and set it on a shelf. "He loves attention. He's not going to want you to leave."

"I don't want to leave." She peered into the goat's eyes. "I don't know how you get anything done around here with all this cuteness."

"It's tough, but somehow I manage." There was a smile in his reply.

"Well, I would stay here all day if I could but I should probably get to the café."

Abe rolled over a wheelbarrow full of hay bedding and started to place it in the pen. "How are things going over there?"

Sunny started to nuzzle Sylvie's back, nibbling on the fur trim of her coat, and Bambino seemed to get a burst of energy. Suddenly the baby goat was on his feet and nosing around her pockets. She tried to focus on Abe with the two goats accosting her. "Okay. I'm still hoping I can convince Jerry to hold on to it."

"I saw that video." He kept his head down as he worked. Was he intentionally not meeting her eye? "The one you did with Royce. Mom showed it to me."

"Oh. Yeah." Teagan had texted her to tell her they'd gotten over a hundred thousand views. "I was a little freaked out." Staring at the camera wide-eyed hadn't been her best look. "But hopefully it'll help bring people in the door."

"I'm sure it will." Abe stepped back into the pen, shooing the goats away from her. "You'd better make a run for it while you can. Or you might never get out of here." He reached out his hand to help her up.

Sylvie planted a kiss on Bambino's head and then put her hand in Abe's. He pulled her up in one swift motion, his grip somehow strong and gentle at the same time.

"Thanks." She had no reason to be breathless. But her lungs seemed too empty. Or maybe too full.

"You're welcome." He dropped her hand and held open the gate for her. "So what're you doing this weekend?"

"Oh. Um." Why had her heart suddenly started doing triple flips? It wasn't like he was asking her out! Was he? "It's the Christmas Ball. On Saturday." Sylvie walked quickly down the hall, but his long legs easily matched her stride.

"So you're going?"

She stepped back into his office, heat closing in on her face. Why was she so nervous? "Yeah. Yes. Mmm-hmm. Sure am." Was she squeaking?

"You're going with Royce." It sounded more like a statement than a question.

"I . . . uh . . . yes." She cleared her throat, absentmindedly patting her pockets for her keys. "Are you going?"

There was a slight hesitation before he answered, a pause as though he was still making up his mind.

"Nah. I probably won't go. They're asking for extra volunteer firefighters to be on call that night. I should stay home in case something comes in."

And what if she hadn't been going with anyone? Would he have asked her?

Abe lifted the crate holding her delivery.

"I'll unlock my car." She reached into her pocket again, but it was empty. Right. She hadn't felt her keys there a minute ago, but she'd been too distracted to notice. "My keys have to be here somewhere."

Abe glanced around the floor. "Maybe they fell out somewhere?"

They retraced their steps back to the pen, where Sylvie saw her keyring dangling from Bambino's mouth. "He stole them right out of my pocket!"

"Told you he was a stinker." Abe unlatched the gate and slipped into the pen, but Bambino took off to the other side. "Goats are actually very playful. And this one's more full of mischief than most." He tried to corner the goat, but Bambino evaded him and trotted to the opposite fence.

Sylvie laughed and slipped into the pen to help. "I had no idea they were such rascals." She made a grab for the goat, but Bambino slipped away, causing her to land on her knees.

"You okay?" Abe helped her up.

She was laughing too hard to answer. She couldn't help it. This baby goat was making fools of them both.

Abe's deep laugh roused a few goosebumps down her right

arm. "Sunny here once figured out how to flip that light switch on and off." He pointed to the electrical box on the wall just outside the pen. "I kept coming in at dawn and all the lights were already on. I couldn't figure out what was going on until I saw her get her front hooves up on the top of the fence and reach the switch with her nose."

"Unbelievable." These animals were much smarter than she'd given them credit for.

"I have an idea." Abe bent to untie his boots and then he walked past Bambino with his shoelaces dragging. Immediately, the goat dropped her keys on the floor and went after the shoelaces.

"He can't resist," he said triumphantly.

Sylvie hurried to snatch her keys off the ground before the goat realized they'd tricked him. "Got them."

They both moved toward the gate, but Bambino playfully head-butted the backs of Sylvie's knees, sending her stumbling into Abe.

"Whoa." He caught her in his arms, his eyes wide, lips parted with surprise.

Her lips parted too. Mostly so she could breathe. Because she was right up against him, this mysterious man who was slowly revealing himself to her, and now her heart was pounding so hard her whole chest ached.

Something changed in Abe's expression, a subtle look of longing that softened his mouth. His face slowly drew closer to hers, and Sylvie's eyelids shut with anticipation. When their lips touched, every synapse in her body fired all at once and she was soaring—or at least her heart was. His lips. Oh, his lips. They were insistent and decisive, guiding hers into a seductive rhythm.

Abe's hands settled on her hips and then slid around her low back. Warmth flooded her then, pouring into every part of her and filling her up. Sylvie laced her fingers together behind his neck, drawing him even closer. Her mouth opened to him and his tongue grazed hers. He tasted of peppermint and coffee and who knew that could be such an intoxicating combination? Sparks flared inside of her, growing in intensity, but then he was gone, pushing her away.

"Sorry," he muttered. "I shouldn't have done that." Abe hastily unlatched the gate. "I know you're hanging out with Royce. That was my bad. I don't know what I was thinking. I wasn't thinking. Okay? We'll forget it happened." He wouldn't look at her. He didn't even wait for her to say something. He kept moving swiftly, ushering her out of the gate and then latching it again after shoving the crate into her arms.

She stumbled out of the barn, her heart reeling. What the heck had just happened?

Fifteen

SYLVIE TURNED INTO THE ALLEYWAY BEHIND THE CAFÉ, her heart still stammering. She couldn't manage to draw in a full breath. And the heat that kiss had generated still spiraled through her, all the way down to her toes.

Abe had kissed her. He'd kissed her! And then he'd run away faster than Crumpet stealing her bra.

She slowed the car to ease into her normal parking spot behind the café, but the space was occupied by a compact SUV. Come to think of it, all of the spaces back here were occupied. She glanced farther down the alley, seeing nothing but a continuous line of cars. No one ever parked here.

She kept going until she could turn onto Christmas Lane. The only spot left was in the little Episcopal church parking lot between two massive diesel pickups. What in the great wide world was going on around here? It was the middle of the week. Silver Bells's streets were never this crowded.

Grumbling to herself, Sylvie wedged her car into the parking spot and climbed out. She retrieved the crate of milk, butter, and eggs from her hatchback and then hiked down the sidewalk and turned onto the alley, her boots slogging through the slush. She finally pushed in through the kitchen door, out of breath and frozen from her fingers to her toes.

"Oh thank God!" Jen was piling muffins from the storage container onto a tray. "We've been trying to call your cell-phone for a half hour."

"Sorry. I had to stop by Abe's to pick up my order because his truck wasn't working. And then there was this baby goat . . ." And a kiss. Abe had kissed her! "I left my phone in the car and got sidetracked." She was still a little sidetracked, truth be told. She hoisted the crate onto the stainless-steel countertop and then went about shedding her winter gear.

"We've already sold out of all the donuts and scones you baked yesterday." Her friend picked up the tray of their backup cherry chocolate chip muffins. "Cookies are running low. And we have one quiche left to cut, but at this rate we'll run out in ten minutes."

"I don't understand." Panic hummed through her. "I made plenty of food yesterday." It was a Thursday, for crying out loud. Their slowest day of the week!

"Tell that to the line of people down the block." Jen cruised to the door, and Sylvie followed her, stepping into the dining room. Every single chair was occupied. And she could see people lined up outside through the windows.

Teagan was checking out to-go orders at the counter, but the baked goods case was only half-full.

Forget the gentle hum . . . now panic raced through her blood. "We don't have enough food to feed all of these people."

"You're telling me." Jen rushed to the baked goods case, unloaded the muffins, and then hurried back, perspiration shimmering on her forehead. "It's been like this since I got here a half hour ago. I'm guessing Royce's live video blew up. But now we'll probably have to close early."

"We can't!" Closing early would only show Jerry she couldn't handle more business. "Okay. Um. Wow," she stammered while they ducked back into the kitchen. "We have to make more food." What could she get ready the quickest? She had a fresh supply of eggs and butter and milk. She could make frittatas and muffins and breakfast potatoes. "We can do this. We have to do this." She staggered past the refrigerator on her way to the pantry and passed by one of the signs Grams had cross-stitched. *Donut worry. Bake it happy.*

"Don't worry," she repeated to herself. "Don't worry." She could handle this. She had to handle this, or she'd lose the Christmas Café. She simply had to take one thing at a time. Unpack the crate, step one. Preheat the oven, step two. "You start on the muffins," she told Jen. "Since they only need twenty minutes in the oven. Let's keep it simple and stay with chocolate chocolate-chip." No time for fancy frostings or labor-intensive prep work.

"On it." Jen already had the mixing bowls on the counter.

"I'll start frittatas." She set two large sauté pans on the stovetop, then started to crack eggs into a bowl. "And after the muffins go in, start a double batch of our special chocolate snickerdoodles. By the time you're done tossing them in cinnamon and sugar, the oven will be free, and they bake at the same temperature."

"Brilliant," her friend said over the whir of the mixer.

The doors swung open, and Claire rushed into the kitchen. "I've never seen this place so busy." Her sister was positively glowing. "In fact, I've never seen any establishment in Silver Bells this busy. It's amazing!"

"I just hope we can keep up." Sylvie rushed to the refrigerator and started to rip out vegetables—peppers and onions and asparagus. Oh! And tomatoes.

"You have to keep up." Claire rolled up her sweater sleeves. "This could change everything."

Yes, she knew that. If she could pull this off—this could be their highest profit in a single day ever. "I don't know how we're going to feed all of these people. There're are only two of us back here."

"Then I'll help you." Her sister walked to the coatrack and tore an apron off the hook. "Why are you looking at me like that? I can help."

"Sorry." But Sylvie had to stare at her sister in that apron to believe what she was seeing. "You don't cook or bake." Manuel did all of the cooking in their house.

"You can tell me what to do." Claire tied the apron around her waist. "Believe it or not, I am pretty good at following directions."

"Okay. Start dicing these." She directed her sister to the cutting board with the veggies.

"Sure. Small dice or what?"

"Small dice." While Claire was busy wielding the knife, Sylvie texted Brando an SOS—*Need help at the café ASAP!*—and then finished whisking milk and salt and pepper into the eggs. They'd simply keep on making frittatas and muffins until they ran out of ingredients.

"Muffins going in!" Jen had finished filling the tins before Claire had even finished cutting the peppers. Jen cruised past them and slid the muffin trays into the oven.

"The pieces don't have to be perfectly symmetrical," Sylvie told Claire. They were on a time crunch here. "No one's going to admire their shape in the frittatas."

"Right." Her sister started to chop faster. "I guess I was wrong about Royce. He's really been great about helping you with the café."

"And he looks good doing it," Jen added.

"Yeah. He has." Sylvie started collecting ingredients for the cookies. But her life was all starting to feel a little out of her control. The crowds at the café. The time she was spending with Royce. The kiss with Abe. It was a whole lot of hullabaloo, as Grams had always liked to say.

"We've got a full house, people." Teagan poked her head in through the door. "But I'm keeping everyone happy with lots of coffee!"

Seeing the girl's wide grin put her at ease. Teagan was great with the customers. They all loved her. "We'll have food out there in less than a half hour," Sylvie promised. "Tell them everything is coming out hot and fresh—right from the oven."

"Got it!" The waitress disappeared again.

"Teagan said it's been like this all morning." Claire dumped the pepper pieces into a bowl. "She called me in a panic to see if I had seen you. Where were you, anyway?"

Busted. Sylvie focused on measuring out flour. They'd need a lot of cookies. "I had to stop by Abe's place to pick up the delivery." Thank goodness she hadn't decided to skip it.

"And you said something about a baby goat?" Jen asked.

"Yes. Bambino." The goat who'd knocked her right into Abe's arms. She could still see his face when he'd caught her, when there'd been a collective pause in the universe right before he'd kissed her.

"You were at Abe's?" Her sister paused with the knife halfway through the onion. "You must've been there for a while."

"Yep!" Ugh. Way too shrill. "I fed Bambino and had to make sure we got the order all squared away." Sylvie squeezed her eyes shut. How many cups of flour had she dumped into the bowl?

When she opened her eyes, she noticed Jen giving her a funny look.

Avoid eye contact. She had to stop thinking about her morning with Abe or she'd never get through this mad rush. "How's the Miss Christmas committee going?" When all else failed, her sister could be easily distracted by talking about her mayoral work.

Listening to Claire cover every detail of the town tradition would be a lot better than trying to pretend she hadn't felt that kiss down to her toes this morning.

"It's going well." Her sister eyed the asparagus as though she wasn't quite sure how to cut it. "You were nominated this year, you know."

Sylvie dropped a full measuring cup and flour poofed onto the floor. "What?"

"We're getting ready to release the list of finalists and you're on it." Claire dropped the knife and made a proud *ta-da!* gesture with her hands over the asparagus.

"I know who I'm voting for." Jen carried a broom over and cleaned up the flour mess.

"I don't want anyone to vote for me. I don't even want to be on the list!" She stole the bowl of vegetables from her sister and started to sauté them on the stove. She'd have to add the mushrooms when Claire finished.

"Well, you are on the list." Her sister went back to thunking the knife through the mushrooms. "And you know as well as I do it takes three nominations to make the list of finalists. So clearly I'm not the only one who thinks you'd make a good Miss Christmas."

"It was probably you and Gramps and Brando."

"I forgot to turn in my nomination form, or you would've have four." Jen started to make another batch of coffee.

"Brando doesn't get a vote since he's not a full-time resident," Claire reminded Sylvie.

"It doesn't matter anyway. I won't win." And that was fine by her. "Finish up those mushrooms, please." She set the mixer to cream butter and sugar for the cookie prep and finished getting the frittatas going on the stove. Right now, she needed to clear her head and focus. She couldn't think about Miss Christmas or Royce or Abe. She had to only think about the café.

While she finished sautéing the veggies, Jen took over the cookies, and Claire washed dishes.

The muffins came out of the oven, and the cookies went in, while the frittatas simmered on the stovetop.

"Help Tegan add the muffins to the baked goods case," Sylvie instructed her sister.

The second Claire walked out, Jen marched up to her. "What happened this morning?"

"Nothing." Sylvie checked the frittatas so her friend couldn't get a good look at her face.

"You were blushing and flustered when you talked about going to the farm." She bumped Sylvie's shoulder. "Spill it."

"Abe kissed me!" she blurted. She had to tell someone. "He kissed me!" And, more importantly, he'd made her feel all sorts of things she'd never felt. Intoxicated. Curious. Exhilarated. In fact, she was still floating.

"Did you kiss him back?"

Oh, she'd kissed him back all right. Some instinct took over that she didn't even know she had. "Yes. But it all happened really fast and then he stopped. And apologized."

Jen winced. "He apologized?"

"Yeah. He said he knew I was hanging out with Royce so it shouldn't have happened." But Abe had taken her from zero to sixty in less than a minute, there was no denying that. What would've happened if he hadn't pulled back? "I have no idea what this means."

"It means you've kissed two men in less than a week." Jen looked impressed. "I need to take notes."

"I don't even know what's happening." Sylvie put on an oven mitt and transferred the frittata pans into the oven.

"Well, which one do you like bett—"

The door slammed open. "I can't believe how many people are out there!" Claire filled herself a mug of coffee. "You might want more than muffins and frittata and cookies."

She almost bit Claire's head off, but looking at the clock, she saw they'd actually made good time. Grilled cheese! She'd stocked up on that new goat milk cheddar Abe had made, and she had plenty of bread in the freezer. "Go out there and add a grilled cheese sandwich to the menu," she told her sister. For the next hour, she and Jen buttered bread and flipped sandwiches while Claire and Teagan handled the food running.

The clock had ticked just past noon when Gramps and Brando wandered into the kitchen. "What's going on around here?" her grandpa demanded. "First your brother drags me all over Jackson shopping. And now all I want is a cup of coffee and I can't even have that without waiting in a line."

"It's a busy day." She snatched an apron off the coatrack and threw it to her brother. "Didn't you get my SOS? We need help."

"We were still in Jackson when I saw it. But count us in." He slipped the apron over his head.

"Thank you!" Sylvie flipped another sandwich. "Claire will

tell you what to do out in the dining room." She had no doubt that her sister had taken over the front of the house and was currently hustling customers in and out as quickly as she could.

"I can pitch in too, sweetie," Gramps offered. "If you need the help."

"That would be great." But first she poured him a mug of coffee. "We could use some help with the dishes."

"You got it." He shot her the rascally grin she'd missed seeing on his face. "And I won't even have to talk to anyone."

"Just me." She kissed his cheek and set him up at the big sink. She peeked once more into the dining room. Though it was crowded, everyone seemed happy. Even the people who'd opted to stand around and eat their muffins instead of getting a seat had smiles on their faces.

Sylvie intercepted Brando after he'd taken an order from a nearby table. "Gramps seems a little happier today," she murmured.

"He grouched about the coffee, but we had a good time in Jackson. He even did a little shopping himself."

"I'm so glad. Hey, I'm happy you came home," she told her brother.

"I am too." He sidestepped her. "Now I'd better go get the muffins for these ladies before they make good on their threat to set me up on a blind date with their niece."

"Good luck with that." She walked closer to the café's main entrance. The line still wound outside the doors.

"Sylvie!" Royce waved at her from the sidewalk. He finished snapping a selfie with a group of teen girls and then slipped inside. "Look at this. Our video worked!"

"Maybe a little too well." She really needed to get back to

the grill so she could flip more sandwiches. "We almost ran out of food." But they just might make it another hour until closing time . . .

Royce waved off her concern. "At least now you know this place could really take off, right?" He waved at a group of his adoring fans outside the window. "We did one video and look what happened."

Yes. Look what had happened. She'd been running around like a headless chicken for the last four hours. She hadn't stopped sweating. And worries kept gripping her by the throat. Was the food tasting okay even though they were rushing everything? Were people going to get fed up and give them terrible reviews online? "We can't keep up with this demand." She was almost afraid to think about tomorrow.

"That's a good problem to have." He slipped his arm around her waist and steered her close to the kitchen door. "You'll have to hire a few more chefs, that's all. And more waitstaff, maybe some food runners. But you can get this place running like a real restaurant."

A real restaurant. The Christmas Café wasn't supposed to be just a restaurant. It was a gathering place, a refuge, a place to feel the holiday spirit, to linger as long as you wanted. She liked to make all of the food from scratch. She liked to know that her food played a part in celebrations and comfort and the joy that permeated these walls. "Everything would change."

Royce had the adorably confused expression down pat. "I thought you wanted to grow the business."

"I did. I do."

But what would she have to give up in the process?

Sixteen

SYLVIE ADDED A DAB OF GLITTERY RED PAINT TO THE PEP-
permint wheel on the life-sized gingerbread house Jerry had
built out of cardboard and attached to a trailer in the late 1990s.

The Christmas Café had been driving this same gingerbread house float down Main Street in the Silver Bells Parade
of Lights for well over thirty years, but the last few years, the
spectacle required more and more massive repairs and up-
grades.

"That's way better." Teagan stood back and admired their
handiwork. "This thing is gonna fall apart someday."

"Well, we might not need a float at all after this year," Sylvie said glumly. Today had been every bit as busy at the café as
the day before, and this time they'd run out of food and had to
close at eleven o'clock. They simply weren't set up for the volume of people coming in, no matter how much planning she
tried to do.

"You really think Jerry is gonna sell the place now that it's
practically famous?" the girl whispered, peering over her
shoulder.

Since they were just about finished with the touchups to the parade float, their boss had stepped outside of his massive garage to wash the rest of the paint buckets and brushes.

"I don't know if the café is famous, exactly." Yes, they'd had a constant flood of ski tourists ever since Royce's live video, but Jerry hadn't said much to her about the increase in business. And they hadn't even been able to accommodate all of the new customers either. They had to turn people away. Was there anything worse for a restaurant? "Actually this afternoon has been a nice reprieve from the worries." Painting and sprucing up the parade float had given her something else to focus on for a few hours. She looked forward to the parade every year. For as long as she'd been working at the café, Sylvie had driven the truck while Jerry dressed in the Santa suit and stood in front of the gingerbread house among the life-sized lollipops. "I don't think—"

A clattering of metal buckets followed by a yelp from their boss cut her off. She and Teagan both dropped their paintbrushes and ran outside to find him hopping around on one foot, cursing.

"Jerry!" She tried to help him limp back into the garage, clumsily guiding him to one of the lawn chairs they'd set up. "Oh goodness. Are you okay?"

"I've been meaning to remove that confounded stump for months." He pulled off his cowboy boot and sock. "I think it's broken. My big toe's broken."

"Sure looks that way." Sylvie glanced at the purple bruising that had already started to spread over the top of his foot. The man also desperately needed a pedicure, but now was probably not the time to make that suggestion. "We should get you to the hospital."

"No hospital," he said gruffly. "At least not tonight. I won't miss the parade."

"I'll go get you some ice." Teagan bounded toward the house.

"We're gonna have to change things up, Syl." Jerry wiggled his toe and then winced. "I can't be walking around on a float now. I'll have to drive the truck, and you'll have to be Santa Claus."

"What?" Sylvie shot upright. "No. No way. I can't do that." She couldn't stand on the float in front of the whole town parading around in a Santa suit. "Teagan could do it—"

"Teagan's the elf." Jerry put his sock back on, his teeth gritted. "Besides, the costume won't fit her anyway."

And he really thought the Santa suit would fit *her*? Sylvie shook her head. She didn't have time to be offended. "Who else can we call?" She would text Brando an SOS but he'd already promised Claire he'd take pictures tonight. "What about Betsy?" His wife would make a great Santa!

Jerry shook his head. "She's already got a spot on the library's float. She'll be reading to some kids."

Lucky her. "Do we really *need* a Santa? I mean, the kids get to see Santa at the ChristmasFest. I think that's enough." There was such a thing as Santa overkill, right? She didn't want all of the kids in town thinking Christmas was *only* about Santa.

"Santa Claus is always a part of our float. We have to carry on the tradition." Judging from the bolo ties and leather vests he'd worn since the seventies, Jerry wasn't a fan of change. "Besides, when I retire and move away, you're going to have to keep the gingerbread float alive, Syl. I won't be around to play Santa Claus so you might as well get used to it."

When he retired and moved away? She gasped. The Christmas Café would still be here when he retired and moved away? "You're not selling?"

The man stood on his good foot, his balance wobbling. "I haven't made a final decision yet, but I'm really impressed with what you've been able to do in such a short time, Sylvie. The café has never been so busy. I can see the value in holding on to it for a while."

"Jerry!" She threw her arms around the man, causing him to stumble and hop again. "Sorry! Oops, so, so sorry!" She helped him hobble back to the chair. "All right. I'll do it. I'll be Santa Claus tonight. I can't believe—"

"Oh, honey!" Betsy, came rushing into the garage with Teagan following close behind. "Look at you. Let's get you into the house so we can ice that toe." She pulled him up and slipped her arm around his waist.

"You come too, Sylvie." Jerry waved her along. "We need to get you all suited up."

Teagan shot her a quizzical look.

"I *get* to be Santa Claus." She linked her arm through Teagan's and practically skipped into Jerry's log house. This would be no problem. She'd saved the café! She could do anything. She could totally pull off becoming good ol' Saint Nick for one evening.

Twenty minutes later her optimism had dried up. "Um . . . I'm not sure I'll be able to walk in these boots," she said to Betsy as she stumbled around her cluttered crafting room testing out the black clompers that matched the outfit.

"Don't you worry." Betsy opened a drawer on a hutch and pulled out sheets of tissue paper, wadding them up. "We'll make those boots fit, mark my words." She gestured for Sylvie to sit on the overstuffed chair in the corner. "You don't have to walk a lot. Jerry usually just stands and waves." The woman pulled off the boots—thankfully, since Sylvie couldn't even *see* her feet, let alone reach them with the pillows strapped around her waist—and stuffed tissue paper into the toes. She shoved them back onto Sylvie's feet and reached out a hand to help her up. "There we are."

"Oof-da." Getting to her feet took so much effort she nearly ran out of breath. "That's a little better, I guess." She shuffled a few steps. She'd at least be able to stand and wave. Walking, however, would not be a good idea. Especially on a moving trailer. Grace wasn't exactly her middle name.

"And now for the finishing touches." Betsy handed over the fluffy white beard and the red velvet hat.

"Right." She pulled the beard on first and then added the hat, glancing at herself in the full-length mirror across the room. "Huh." She really could pull off Santa. No one would even know it was her under all these layers.

"You make a perfect Santa," Betsy said, looking quite pleased with herself. "Ta-da!" She opened the crafting room door and nudged Sylvie out into the living room, where Jerry and Teagan sat.

"Wow." Teagan gave her a quick appraisal. "You look like the big guy himself." Of course, Teagan looked extra adorable in her green-and-white-striped leggings and green jumper.

"Thanks." She didn't care much how she looked, really, but walking across the room proved to be a big problem.

"We'd best get a move on." Jerry eased out of the chair, his cursing earning him a glare from his wife. "Good thing I broke my left toe and not the right, or Teagan would be driving tonight."

"I'd love to drive!" The girl led the way outside, where the float trailer was all rigged up to Jerry's truck and ready to roll. "I have my permit, you know."

"I'd rather have Jerry drive." Sylvie waddled along behind them, turning sideways to maneuver herself down the porch steps so she didn't face-plant. "No offense." Between the boots and the hefty padding around her middle, she had enough trouble staying upright without a brand-new driver behind the wheel.

"Let's get you in the truck." Betsy opened the back door of the extended cab, and Sylvie climbed up with the woman shoving and supporting her from behind. "There we go. I don't think the seatbelt will fit around you, so you'll have to skip it."

"I wouldn't mind skipping this whole thing," she muttered. Her first order of business as the new boss lady might be to nix this old-school float.

"What's that?" Jerry turned around from the driver's seat.

"Nothing!" she sang.

Teagan climbed in too and Betsy said goodbye, telling them she would see them at the parade in a few minutes.

As they drove through town, Sylvie peeked out at all the people already crowding the sidewalks on Main Street. It sure looked like a bigger crowd this year. Kids were everywhere, all bundled up in their snow pants and hats and mittens, their smiles big and their cheeks pink.

They stopped at the staging area, and both Teagan and Jerry were out of the truck before Sylvie could ask for some assistance.

"Don't worry, I've got this," she called to no one. *Easy. Take it slow.* She opened the door and went to swing her leg out, but the momentum threw off her balance and she toppled out of the truck, landing on her butt in the snowy street.

"Sylvie? . . . Is that you?" Abe appeared over her.

"Yes, it's me." Of course the first time she'd see him after their kiss she was dressed as a jiggly old man! She held out both arms so he could help her up, and she finally managed to get her legs under her, grunting and red-faced. At least the man was strong.

"Looking good." He pulled the beard away from her chin. "I almost didn't recognize you."

And she almost didn't know how to respond to him. There was no hint from his expression that he'd kissed her. No awkwardness or hesitation. And yet here she stood, heart going a hundred miles a minute, a telltale warmth burning at her very center. Annoyance flickered. How could he stand there and pretend nothing had happened? Maybe that kiss hadn't struck him the way it had her.

"I thought Jerry usually played Santa."

"He does." She was starting to sweat. And her heart thumped harder. The tingles were back too . . . spreading through her. And Abe stood there with his typical neutral expression.

"Jerry broke his toe an hour ago, so I've been called into service." She readjusted the bowl full of jelly protruding over the belt and pulled the jacket away from her neck to get some airflow. "This is going to be a disaster. I can hardly walk in this getup." And now, standing here, she felt almost lightheaded.

"Don't worry. I'll be right behind you." He gestured to the goats that were harnessed into a lighted sled behind them. "And so will Sunny. She's our lead sled goat."

"Sled goats," she marveled. "Do they really pull that thing?"

"They love it." He seemed to have no problem looking directly into her eyes even though she had to keep darting her gaze away to stop herself from getting overwhelmed. "Dad started working with them last year, but he's had a tough time this month. So I'm stepping in."

"Well, I'm glad you're here. You'd better be ready to catch me if I fall off this thing." Judging from how the goats were currently wandering and pulling against each other and bleating as though they were irritated, she wasn't the only one who was going to have her work cut out for her tonight. Maybe people would be too focused on Abe's spectacle to notice her stumbling clumsily around the gingerbread float.

"I'll catch you." Ah-ha! There was a flash in Abe's eyes, a striking intensity only for a few seconds, and then his gaze was guarded again. He *did* remember the kiss. But maybe not as fondly as she did . . .

"Sylvie, we've gotta get ready," Jerry called from the float. He hobbled over, using a carved walking stick for support. "Teagan is already in place."

"Right." She readjusted her fluffy white beard. "I guess I'll see you out there."

"I'll be keeping an eye on you." A slow simmering grin heated up Abe's eyes, but before she could translate what it meant, Jerry escorted her up the trailer steps, her unbalanced weight shifting side to side.

"Now remember," Jerry started, "it gets pretty herky-jerky with all the stopping and starting, so try to keep yourself balanced at all times."

"Sure. No problem." She wasn't even balanced walking down the street on a normal day. Sylvie quickly glanced around for anything she could potentially use as a chair.

Didn't the big man spend a lot of his time sitting? She really didn't want to fall on her butt in front of the whole town tonight.

"Act jolly!" Jerry left her standing in front of the gingerbread house among the life-sized lollipops. Maybe if she held on to the PVC-pipe candy canes, she wouldn't fall over. Yes, that's what she'd do. She'd act jolly while she stood still and held on for dear life.

"Knock 'em dead, Sylvie," Abe called as he climbed onto the low sled behind her.

"I just hope I don't knock myself dead," she muttered.

Behind Abe, other parade floats lined up. Dusk had settled, so now the lights twinkled brightly. Her sister would be on the town council's float somewhere near the front of the line. But Sylvie couldn't get too distracted by all of the other displays. She had to focus on staying upright.

Somewhere nearby, the local high school band was kicking things off.

"You ready?" Teagan called up, a pouch of candy slung over her shoulder. Her main job was to walk next to the float and toss goodies to the kids lining the streets.

"I'll never be ready."

Jerry honked his horn twice, a signal that they were getting ready to move. Sylvie tightened her grip on the fake peppermint stick and braced herself.

The trailer lurched forward, causing her to shift, but she stayed upright and even pried one of her hands away from the PVC so she could wave while they slowly rolled along Main Street.

"Santa, Santa!" kids cried, madly waving their arms.

"Ho, ho, ho!" she called in her deepest voice. This was actually kind of fun. "Merry Christmas!"

More kids cheered, and Sylvie decided to let go of the peppermint stick to venture a little closer to the edge of the float. Teetering in the boots, she waved both hands. And look at how happy everyone was! The kids were jumping up and down, and then scrambling to collect the candy Teagan threw out. Even the adults wore big grins, waving at her like they were remembering their own childhood magic.

"Merry Christmas!" she yelled again. "And to all a good ni—"

The trailer stopped abruptly, pitching her forward. She flailed, trying to grab onto the nearest peppermint stick, but the PVC pipe dislodged and the momentum sent her overboard. She flew off the trailer and took out Abe on the sled behind, both of them rolling to the snow-covered street in a heap.

"Santa!" A little girl started to run toward her before being corralled by her mother.

Sylvie found herself staring into Abe's eyes. His face was inches away. She gasped in a deep breath, but couldn't seem to steady her heart.

Abe was breathing harder too, she was sure of it. His gaze drifted down to her lips—yes, ladies and gentlemen! He was staring at her lips with intrigue burning up his eyes and then his mouth moved, one corner hiking up into a sexy little grin. Ah-ha! The kiss had gotten to him too.

And now it was happening again, that same strong pull between them, but Abe abruptly sat up. "Are you okay?"

No, she was not okay! She'd made a fool out of herself in front of the whole town, just as she'd feared. And worse than that, she'd practically been silently begging for him to kiss her again, and he'd bailed. Again. "I'm fine."

A few feet away, the goats were bleating and squawking

while they seemed to disagree on which way to pull the now-sideways sled.

As for the rest of the crowd . . . a hush had fallen over the streets minus the band's festive rendition of "Frosty the Snowman."

Abe scrambled to get up and then took her hands to pull her to her feet. Underneath all that beard, her cheeks were on fire. Everyone was staring . . . *gawking*. Had they all seen it? The way she'd stared at Abe? The way he'd distanced himself from her so fast? Maybe not. Probably not. But she still felt exposed somehow . . .

"I'll help you get back on the float." He reached out his hand to her.

But she turned away. "I don't need help." Sylvie climbed her way back onto the float without any assistance, thank you very much. And then she took a bow because, why not? Everyone was staring, and she had to own this moment. She was Santa Claus, after all.

Applause started—anemic at first—but then it picked up when she started waving. The crowd on the street clapped and cheered. Abe joined in, his eyes steady on her, even though his goats were dragging the sled toward the crowd. He caught her eye and smiled that real smile—the one she used to have to work so hard for—and then he whistled for her too.

Sylvie waved again, calling out a hearty, "On Dasher, on Dancer, on Comet and Cupid!" while the truck lurched forward. What had she been so nervous about, anyway? The worst had happened—she'd fallen in front of the whole town. But then she'd gotten back up all on her own. She'd gotten back up and, right now, *she* was the starlet of Silver Bells.

Seventeen

"DON'T GIVE ME THAT FACE." SYLVIE PLANTED A KISS ON Crumpie's nose.

Her dog sat on her bed with his shoulders hunched, staring up at her through those dark puppy eyes with his brows in a forlorn crease.

"I have to go to work," she reminded him. "So I can pay your Chewy tab." Yes, she'd been working a lot more this month. She used to cart her dog along with her—but that was before business had taken off. Now she couldn't take the extra time to walk him and make sure he didn't try to sneak into the sugar cabinet during the day.

"Come here." She pulled Crumpet into her arms, cradling him while she walked down the hallway.

Halfway to the kitchen, Sylvie stopped. Why were all the lights on? And was someone banging around in *her* kitchen? She glanced at her watch. Gramps wouldn't be up for another half-hour yet. That only left Brando or an intruder. She crept quietly until she could get a good look around the corner.

Her brother stood at the stove stirring something in a

cast-iron skillet. "What is happening?" Sylvie stepped fully into the kitchen and set Crumpie in his seat.

Brando lifted the skillet off the burner and used a spatula to scrape scrambled eggs onto an empty plate he had waiting. "I made coffee this morning." He gestured to a steaming mug. "And eggs too."

Sylvie inspected both suspiciously. They *looked* okay. The coffee wasn't quite as dark as she liked it, and the eggs had a slightly runny texture, but they looked edible at least. "I don't understand."

He shrugged, playing it cool. "I woke up early and put my laundry in and then figured I would make *you* breakfast for once."

She walked to him and laid her hand across his forehead checking for a fever. Either he was sick or there'd been an alien abduction last night.

"What? I'm not a total parasite, you know. I can help out around here." Brando sidestepped her and went to the refrigerator, where he pulled out the orange juice and took a big swig right from the carton.

There was the younger brother she knew and loved.

"Want some OJ?" Brando held out the carton in her direction.

"Nope." She wouldn't be drinking any more of that, thank you very much. "You can go ahead and finish it." Out of habit, she started to eat her eggs over the sink but . . . she actually didn't have to rush around since someone else had cooked. So she sat down at the table next to Crumpet and scraped some of her eggs into his dish. "These don't taste half bad." A little more salt and maybe a pinch of pepper but not bad.

"I'll take that as the highest compliment coming from you."

Brando set down her coffee and then sat across from her. "So I've been thinking . . . I'm going to stick around here for a while. And I should probably find my own place so I can give you your office back."

Coffee nearly spewed from Sylvie's lips. There were so many things in that sentence she could react to but most importantly . . . "You're staying in Silver Bells?"

Brando handed her a napkin from the holder at the end of the table. "I don't know about permanently. But you were right about the pictures. People like them. I've already gotten a ton of requests for family portraits. And someone even wants me to shoot their outdoor wedding in the spring. This is what I want—to capture moments in people's lives. I can do that here."

"That's great, Brando." Sylvie took another sip of coffee. "That's really great."

Her brother's grin faded into a more serious expression. "I don't think I would've taken a shot if it wasn't for you. So thanks, Syl. Thanks for always putting up with me at your house and thanks for seeing something good in me."

Aww. Good thing she'd opted not to wear mascara today.

"You're a lot like Grams. You know that?" Brando's tone turned nostalgic. "She always saw the best in people too."

"I think that might be the best compliment I've ever gotten." She snatched another napkin to dab at her eyes.

"Don't get used to it." He stood and collected her empty plate. "I'm still your brother. Annoying you is part of my job description. So what've you got going on today?"

"I have that preproduction meeting for the movie scene this morning." She gulped more coffee. She'd need all the help she could get to make it through the planning session for her big scene. Thankfully, everyone had agreed to meet at the café. "I'm so nervous. I don't fit in with all of them. And what if I trip and spill the food or something?"

Brando turned away from the sink and regarded her thoughtfully. "You're great at seeing what other people are good at. Now it's time to see it in yourself."

Why was that so hard to do? "Yes, well, thanks for the advice." Talk about a role reversal. "But I'd better get to work. I have about five hundred brandied mince tartlets to whip up after the meeting, so I don't want to be late."

"Let me know if you want help," Brando called while she bundled up.

"Yip!" Crumpet raced to the front door. "Yip! Yip!"

"Sorry, baby." Sylvie stepped into her boots. "You'll have a great day with Uncle Brando."

"Yeah, we will." Her brother came and scooped up the dog. "You wanna go on a walk?"

"Thank you," she called over Crumpie's excited howls.

She hadn't taken two steps down the porch stairs when Marion came strutting down the sidewalk. "Are you really dating Royce Elliot?" The woman paused and blocked the path to Sylvie's car.

Why did she have a sneaking suspicion that Marion had been waiting around the corner for her to come outside since dawn? "Um. No. We're not *dating*. We are friends." She moved around Marion and clicked the unlock button before opening the door to locate her snow brush so she could sweep the few new inches off her windshield.

"Are you sure about that?" Marion was high-stepping in place, the sun reflecting off her silver puffer jacket. "Friends don't look like this." Marion scrolled on her phone and then held out the screen in Sylvie's direction.

She approached the sidewalk and squinted, studying the grainy picture of her and Royce all snuggled together on that sleigh ride weeks ago. "You took a picture of us?"

"No. Not me." The woman tapped the screen, zooming out. "This was posted on one of those entertainment blogs, sweetie." She pointed to the title of an article: "Royce Elliot Finds Real Christmas Romance."

Sylvie's blood burned hot. "Who did that? Who took a picture without me even knowing?"

"He's a celebrity." Marion's tone was the definition of know-it-all. "People are taking pictures of him all the time."

"Let me see that." Sylvie grabbed the phone out of her hand.

Holiday Channel heartthrob Royce Elliot was spotted out and about with a mystery woman in the small town of Silver Bells, WY, where he's filming his latest Christmas rom-com. No word on who the new flame is yet, but don't they look cozy?

"This is ridiculous." She handed the phone back and tossed her scraper into the car with a layer of perspiration itching on her forehead. "I'm not his *flame*. We've gone out a couple of times but—"

"So you are seeing him?" Marion's eyes were bulging. "This is incredible! Sylvia West, dating a movie star!"

"We're not—"

"Don't worry!" The woman marched onward, swinging her arms like a speed skater. "I won't tell anyone! Your secret's safe with me!"

Now there was a lie if she'd ever heard one. By sunset the whole town would think she and Royce were engaged.

"We're not dating!" She didn't know why she even tried. Marion likely couldn't hear much through her earmuffs anyway.

Sylvie climbed into her car and stewed the whole way to

the café. How dare a total stranger decide that she's Royce Elliot's new flame? Were there photographers lurking everywhere? Why hadn't she seen any? Her eyes narrowed and scanned the streets, but with temperatures hovering near ten degrees, no one was venturing out. "Might be nice if someone would *ask* if I'd like to be his new flame before publishing an article," she muttered, wedging her car into the narrow alley behind the café. This week she'd learned that a kiss didn't mean she was someone's flame.

Even if she might like to be.

On that note, Sylvie climbed out of her car.

Once she'd gotten settled inside the kitchen, she unlocked the restaurant and went about making a huge pot of coffee for the cast and crew members that would be attending the meeting. She'd just finished setting her favorite variety of pastries on a tray when Royce came sauntering into the kitchen.

As usual, Sylvie did a double take. Pretty much every woman who passed the man on the street did a double take. And for some reason this morning he looked dressed up, wearing gray slacks and a white button-up shirt. "Hey. Everyone's here. We're just getting settled at the tables."

"Great." Her pitch didn't quite reach enthusiastic. "The coffee's almost done."

"Okay." Royce was looking at her with a quizzical slant to his head. "Are you ready for the meeting?"

"Yep." *Nope.* She gestured to the tray. "I thought everyone would enjoy a muffin or scone." They didn't have too many to spare with the crowds as of late, but she'd stayed late last night to make an extra batch of each. "I'll join you all as soon as the coffee is done brewing."

"Oh." The man continued to stare at her, as though trying to work out some puzzle.

"What? I don't seem ready?" Was he picking up on the nerves coursing through her? She'd thought she was doing a good job hiding them.

"It's just that . . ." Royce visibly hesitated. "Um, well, this is kind of a professional meeting. I mean, most people dress up a little—like, business casual."

Sylvie looked down at her straight-leg yoga pants and her light-up Rudolph sweatshirt, humiliation igniting her cheeks. "I'm working all day, so I wanted to be comfortable." No one had mentioned business casual to her. Why in the world would they dress up for a quick meeting? "This is what I always wear to work." Because she had a real job. She didn't pretend to be someone else for a living!

"Yeah. Sure." He put on a camera-ready smile. "That's fine. No worries."

No worries? She hadn't been worried at all until he'd called out her appearance.

"You look great. Love the sweatshirt." He squeezed her arm and walked away. "I'll meet you out there," he called before ducking out the door.

Oh, sure. He wanted to meet her out there. Great. She had to walk out there by herself dressed like a holiday novelty while the rest of the cast and crew wore their business casual finest. *Oh well.* "Let the awkwardness begin," Sylvie muttered, taking the coffee carafe and the tray of pastries through the door. Hopefully with such a delicious assortment of goodies, no one would notice or care what she was wearing anyway.

No one seemed to gawk at her when she stepped into the dining room. Everyone milled around, chatting and snapping selfies with the decor.

She hurried the pastries and coffee to the table she'd set up last night and then rearranged the mugs and napkins so she didn't have to talk to anyone.

"Sylvie! Look at this spread." Jun walked to the table. "You didn't have to go to all this trouble."

"I didn't mind." She held her head high, bracing for the woman's judgment, but the producer offered her a warm smile.

The woman selected a lemon chai muffin and plopped it on a plate. "We could not be more thrilled about you doing that viral video with Royce. Genius. After all of the chatter, viewers are going to be searching for your face in the film. In fact . . ." She waved to a man Sylvie had yet to meet, beckoning him to join them. "This is Seth, our makeup artist. He wanted to chat with you about some ideas."

Sylvie tried to smile. Seth looked nice enough . . . friendly brown eyes behind round rimmed glasses, a welcoming smile. "Nice to, uh, meet you, Seth." From his fringy red-streaked hair to the collection of intricate tattoos peeking below his rolled-up sleeves of a trendy fitted blue satin suit jacket, Seth clearly had her Rudolph sweatshirt beat.

"We might need to do an eyebrow intervention." Seth's eyes had narrowed. "Do you have time later today?"

"No." She took a step back. "I'm all booked up today, I'm afraid. And I like my eyebrows."

"Hmm." His gaze continued to scrutinize her. "Well, I can see, makeup is going to take a while. We'll need you here for the scene at least two hours early."

Two hours?

"She can do that, right, Sylvie?" Jun flagged down a woman who was walking past. "And this is Vera, our costume designer."

"What a joy to meet you!" The older woman rushed to Sylvie and pumped her hand up and down. "I absolutely love your baked goods. I've never tasted scones as light and fluffy in my life. They are to die for!"

"Thanks." Sylvie managed to take the first full breath she'd inhaled since she'd walked in here.

"I have your costume all ready." Vera beelined to a clothing rack that had been set up in the corner and rushed back to hand her a garment hanging in a bag along with a shoebox.

"Is this a *dress*?" She held up the bag to inspect the ensemble.

"Yes," Vera said excitedly. "This film is full of nostalgia so we wanted a vintage Christmas-themed ensemble for our favorite baker and waitress."

"It's going to be perfect," Jun insisted, and then she stepped away. "Excuse me, we need to go discuss some lighting issues."

"Mmm-hmm." *Keep smiling.* Sylvie set the shoebox down on the nearest table so she could get a better look at the garment. "Oh my." The dress had all the makings of a carhop-style waitress uniform, complete with a full skirt, and a plaid collar to match the shiny red and green material. "This is . . . uh . . . wow."

"It's perfect. Right?" Vera untied the plastic protecting the outside. "This scene will take everyone back to a different era."

Sylvie could feel her smile morphing into a grimace. She was all for vintage charm, but, with its frills and ruffles, this hideous ensemble looked like something a celebrity might wear to a costume party. God, she almost didn't even want to look at the shoes. Sylvie pried open the shoebox and peeked inside. "Oh, I can't wear those." Christmas plaid stilettos? For a server at a restaurant?

"Why don't you just go try everything on and see how it all fits?" Vera said, with an overly polite wrinkle in her nose. "Then we can make a decision."

"Fine." But she could tell the woman right now this ensemble was not going to work for her. None of this was working for her. Except it was too late to back out of the commitment now. She marched into the bathroom and locked herself in to squeeze herself into a dress that was much too high above her knees and much too fitted for her liking.

Staring at herself in the mirror, Sylvie buttoned the collar as far up as it would go, hoping to conceal the cleavage the cut encouraged. "Lord help me," she muttered as she stuffed her feet into the death spike shoes.

Teetering, she opened the door to step out, but Royce met her there.

"Wow. Look at you." A spark of appreciation lit his eyes.

"Yes. Look at me." She looked like a newborn colt learning how to walk for the first time. And this dress—it was all of twenty degrees outside, and she was parading around in here in a skirt that hung a good five inches above her knees. "I feel ridiculous."

"Well, you look amazing." The actor proudly offered her his arm. "You are going to be the best waitress extra in the business, Syl. Trust me."

Trust was a shaky thing. She didn't fully trust Royce. And yet for some reason it was still hard to resist his charm.

Vera watched her intently as they approached. "You're right about the heels," she said, already tapping on her phone. "You can't walk in them to save your life. I'll find you some flats stat."

"That would be great." Now, if they could just burn the dress, she'd be good to go.

"The dress is perfect, though." The costume designer moved around her, looking from all angles. "It fits you like a glove."

Yes, like a tight, itchy, obnoxious glove.

"I'll work on the shoes." Vera charged to the clothing rack again.

Letting out a sigh, Sylvie stepped out of the death spikes so her feet could be grounded again.

Royce faced her. "You're going to be the star of the scene in that costume, Sylvie."

"I'd rather not be the star." She didn't shine when she had to put on an act. Her most sparkling moments happened behind the scenes. In her kitchen. With her family and the few close friends who really knew her. Those were the times she could be her brightest self.

"Don't worry. I'll make you a star." Royce aimed that eye-catching grin at her.

"Actually, I don't need you to make me anything." Not a star, not his flame, and definitely not his project.

Eighteen

SYLVIE PICKED THROUGH THE CLOTHES HANGING IN HER closet.

"Nope, no . . ." She counted a total of three dresses. The simple navy A-line she'd worn to Grams's funeral, which she hadn't even been able to bring herself to try on since. The pastel pink empire waist monstrosity her mom had bought and sent her from Florida because "it had been on sale and it would look so lovely on you." Needless to say, that sale tag still dangled from the armpit. And her third option was the deep wine-colored off-shoulder bridesmaid dress she'd worn in her sister's wedding.

She pulled the hanger off the rack and laid the floor-length garment out on her bed. As far as bridesmaid dresses went, it wasn't terrible. And it appeared this was her only option unless she wanted to wear her yoga pants to the Christmas Ball. "What d'you think, Crumpie?"

Her dog was currently sprawled on the window seat gnawing on one of the Christmas plaid death spikes that matched her costume for the movie scene. Vera had insisted she take them home so she could practice walking in heels just in case they couldn't find something more suitable, but Crumpie had decided to exercise his jaws instead. And she hadn't stopped him.

"Let's see if this still fits." Sylvie undressed and unzipped the side zipper on the bridesmaid dress. The waistline was too small to fit over her hips so she hoisted it above her head and tried to shimmy her body into the chiffon, but halfway down, her hair snagged. "Oh no. Oh geez." She tried to pull on the fabric, but her hair had become one with the zipper. "Ah! Help," she squeaked, dancing around. She couldn't see anything through the fabric.

"Yip!" Crumpet latched his teeth onto the hem of the dress and started to pull, which only made it harder to maintain her balance. "No, Crumpie, easy. No—"

A knock sounded on her door. "Syl?" her brother called. "Some guy just delivered a package for you."

"Come in and help me!" While Brando opened the door, she did her best to shimmy the dress down enough to cover her underwear.

"What're you doing?" her brother asked in the same tone he'd used those few times he'd caught her doing Zumba videos in her room when she was fifteen.

"I'm stuck!" She tried to follow the sound of his voice, but ended up stubbing her big toe on the bedpost.

"I don't understand." It did not sound like her brother was moving to come to her aid.

"The zipper snagged my hair and now I'm stuck," she growled.

Crumpet was still playing tug of war—shredding the hem of the dress from the sound of things.

"Well, what d'you want me to do about it?" Brando asked warily.

"Just untangle my hair," she shrieked.

"Fine." Footsteps stomped close by. "How did this even happen?" he demanded, tugging at her hair.

"Ow! Take it easy." Sylvie elbowed him through the dress. "I'm trying to get ready for the ball." In hindsight, she probably should've decided what she was going to wear a week ago like most people did. But she'd been too busy.

Her brother pulled on her hair. "I might have to use the scissors."

"Don't you dare." She could not show up at the biggest Christmas event in Silver Bells with a chunk of her hair missing.

Brando continued messing with her hair and the zipper, muttering curses. "There." With one final tug, he freed her.

"Thank you!" Sylvie yanked the dress all the way down but had to do some more shimmying to get the garment in place. "Whew." Talk about a calorie burner.

Seeming relieved to see her face, Crumpet let the hem of the dress go and hopped back up to continue dismantling his new stiletto.

"That dress looks a little too small for you," her brother said on his way out of her room.

She took back everything she said about being proud of Brando. "Who's the package from?" She picked up the box that he'd set on her dresser.

"Dunno. Some courier service from Jackson brought it." He disappeared down the hall.

A courier from Jackson? She opened the card that had been attached to the outside of the box.

Looking forward to tonight. —Royce

A great sense of foreboding welled up inside of her, forcing her to hold her breath. Surely Royce hadn't gone shopping for her. Surely he wasn't trying to tell her what to wear. She ripped open the box and found a chic fitted black dress with a plunging neckline folded up in some tissue paper along with a pair of beautiful red patent-leather ballet flats. Sylvie pulled the dress out of the box and held it up.

"Is that what you're wearing tonight?" Claire—Sylvie hadn't even realized she was over—sailed into the room and stole the dress out of her hands. "Oh my God. It's divine."

Sylvie sank to the bed. Yes, the dress was divine. She could tell it was expensive just from the feel of the fabric in her hands. "What're you doing here?" she asked her sister instead of answering the question.

"Oh, you know . . ." Claire sat next to her, still admiring the dress. "I thought maybe you needed a little help getting ready for the ball tonight."

"I'm getting a lot of help." She hadn't meant to sound so bitter. But really . . . Royce had sent her a dress to wear. He probably wanted to make sure she didn't show up in her light-up Rudolph sweatshirt.

"You spent eight hundred dollars on a dress?" Her sister gawked at the price tag dangling from one of the straps.

"*I* didn't spend anything." She handed over the card from Royce.

"Wow." Claire set the dress on the bed and picked up the shoes. "How thoughtful. I mean, he must've known that you hate figuring out what to wear."

"Or he doesn't want to be embarrassed by me tonight."

After the Rudolph sweatshirt situation, she had her doubts that his motive was pure thoughtfulness.

"Don't be silly." Her sister nudged her shoulder. "What're you waiting for? You have to try this on! It's absolutely beautiful."

"Fine." She stood up and brought the dress into her closet. Instead of hoisting the old bridesmaid dress over her head again, she forced it down over her hips, letting the seams rip. Crumpet had trashed the hemline anyway.

The black dress went on perfectly and easily and, even worse, the material felt like butter against her skin. She begrudgingly walked out of the closet, and Claire gasped.

"Oh my God, Syl. It's fabulous."

It felt fabulous on, but she eyed the dress in her full-length mirror. Her sister was right. It was beautiful. It flattered her curves and had this elegant drape effect in all the right places. But the neckline was so low she wanted to put on a scarf and . . . well, she felt uncomfortable. But maybe it wasn't the dress as much as what it represented.

Claire pushed off the bed and approached her, smiling happily while she fussed with the straps. "You're like Cinderella, and Royce is your fairy godmother," she joked.

Sylvie turned to get a view of the dress from the back. Damn it. This angle looked every bit as good as the front. But . . . "I've never liked Cinderella."

Claire started to dig through the jewelry box on her dresser. "Really? What could you possibly have against Cinderella?"

"It's the story I don't like." When Sylvie sat on the bed, the magic dress didn't even wrinkle. "I mean, instead of dressing her up all fancy and perfect, her fairy godmother should've been like, 'Girl, you are good exactly the way you are. You go to that ball and you dance exactly how you want to dance and you show all those snooty elites that you're a diamond. Screw the glass slippers. They're not practical anyway.'"

Her sister dropped the earrings she was holding and turned to face her. "I guess I never thought of the story like that."

"Well, it's always bothered me." Because even as a little girl the message had come through to Sylvie loud and clear. *You're not good enough the way you are.* "Why should Cinderella have to transform into something else to be loved? I mean, that's the whole theme of the fairy tale. Let me change you into something lovable. And then she has to run away and hide before midnight strikes, or people will see her for who she really is." Clearly a woman hadn't written that story. "And then the prince comes around and he doesn't even *recognize* her." Once she got going on this topic it was hard to stop. Some people had their political soapboxes, but she had her Cinderella soapbox. "Seriously? The prince danced with her all night—he wanted to marry her even—but he couldn't be sure it was her until the slipper fit?" Was she the only one who saw something wrong with that picture?

"Oh my God." Claire sank back to the bed, her expression stricken. "You're totally right. The Cinderella story *sucks*."

Sylvie looked in the mirror again. Her hair was still all ratted from the dreaded zipper. And there were a few newer hairline wrinkles around her eyes that she could likely conceal with makeup. Her waist wasn't cinched and her arms weren't toned. But those things simply didn't matter to her. They never had.

"The thing is . . . I like who I am." Maybe she hadn't been

THE CHRISTMAS CAFÉ ❈ 219

sure how much she liked herself before the last few weeks. But none of this felt like her. The live videos and the entertainment blog articles and going out with a movie star who did care about all of those things. Royce cared about appearances a lot. This dress showed just how much he cared. "This is a very pretty dress, but it's not me. It's not something I chose for myself."

Claire hopped up. "I like who you are too. I always have. You can't wear that dress tonight."

Sylvie looked around her room. "I have nothing else to wear. I guess I just won't go."

"I know!" Her sister linked their arms together. "Let's go look through Grams's things. Maybe you'll find something in there."

"I love that idea." It had been months since she'd looked in the boxes they'd stored in the garage rafters. And poring through those boxes never failed to produce a flow of memories that brought Grams even closer. "But we need to ask Gramps first." Looking at Grams's boxes and actually *wearing* something that had belonged to her late grandmother were two different things.

They found their grandpa and Brando facing off over the chessboard at the kitchen table.

"Your move, kid." Gramps had his eyes locked on the board, already calculating his next move. He'd always loved strategy games.

"Hey, we're going to look through Grams's boxes to find something for Sylvie to wear to the ball tonight," Claire announced.

Sylvie shot her sister a glare. Would it kill her to show a little more subtlety? "What she means is, would you mind if we took a look to see if any of Grams's old dresses fit me?" She looked down at the dress Royce had sent. "This one doesn't feel like me. And I just know Grams would have had something perfect."

Her grandfather peered at her over his glasses, which had slid down his nose. A slow wistful smile spread across his face. "I think that's a wonderful idea."

He started to get up from the table, but Brando lurched to his feet. "I'll go get you the boxes."

Sylvie shot her brother a grateful smile. Gramps might think he was still able to climb a ladder, but she'd rather he didn't, just to be safe. "Thanks. We'll be in my room."

She and Claire hurried back down the hall.

"What're you going to tell Royce about the dress?" her sister asked as Sylvie slipped it off in the closet.

"I'm going to thank him and tell him it wasn't right for me." Maybe his intentions had been good, but she needed to pick her own dress, something that represented her. "He can return it." She threw on her robe and stepped out of the closet so she could hang the dress back on the hanger. "I might have to keep the shoes, though." Because they were red and shiny and flat and completely adorable, and she didn't have enough willpower to turn down such perfect shoes.

Claire carefully folded the black dress and nestled it into the box. "Maybe we'll find a classic Grams dress that matches them."

"I sure hope so." Wearing one of her grandmother's outfits would be almost like bringing her along to the Christmas Ball. Having a part of Grams there would fill her with the confidence she'd been grasping at ever since she'd lost her.

"Special delivery." Brando set a stack of three boxes labeled *clothing* on the floor and did an about-face. "That's the extent of my abilities to help Cinderella prepare for the ball."

Sylvie shared a horrified look with her sister and then called down the hall, "I am nothing like Cinderella!" She slammed the door for effect, and both of them broke out laughing.

"Poor Brando." Claire opened the first box. "He has no idea what he missed earlier."

"I'll be sure to give him the full rundown of my Cinderella diatribe later." Sylvie pulled one of her grandmother's sweaters out. "Oh, wow. Do you remember this sweater?" She brought the cardigan closer and inhaled deeply. "It still smells like her." Like the cheap Avon Sweet Honesty perfume she'd worn every day—all honey and vanilla.

"She wore that sweater all the time." Claire smelled the fabric too. "Oh, I miss her so much sometimes it hurts."

"You do?" Sylvie gazed into her sister's teary eyes. Tears! Claire had tears!

"Of course I do." Her sister dabbed at the corners of her eyes with her shirtsleeves.

Sylvie continued to stare at her without blinking. "But you don't seem to miss her. I mean, you've never said anything and I didn't see you cry—"

"I cried a lot." A tear rolled down her sister's cheek. "But I'm the oldest. I need to get things done. That's my job. I can't let emotion distract me from doing what needs to be done."

"Claire . . ." She threw her arms around her sister, the sweater wedged between them. "You don't have to pretend you're fine all the time. It's okay to bawl your eyes out. Trust me. I do it all the time."

"But I can't," her sister blubbered, crying harder now. "I

can't, Syl. I have to be strong. Everyone needs me to be the strong one."

"No. We don't." She hugged Claire tighter. "You can be strong sometimes and I can be strong sometimes and Brando can be strong sometimes. We can take turns holding each other up."

"Well, that's good," her sister's voice was muffled against Sylvie's shoulder. "Because this whole adoption process has me crying every day. And worrying about everything. What if we don't get picked? What if—"

"It will all work out." Sylvie let Claire go so she could stare into her sister's eyes and show her steadfast faith.

"I want to believe that," her sister whispered.

"I believe it enough for both of us." This time, she could be the strong one. She could hold her sister up through this process. From everything she'd heard, adoption was a roller-coaster ride. But she was proof it could all work out great.

"Okay." Claire wiped her eyes and sighed deeply. "Okay. Thank you." She turned her attention back to the open box. "Now let's find you something to wear."

Not so fast. Claire's old habits of dodging her emotions seemed to die hard. "We can move on as long as you promise that you'll come to me when you need to talk. Or cry. As you know, I'm very good at crying."

"I will. I promise." It was hard to judge the sincerity of the promise since her sister had started rifling through the box again, but Sylvie would take it.

"Oh! This! Look at this!" Claire pulled out a wrinkled emerald green dress.

Sylvie touched the fabric, running her fingers over the chiffon layers on the skirt. The embroidered dotted swiss gave the garment a charming vintage look. "I remember she wore this one to the Christmas Ball years ago. When we were little."

"Yes." The memories flashed through her mind. "She looked radiant in that dress."

"And so will you." Claire handed it to her and then jumped off the bed, urging her to the closet. "Try it on! I know it's going to be perfect."

"Maybe . . ." Sylvie closed herself in the closet, but she already had a feeling too. She shed the robe and stepped into the green beauty, effortlessly pulling it up over her hips. "Zip me up!" She rushed out and stood in front of her sister, and then spun to face the mirror. It needed a good steaming, but she swore she heard angels singing. Maybe not out loud but in her heart. The dress fit more than her body. From the sweetheart neckline to the fitted bodice to the full skirt that hit just below the knees. It fit *her*.

"This is the dress." It was her and it was Grams and it was perfect.

"This is the dress!" Squealing, Claire ushered her out the door, down the hall.

Gramps now sat on the couch in front of a fishing show.

"Ta-da!" Her sister nudged her into the living room and Gramps turned off the TV.

"You are a vision, my dear."

"I can't believe how well this fits." She turned around slowly, still marveling that the dress her more petite and shorter grandmother had worn also flattered her figure.

"Your Grams loved that dress." His gaze looked past her as though he was seeing his late wife. "She wore it the first night she was given the Miss Christmas title."

"I'd totally forgotten that." She'd been so little that her

memory of the night was blurry and surreal. "I remember thinking she looked like an angel." Because her grandmother had positively glowed at the ball.

Gramps nodded. "She found the dress in a consignment store in Jackson. One of them real fancy places. Still had the price tags on it, and it was a real expensive dress for those days." He stood and offered Sylvie his hand and then twirled her around while Crumpet danced at their feet. "She said it was meant to be. And you were meant to find that dress today. She'd be thrilled that you're wearing it tonight."

"Oh my God, what is with all this crying?" Her sister dabbed at her eyes. "It's like now that I started I can't seem to stop. But I have to." She gasped in dramatic Claire fashion. "I have to go! I have to get ready too!"

Sylvie managed to get a quick hug in before her sister zipped out the front door. She still had to steam the dress but she couldn't walk away quite yet.

"Hey, Gramps." She went back to him and gave his hand a squeeze. "Are you sure you don't want to come with us tonight? Royce wouldn't mind." He genuinely seemed to like her grandfather. And she didn't exactly need to spend time alone with the man.

"Nah. I'll stay home and babysit the rug rat." He sat back on the couch and patted his lap for Crumpet to hop up. Gramps loved that dog every bit as much as she did.

Sylvie hated to leave him, especially since Brando would be taking pictures at the ball tonight. "Well, I won't be late, so maybe we'll have time for a movie when I get home."

"You just go and have a good time." Gramps clicked the TV back on. "We'll be fine."

"Anyone know how to tie a tie?" Brando walked into the room fidgeting with the fabric around his neck.

"Well, look at you." She couldn't remember if she'd ever seen her brother wearing a suit. Maybe their mother had forced him to wear one to his senior prom.

"It's all in the knot." Uttering a groan, Gramps pushed off the couch again, helping her brother weave the tie into a neat knot.

"Who's your lucky date?" Sylvie couldn't help but asking.

"No date for me. It's all business since Mrs. Wingate hired me to take pictures." He shot her a devilish smirk. "I'll be sure to catch you crossing your eyes or getting your hair stuck in your zipper again. Maybe the shot would make the paper."

"And I'll be sure to pay the local Jazzercise club to hound you until you've danced with every single one of them." Jen would jump at the chance.

"No!" Her brother's wide eyes filled with horror. "Not the Jazzercise ladies. Last time I was in town one of them pinched my butt at the market."

"Just imagine how much they'll enjoy slow dancing with you, then." Sylvie broke into a laugh that rivaled the evil stepmother's.

"I'll make you look perfect in every picture." Her brother lifted his camera off the kitchen table.

"She doesn't need anyone to make her look perfect," Gramps told him, his eyes twinkling. "Sylvie is beautiful exactly the way she is."

For once, she believed him.

Nineteen

ROYCE WAS QUITE THE GENTLEMAN WHEN SHE EXPLAINED to him about Grams's dress. "You'd look lovely in a paper bag," he said, his eyes shining. "So this ball is a pretty big deal, huh?" He pulled away from the curb and glanced at the navigation map.

"It's the biggest event of the year in Silver Bells." Now that they were on their way, anticipation simmered inside of her. While another year she may have dreaded it, this year she was ready. She was ready to feel Grams's presence. She was ready to step back into a tradition that had once been so much a part of her.

"I've never been to a Christmas ball before." Royce slowed behind another car. Already a line of trucks and SUVs trailed down the street as people searched for parking a block away from the Wingate home.

"There's a lot of dancing. And food." Sylvie watched the house come into view, all lit up and crowded with people streaming inside. "And then they always announce the winner of the Miss Christmas honor too."

"There's a beauty pageant?" Royce looked at her in disbe-lief.

"Not exactly. It's more like a title bestowed on the person who displays the most Christmas spirit in town. But in recent years it's turned into more of a popularity contest than any-thing. No one has to parade around in swimsuits or anything, though."

"Thank God for that." He stopped the car near the side-walk in front of the house. "You can get out here. I'll park and meet up with you inside."

"Why, thank you." Door-to-door service would be nice. She loved the ballet flats, but they didn't have any traction for the ice.

Sylvie climbed out of the car and made her way inside, taking her time to admire all of the lighted details on the way up the front walk—the lighted peppermint sticks lining either side of the concrete, the gingerbread people peeking out from behind trees. The scene took her back to when she'd walked this path with Grams and they would ooh and aah over every detail.

Happiness poured into her heart as she climbed the stone steps and ducked in through the front door. The foyer had been transformed, with garlands outlining the grand curved banisters and white Christmas trees standing in each corner.

"Sylvie." The elder Mrs. Wingate stood sentry as the greeter. She looked as elegant as ever, her white hair perfectly coiffed and her red lipstick stubbornly intact. "How wonder-ful to see you. And that dress. It belonged to your grand-mother, didn't it?"

"Yes." She slipped off her coat and hung it on one of the racks so the woman could get a better look.

"How I miss her." Mrs. Wingate's smile was every bit as warm as Grams's. "Especially this time of year."

"Me too." But she was learning to live with the missing. Learning to step out on faith and live in a way she knew would make Grams proud.

"Sylvie!" Beth Wyman waved from across the foyer.

Well, well, well. A warm greeting from the Starlet Sisters.

"Hi!" The woman rushed over, with Vicky and Alicia close behind. "So nice to see you here," Beth gushed. "I love that dress. It's very retro."

"Yeah. Uh. Thanks?" A compliment!

"Hey, sorry that took so long." Royce had snuck up next to her.

"So what do you think about our little town's festivities, Royce?" Vicky asked, twirling one of her brown spiral curls around her finger.

Ah. Now this little ambush made sense.

"I'm impressed." Royce looked around. "For such a small community, there's a lot of Christmas spirit here."

"Well, we have so much to offer in Silver Bells," Alicia murmured. "Hopefully you'll be staying a while so you can get a little taste of everything."

Sylvie's eyes rolled. Or every*one.*

"We'll have to get together sometime soon," Beth said to Sylvie.

Was she joking? They'd never gotten together. She'd never been of interest until Royce walked into the picture. But she had no desire to stand here and pretend they were her friends. "I'm pretty thirsty," she announced.

"Then let's get you something to drink." Royce took her arm. "It was nice talking with you, ladies."

"You too." Beth fluttered her fingers in a wave. "Sylvie, let us know when you're free for a girls' night."

Without answering, she let Royce escort her into the main living room. The massive space had been cleared for the band and the dance floor—what do you know, right in front of the fireplace. Some couples were already out there, holding each other close while they swayed to Bing Crosby. From the beautiful stone hearth adorned with greenery to the gigantic tree that almost reached the top of the vaulted ceiling to the many wreaths hanging on the walls, this room was a true Christmas paradise.

"You sure seem to have a lot of friends." Royce swiped two glasses of champagne from a passing waiter and handed one to her.

"I don't actually." She sipped from the elegant stemmed glass. "They're only talking to me because I'm here with you."

"No way." His innocent dismissal had to be an act because he wasn't that stupid.

"It's true. Those three women mostly ignore me." Not that she minded. She'd rather be ignored than have fake friendships.

"I can't imagine anyone ignoring you." He took the glass out of her hand and set them both on a nearby table, and then led her to the dance floor. "You're lovely. And very kind. And funny. And talented. I'm lucky to be dancing with you." Royce pulled her closer.

Well, that made her smile.

They swayed to the soft jazzy version of "Baby, It's Cold Outside," with him humming along. This moment was ethereal—almost dreamlike. Except that everyone was pretending not to stare at them. And she caught snippets of whispers as they moved around the dance floor.

Royce gazed down at her with a grin that was as clueless as it was seductive. "Smile, Sylvie. Everyone's watching us."

Clearly, that was what he wanted. Everyone watching. He smoldered and smiled and charmed and relished the attention. In fact, the expression he wore now was completely different from the way he'd looked at her in the sleigh or at the movie. And it was very different from how he'd looked at her when she'd been wearing her light-up Rudolph sweatshirt.

"Do you remember what you said to me on the sleigh ride?" Sylvie felt the smile melt off her face. "Right outside of this very house?"

"Can't say that I do." Royce kept his smoldering grin intact.

"It was about how when someone's gone, their magic lives through you." She stopped dancing. "We were talking about my Grams."

"Oh, right." He pulled her into motion again. "Sure. I remember that."

"You also said those same things in a movie I watched. Was it a line? Something you'd memorized for a film?"

His grin faltered but he kept right on dancing. "I don't know. I can't remember every line from every movie." He twirled her around. "It doesn't really matter, does it?"

It did matter. Words were meaningless if they were simply recited from a script. If there was no substance behind them. She wanted substance. "I don't need all of this." The attention and the looks and the people pretending to be her friend. "I don't need lines from a movie." God, what was she doing here? With Royce? What was she doing here with him when Abe was at home? He might not know exactly what to say, or even say much, but he showed up every time she needed someone. And when he did talk, she knew she could trust what he said.

"Stop." Sylvie put on the brakes again. "We need to go somewhere and talk—"

"All right, ladies and gentlemen." Claire walked across the stage in front of the band as the song ended. For crying and rushing out of her house earlier, Claire sure looked as put together as always in that long fitted black dress with a tasteful slit up her right thigh. "As you know, every year we like to kick off this party with a special announcement."

Murmurs went around the room as everyone closed in toward the stage.

"We're thrilled to announce this year's Silver Bells Miss Christmas."

Applause broke out around her, but Sylvie stood frozen. Suddenly she had a bad feeling.

"Can't wait to find out who won," Royce joked.

She could wait. She didn't want her sister to call her name. She didn't want to walk up across that stage pretending to be thrilled that she'd won the Miss Christmas title when the only reason was the man standing next to her.

"As you know, the Miss Christmas tradition dates back to the very first Wingate family ball in the year 1946," Claire recited. "At that first ball, the town named the late Miss Irene Wingate as Miss Christmas for her spirit, generosity, and commitment to making the holidays magical. Now, each year since, the town has celebrated this same tradition. And this year, we have chosen someone very special."

No. Sylvie started to back away. *Don't you dare—*

"Our Miss Christmas title this year goes to none other than my sweet sister, Sylvia West." Claire was clapping right into the mic, louder than anyone else. Everyone in the room cheered like they meant it. But they didn't.

"It's you." He nudged her toward the stage. "It's your big moment."

"No. This is not *my* moment." Humiliation pinched her cheeks. This was his moment. He'd won the popularity contest. Not her.

"Come on up, Sylvie." Her sister waved her to the stage.

It was customary for Miss Christmas to address the crowd, to offer a gracious acceptance speech. But she couldn't. She couldn't pretend. "I have to go." She whirled and ran but it felt like she was moving in slow motion, like one of those dreams where you were trying so hard to get away but your body couldn't move fast enough.

"Sylvie?" Royce called behind her. "Hey! Come back! What's everyone going to think?"

She didn't care.

When she hit the foyer, she slipped and the right ballet flat popped off her foot. So much for being nothing like Cinderella. Sylvie uttered a frustrated grunt and kept running. Across the foyer, out onto the icy sidewalk. Cold! So cold on her bare foot!

"Syl?" Brando charged out the door behind her. "What's wrong?"

"I have to go. Please get me out of here, Brando." The tears were rolling now, hot and fast. "I lost my shoe inside."

"No worries." Without another question, her brother knelt in front of her. "Climb on."

He gave her a piggyback down the sidewalk just like he used to when they were teenagers, all the way to his old Jeep that smelled like coffee and pine trees and then he shoved a bundle of clothes and books out of the front seat to make room for her.

"I take it you didn't want to be named Miss Christmas this year?" he asked as they pulled away from the curb.

"They should've given the title to Royce." She rubbed feeling back into her frozen right foot. "He's the only reason anyone voted for me."

"I voted for you, even though Claire said my vote wouldn't count." He took his hands off the wheel to shimmy out of his coat and then handed it to her. "And I didn't vote for you because of Royce, either. But because you are Christmas. You're giving and you're joyful and you're selfless."

Oh man. The tears started up again. "Thanks."

Since this was Brando, avoider of all emotions and tears, he eyed her bare foot. "I thought you said you were nothing like Cinderella. But it seems to me the *shoe* fits . . ."

Ha. She shot him an evil stepmother glare.

Brando parked the Jeep in front of her house and came around to her door. He piggybacked her up the front walkway and into the house and then set her feet on the floor. "My good deed is done for the year. Now you can never threaten me with the Jazzercise club again."

Sylvie took off her brother's coat and tossed it to him. "We'll see about that."

"Yip! Yip!" Crumpet barked at them from the other side of the living room.

"Hey, pups." She went to scoop him into her arms, but the dog dodged her and ran to the back door.

"Yip! Yip!"

What was that high-pitched bark? He sounded . . . panicked.

Sylvie looked around. The lights were all on and *Miracle on 34th Street* blared on the TV. "Where's Gramps?" She turned to her brother, her pulse starting to echo in her ears.

"I'm sure he's in his room." Her brother disappeared down the hall.

"Yip! Yip!" Crumpet stood on his hind legs and scratched at the back door with both of his front paws again. "Yip!"

"What is it?" Something was wrong. Something had to be wrong.

"He's not here," Brando said when he came back to the living room. "Maybe he ran an errand."

"No. The TV is on. Crumpet's not in his playpen." She ran for the back door, slipping her boots on. "He must be in the garage."

Why would Gramps be in the garage at this time of the night? The pathway wasn't even lit! What was he thinking? She plowed through the snow covering the rickety deck. Yes, the lights were on in the garage. He must've gone to get something . . .

"Gramps?" She opened the garage door and stepped fully inside—

He was on the floor. Her beloved Gramps was lying still on the dirty concrete floor next to the fallen stepladder, a pool of blood spreading around his head.

"No! No, no, no." She fell to her knees beside him, blind and boneless, the fire of adrenaline rushing through her.

Brando crouched next to her on the floor, already on his phone, already talking to someone, maybe telling their address, but Sylvie couldn't hear past the rush of blood inside of her and she couldn't breathe.

"Gramps," she whimpered, taking his face in her hands. "Wake up. I don't understand." She looked around, blinking the barrage of blinding tears away. "What happened? I don't understand."

Her brother pointed to the stepladder. "It looks like he tried to climb the ladder to get to Grams's boxes again." Her brother felt for a pulse. "His heartbeat's strong and he's breathing. That's a good sign."

Sylvie squeezed her grandfather's hand. "Wake up," she murmured over and over. "Please wake up. Don't leave me. Please." He couldn't die like this. This couldn't be the last few minutes she got to spend with the man who'd taught her what love looked like.

"I'm going to get him some blankets." Brando was already halfway to the door. "The ambulance should be here any minute."

"You're going to be okay." She ran her hand over her grandpa's wispy white hair. "Do you hear me? You're going to be okay. I need you to be okay. The ambulance is coming." But she couldn't do anything for him. She couldn't help him the way he always helped her. Utter despair washed over her.

There was nothing she could do but hold his hand and wait.

Twenty

"TUCK THIS IN AROUND HIM."

Brando knelt next to her and shoved a blanket into her hands. "I hear the fire truck. I'm going to meet them." He disappeared again while Sylvie tucked the blanket in around Gramps's motionless body.

"We're going to keep you warm," she whispered. "Everything's going to be all right." How many times had her grandfather told her that while he hugged her in his safe embrace? She would give anything to feel his arms around her now, to hear the gruffness of his voice while he reassured her. But she would be his strength this time. She would take care of him the way he'd so often taken care of her.

Red flashing lights lit up the inside of the garage. Voices outside grew louder, closer.

Two of Silver Bells's finest volunteer firefighters, Emily Andrews and Garrett Naylor, rushed into the garage first, followed by Brando and . . . Abe.

"Okay, Sylvie. We'll take over." Emily crouched next to her, laying down a bunch of equipment while Garrett moved into position across from them.

She didn't know either of them well, but Emily had been a nurse and Garrett was a living legend in town for all of his precarious backcountry emergency extractions with the search and rescue team. Gramps was in good hands.

And yet it shook her to watch them go to work on him, taking his vitals, shining a light into his eyes.

"He's not waking up. Why won't he wake up?" She wanted to cry but her emotions were as frozen as her body.

"Come here, Syl." Abe knelt and threaded his arm around her waist, prodding her to stand. "They're gonna take good care of him. I promise. And the ambulance is only five minutes out."

A few feet away, Brando was on the phone again. Maybe talking to Claire?

"I shouldn't have left him tonight." Her knees felt weak under the weight that was slowly crushing her. "I should've stayed home with him to watch a movie." Would she ever get to watch a movie with him again?

"You found him." Abe enclosed her in his arms, drawing her close, sheltering her. "You found him in time. That's what matters. You and Brando saved him. Now he can get help."

She rested her forehead against his chest. Emotion built inside of her, straining her lungs, but she could only manage to breathe in little painful gasps. Being this close to him allowed calm to start filtering into her chaos.

"I need you to breathe with me. Okay?" Abe murmured against her hair. "Take some long deep breaths with me. Listen." He inhaled and the rise of his chest coupled with the faint pulse of his heart gave her something to hold on to. Sylvie breathed too. With him. Slow, long breaths that settled some of the chaos inside.

"That's it." Abe rubbed her back and whispered into her hair. "You can do this."

She could do this. She could. Sylvie lifted her head, looking into Abe's eyes with all of the gratitude in her heart. While they loaded Gramps onto the stretcher, she stepped out of the way and stood next to Abe, her hand finding his.

Brando came around to stand on the other side of her. "Claire can't get her car out—she's blocked in—so I have to go pick her up from the Wingate Mansion."

They didn't have time to find Claire at the Wingate Mansion! "But we need to get to the hospital right away."

"I'll give you a ride," Abe offered. "I've got my truck. I was at home when the call came in, so Emily asked me to meet them here in case they needed more support."

"That would be great." Tears pushed against her eyes again. "Thank you."

The EMTs rushed the gurney out the door, and Sylvie followed quickly so she could squeeze Gramps's hand one more time before they put him in the ambulance.

"We're taking him to County," the driver said after shutting the doors.

"We'll meet you there." She hugged her brother tight and then quickly went into the house to put Crumpie in his playpen.

"I can come back and get Crumpet after I get you to the hospital." Abe held open the front door for her. "That way he won't be alone too long."

Another thank you seemed inadequate. "That would mean a lot to me." Knowing Crumpet was being taken care of would allow her to solely focus on Gramps.

Abe led her to his truck parked along the curb and helped her get settled in the passenger's seat.

"I'll probably be the only person at the hospital wearing a fancy dress," she said when he was seated next to her. A fancy dress and snow boots.

Abe turned up the heat and pointed the vent in her direction. "I love the dress. It looks like it was made for you."

Tears made everything shimmer. "It belonged to my Grams."

"Your grandma was a special person. Your Gramps is too." Abe had the most comforting manner of speaking. His cadence was unhurried and thoughtful. "After I got back, your Gramps started to show up at the farm every Tuesday and Thursday morning to help do whatever needed done."

"I didn't know that." She remembered that he'd gone out on Tuesdays and Thursdays but he'd always simply said he was helping a friend. "That sounds like him, though."

"Yeah." He made the turn out onto the highway. "Walt would come to the farm and find me working—in the barn or out in the pens, and he'd quietly pitch in till the work was done."

"He has always been a hard worker." And her grandpa would never tell a soul about the good deeds he did.

"You're a lot like him." Abe slid a glance her way. "You're a lot like your Grams too. You have their spirit about you, Syl. You're their legacy."

It was a good thing Abe didn't seem to mind her crying because she couldn't stop. "They've both given me so much," she sniffled.

"How did you know to go home and check on him?" Abe leaned over to open the glove box and handed her a neat package of tissues.

"Oh . . . that's a story." She wiped her eyes and blew her nose and then let the whole sordid tale spill out while Abe listened intently and made sympathetic faces. "I couldn't go up on that stage in front of everyone and pretend I didn't know the real reason they chose me. So I ran." She'd embarrassed herself. She'd probably embarrassed Claire and Royce too. "I made a scene, that's for sure."

Abe seemed to consider that statement. "Don't get down on yourself for walking away. Sometimes that's the best thing you can do." He exited the highway, and she liked him even more for his blatant disregard of the speed limit.

They were close to the hospital now. And the images of Gramps lying in that pool of blood came back, raising her blood pressure. But like Abe had said, she could do this. She could be strong for Gramps and face whatever she needed to face to be with him.

"If you want the truth, I think the whole Miss Christmas thing is a bunch of malarkey," he grumbled. "Everyone should be doing their best to show some generosity and goodwill all the time—not to score points for some stupid title."

Sylvie turned in her seat to face him. "That's the best thing about you, Abe." She waited until he looked at her. "You're genuine in everything you do." He didn't try to impress anyone. He didn't even seem to care much what people thought. He'd driven a goat sled in the Christmas parade, for crying out loud, and that had been one of her favorite nights ever.

He pulled up in front of the emergency room doors, shoulders bent into a shrug. Clearly he didn't know what to say after the compliment, which made Sylvie smile.

"Will you come in with me?" She wasn't sure she could do this alone.

"I'd be honored to." Abe covered her hand with his and squeezed, somehow the perfect gesture for the moment. "I'll go park the truck, be right there."

"Okay." She climbed out and walked through the doors, grasping at the sense of calm she'd had in the truck with Abe. It was eerily quiet in the waiting room. Only two other people sat there, on opposite sides from each other, both with their gazes glued to their phones. Sylvie approached the reception desk with her hands knotted nervously together. "I'm looking for my grandfather. He was brought in by ambulance."

"Yes, of course." The woman had an easy, friendly smile. "The nurse was just out to see if anyone had come yet. I'll call her back, if you'd like to take a seat."

She nodded and backed away from the desk but didn't sit down.

"Hey." Abe approached from behind her. "Any news yet?"

She shook her head. "Waiting for a nurse to come out." Was that a bad sign?

She didn't have time to worry more before the double doors to her right opened and a nurse scurried out.

"Sylvia West?"

"Yes." Her throat closed.

But the woman smiled. "Your grandfather said you'd be here soon."

He said. He said! "He's awake?"

"Yes ma'am." The nurse—Nadine, according to her name badge—smiled. "He regained consciousness in the ambulance. They've taken him down for a CT scan now, and I'm sure the doctor will be out to chat with you as soon as we know something."

"Thank you!" It was all Sylvie could do not to hug the woman. "Thank you so much. Thank God he's awake."

"We'll be back out shortly," she called, already going back through the double doors.

A sigh relieved the knot of tension in Sylvie's chest. Gramps was awake!

"That's great news," Abe agreed. "Hopefully you can see him—"

"Sylvie!" Claire dashed into the waiting room and flew at Sylvie, her arms outstretched. They embraced, holding on to each other while they cried. "What's going on? Have you heard anything?" her sister whimpered.

"He's awake. And they took him for a CT scan." Sylvie looked around for Abe but only her brother and sister stood with her, fear evident on their stony faces.

Where had Abe gone off to?

"Have you seen the doctor yet?" Brando asked. "What have they said? How bad is he?"

Sylvie gave up looking for Abe. "I haven't seen the doctor, but a nurse came out and said they'll come back after the scan."

"But he's awake." Brando seemed to say the words to reassure himself.

"What was he thinking, climbing up a ladder?" Claire cried. "I'm so glad you left the ball. Thank goodness you found him. He would've frozen out there."

Yes, Sylvie was glad she'd run out on the ball, but she probably owed her sister an apology. "I'm sorry I took off like that and left you standing up there."

"I get it."

Their brother made a snorting noise.

"Okay, fine." Claire rolled her eyes. "I didn't get it, but Brando explained everything to me and your feelings make complete sense." Her pretty blue eyes fretted. "As long as you know I didn't nominate you for Miss Christmas because you were spending time with Royce. There's truly no one more deserving. I wasn't trying to humiliate you, or show off the fact that you were dating Royce."

"I know." Claire's skill set was more forging ahead than thinking things through. "I hope things didn't get too awkward after I left."

Claire shared another look with Brando. "Um. Well. No. It didn't get awkward. Because Royce accepted the award on your behalf. He gave a great speech and everything . . ." She looked a little sheepish.

"Unbelievable." Actually, it wasn't unbelievable, which was the exact problem. "I'll bet he gave a great speech." Award-worthy even.

"Apparently he told everyone you got an emergency call and had to leave," Brando added, voice dripping with irony.

"I guess I'm not surprised. He's quite the actor."

Abe reappeared from a hallway and sauntered to their corner balancing a coffee carrier filled with to-go cups. "I thought you all could use some fuel. We've got fully caffeinated hospital coffee. I hope you like it black because there was no more creamer. And here are a few snacks too." He set the carrier down on a small end table and grinned, pulling candy bars out of his coat pockets.

"How thoughtful of you." Claire gave Sylvie a good long amused glance.

"Very thoughtful," she agreed, taking one of the cups. "Thank you." Her heart started a slow melt when she looked at him, and now she knew exactly what that light-headed feverishness meant when Abe got close. She adored his pensive dark eyes and his plaid trapper's hat and his quiet thoughtfulness and the sly grin he seemed to save only for her. Actually, she adored all of him. "You can sit here." She patted the empty chair next to her and welcomed that tingly warmth spreading through her.

"Thanks." He sat with them and snagged one of the coffees.

Brando popped some M&M's into his mouth. "Remember that time Gramps hooked up a zipline from their second-story window to the tree in their backyard?"

"That was so fun!" The memory cracked Sylvie up. "He told me to climb out the window and hold on and he'd catch me so I didn't hit the tree." And she hadn't!

"Seriously? He let you climb out the window?" Abe held out half of his KitKat for her to take.

Don't mind if I do. "He sure did."

Claire shook her head. "I thought Mom was going to have a heart attack when she found out."

"It was so fun, though." Sylvie remember feeling the wind in her hair as the zipline carried her down to the yard. "Gramps loved fun. He always had the best ideas. And he was never as worried about anything as our parents."

"Why do you think I liked spending the weekends with Gramps and Grams so much?" Brando collected their empty coffee cups and threw them in the trash. "He used to let me sled down their stairs in a laundry basket."

Over his shoulder, Sylvie saw the doctor coming. She stopped laughing and jumped up so abruptly that her chair knocked into the wall behind her.

"Sylvie West?" The woman greeted her with a handshake. She nodded and introduced her siblings as well.

The doctor wore a businesslike expression, but a slight smile softened her expression. "Your grandfather told me you'd be the one in the fancy dress."

Her breath caught. He remembered what she'd been wearing. "So he's going to be okay?"

"So far our tests indicate your grandfather has a concussion," the doctor said. "Right now, we're not concerned." She paused while Sylvie hugged Claire. "He also has a few bruised ribs. As far as we can tell right now, there's no memory loss. He even remembers climbing the ladder in the garage."

"That's wonderful." Sylvie shook the doctor's hand again. "Thank you so so so much."

The doctor smiled. "He wants to go home as soon as possible, but we'd like to monitor him through the night."

"Of course you're keeping him overnight," Claire insisted. "There's no way we'd let him go home tonight."

Sylvie had to agree. They couldn't take any chances.

"Can we see him?" Brando asked.

The doctor waved for them to follow her, but Abe caught Sylvie's hand. "I'll pop out now and go take care of Crumpet. He can come to my house and hang out with Bambino as long as you need."

Sylvie was fully aware that Brando and Claire and the doctor were waiting for her by the double doors, but she paused so she could properly look into Abe's eyes. "I keep thanking you but it doesn't seem like enough."

"I like being there for you, Syl." His fingertips brushed hers, but he didn't fully take her hand. "So let me know what you need. Whenever. Anytime. I'll be there."

She couldn't simply thank him again so she hugged him, holding on a few seconds longer than would've been considered only friendly. Oh, he smelled good. Like a subtle cologne scented with cedar and sage.

"Keep me posted." He brushed a kiss on her cheek as she

pulled away. Such a small gesture but filled with so much tenderness.

"I will." Her smile burned from within her. A new energy carried her down the hall as she followed the doctor and her siblings to her grandfather's room. He was sitting up in the bed with his arms crossed and his eyebrows grumpily furrowed, likely anticipating the lecture he was about to get from Claire.

"Thank God you're okay." Sylvie made sure to speak first and then flew to the bed to give him her gentlest hug.

"I slipped and bumped my head, that's all," he grouched. "I don't know why everyone's making such a fuss."

Because two hours ago he'd been unconscious and lying in a pool of blood . . . but she decided to keep things positive. "We love you and we're allowed to make a fuss."

"You've a very lucky man, mister," Claire added.

Sylvie sat by him on the bed and held his hand. "Luck has nothing to do with it. He has the best guardian angel watching out for him."

Grams was still watching out for all of them.

Twenty-One

✿ ✿

SYLVIE SAT UP AND STRETCHED IN THE CHAIR SHE'D SLEPT in all night, trying to straighten the serious cricks out of her neck.

She did her best to hide the winces behind a chipper smile. Gramps had tried to send her home multiple times throughout the night, but she couldn't stomach leaving him alone. She wouldn't have slept anyway knowing he was alone and still hurting. Even if staying meant she was still wearing a now very wrinkled fancy dress.

"You didn't have to stay here." Gramps was currently eyeing the tray of eggs and bacon and toast that an orderly had delivered twenty minutes ago. The poor man had to be hungry, but she recognized the stubborn lift to his chin all too well.

Her grandfather hated hospitals. After what Grams had gone through in her cancer fight, Sylvie didn't blame him. It didn't matter that this place had recently undergone a major renovation and everything from the floors to the furniture looked brand-new. He'd spent most of the time they'd been awake pointing out the flaws in the place—the ugly color of the curtains and the antiseptic smell, using them all as justification for why he would never feel better as long as he was stuck in this "hellhole."

"Of course I had to stay." Ouch! She couldn't turn her head fully to the right without shooting pains. "I would've spent all night worrying about you. So I might as well be here, where I can see you."

"You heard the doc." Her grandpa crossed his arms, shoulders sagging into an irritated shrug. "I'm gonna be fine. I have a hard head."

Truer words.

"Where is the doc, anyway? I'm ready to get outta here." Gramps pushed the tray of subpar breakfast away. "First they don't let me sleep a wink all night and now they bring me this sorry excuse for food."

"I'm sure the doctor will be along shortly." She certainly hoped so. For all of their sakes. "Let's try to relax for a while."

"Ha. Relax?" Her grandfather gestured to the monitors still attached to his arm. "No one wants you to relax around here. All these noises, and people coming in and out . . ."

"Taking good care of you," Sylvie interjected. "The nerve!"

Gramps slumped against the pillows again. Her point had been taken. "I don't mean to be such a grump. I'd just rather be at home resting in my own bed is all." His expression softened. "You haven't said much about last night. How'd the ball go?"

"The ball was fine. But I wanted to leave early. And it's a good thing I did." She gave her grandfather a pointed look. "What were you doing in the garage, anyway?"

His eyes immediately cast down. "I was looking for the

photo album of my first Christmas with your Grams." His fingers fidgeted with the hem of the sheet that was folded over his chest. "I couldn't remember what we made for dinner or what the tree looked like that year." He raised his gaze to hers. "I was afraid I was forgetting her."

The desolation in his sad stare gave her heart a painful squeeze. "You can't forget her because she's still so much a part of you." Grams was everywhere. In this town, in their home. "That's the beautiful thing when you're married to someone for over fifty years. You become so entwined with them, your souls are threaded together even though you're separated."

"I saw her." Gramps seemed to hesitate. "I was having a dream, I guess, while I was knocked out. But it sure seemed real."

Sylvie's breath caught and goosebumps scattered down her arms. "Did she talk to you?"

He hesitated again, eyes shifting and his mouth pinched. Finally, he nodded. "She looked at me, and she said, 'It's not your time. You still have someone important to love.'" He shook his head slowly back and forth as though trying to make sense of the vision. "She must've been talking about you. Or Claire and Brando. Or maybe the child your sister is going to adopt. The truth is, I have a lot of people left to love."

"Maybe she was talking about all of us." Or maybe Grams was sending him someone special. Someone who needed a hope-affirming love every bit as much as Gramps did right now. "I think that's beautiful—"

A text chimed in on her phone. She lifted it off the table next to her and grinned at the screen. Abe.

Hope you managed to get some sleep. These two are inseparable.

He'd included a picture of Crumpet and Bambino lying on his couch together.

She couldn't help but laugh. Of course Abe let a goat on his couch. Why not? "It looks like Crumpie has made a new friend." She showed Gramps the screen.

He chuckled too. "Those two look like trouble."

"Double trouble," she confirmed. "That goat stole my keys right out of my—"

"Knock, knock." A woman poked her head in through the open door . . . and she had a dog! A beautiful dog, like a golden retriever but with a lighter and shaggier coat.

"Come in." Sylvie waved the woman into the room, already scooting out of the chair so she could meet the beautiful pup who calmly walked in and instantly sat next to Gramps's bed.

"Hi, buddy." Sylvie crouched in front of him—or her—stroking the dog's silky fur. She gazed up at the woman. "Sorry, I'm happy to meet you too, I swear. I just love dogs."

"I'm the same way." The woman smiled down at her, and Sylvie was struck with how warm she seemed.

"I'm Dottie and this is Matilda." She gave her dog's ears a scrub. "Tilda is a certified therapy dog so we volunteer here at the hospital a few times a week visiting patients." Dottie's long white hair fell in waves around her shoulders and made her seem younger, but the hard-earned lines around her mouth and eyes hinted at a long-standing wisdom. In fact, Sylvie would bet anything she was right around Gramps's age.

"Matilda is so soft," she mused, standing back up to greet the woman properly. "I'm Sylvia West, and this is my grandfather, Walt."

"It's very nice to meet you both." Dottie turned to Gramps, who was eyeing the dog like he wanted to pet her but was too stubborn to admit anything about this hospital could be positive.

"Would it be all right if we stayed for a short visit?" Dottie asked, more kindly than politely. "Tilda loves to put her paws up on the bed to greet people, but she knows she has to be invited first."

"We'd love that," Sylvie said before Gramps could say something negative about the hospital and send these two away.

Dottie focused her attention on Gramps as though awaiting his permission.

"I suppose it wouldn't hurt," he mumbled. "Since I'm stuck in here for God knows how long anyway."

Sylvie let out a laugh to compensate for his gruffness. "So what kind of dog is Tilda?"

"We're not sure, exactly." Dottie patted the very edge of Gramps's mattress, and Tilda moved her paws to the bed so he could reach her.

Even in his mood, he obviously couldn't resist petting the sweetheart.

"There is definitely some golden in her." Dottie sat in the other chair near the door while Gramps and the dog bonded. "She has the golden temperament for sure. But I also believe there's some spaniel in her as well."

"Well, she's simply beautiful." And Sylvie couldn't quite believe how well-behaved. If Crumpet were in this room, he'd be yipping and playing tug-of-war with the bed sheets and probably walking all over Gramps's bruised ribs. "Where'd you find her?"

"Oh, she rescued me about four years ago, after I lost my husband," Dottie said with a smile that blended happiness and sorrow. "Someone had turned her out on the side of the road, the shelter told me. At first she was very timid, but she warmed up quickly with a little love."

Yes, everyone warmed up quickly when they were offered a little love. She snuck a peek at her grandfather.

"The dog sure seems to have a good trainer."

Sylvie tried to hide her surprise. Gramps finally spoke! And he'd complimented Dottie.

"Our little rescue pup at home could learn a lot from Tilda." Her grandfather shot her a scolding glance.

"Crumpet is a pug/chihuahua mix," Sylvie explained. "He's very . . . *spirited*. And he also has selective hearing sometimes."

"Most of them do. I do some dog training on the side. Just for fun in my retirement." Dottie reached into her pocket and handed Sylvie a card. "I'd be happy to come and meet Crumpet and give you some pointers anytime."

"Really? That would be amazing." This woman was perfect for Gramps. Perfect! Okay, maybe she was getting ahead of herself. They didn't exactly know much about her. And she didn't have much time to find out. "So, Dottie . . ." She slipped the card into her wallet. "What else do you do for fun besides hanging out with dogs?"

"I love to read," she answered without pause. "And I'm happy doing anything outdoors, really. I like to garden and hike. Recently I've even taken a few fly-fishing classes."

"Is that so?" Sylvie felt her smile grow. Yep, perfect!

"You catch anything?" Gramps sat up a little straighter against his pillow, now fully engaged in the conversation.

"I did actually." She had the most wonderful laugh too. "I was so surprised. The guide took me out on the river, and on my first cast I managed to bring in a rainbow trout." She pulled her phone out of her pocket and showed Gramps a picture.

"Wow, that's not a bad one." He took the phone, inspecting the picture closely.

And that was Sylvie's cue.

"You know, I could really use a cup of coffee." She was already on her feet. "Would you two mind if I stepped out for a minute?"

"Not at all." Dottie turned her attention back to Gramps. "I caught six fish that day, believe it or not. That's probably why I got hooked."

They both chuckled at the pun, and Sylvie walked out of the room practically humming the "Wedding March." Maybe Gramps had dreamed he'd seen Grams, but Sylvie liked to think he'd really seen her . . . that Grams had been with him when he was cold and bleeding. That she knew he needed someone special to heal his heart and here came Dottie.

Coffee, this time blessedly with creamer, in hand, Sylvie turned the corner and ran smack into—

"Royce?"

"Hey." He halted abruptly. "Sylvie. I'd spot you anywhere in that dress."

It was a little too early in the morning for a smile with that kind of wattage. "What're you doing here?" She hadn't heard from him all night—not even one text after she'd run away and he'd apparently taken her place on the stage.

"I brought these." He held up a bouquet of red roses that had been hanging down at his side. "The waitress at the café told me about your grandfather. How's he doing?"

"He's doing very well." She stared at him, trying to determine what it was that she felt. Not anger necessarily. But she wasn't overjoyed to see him either. "I think we'll be able to head home pretty soon."

"Good. That's great." He handed her the bouquet. "You don't have to worry about the scene at the ball. I accepted the award for you, and no one even knew why you ran out."

So . . . what? He thought he'd saved her from public humiliation? "I didn't ask you to do that." Had he even thought of following her out? "I left because I didn't want the award. I don't want it."

"I know. Who cares about the stupid award?" He stepped closer to her. "I just wanted to save you from a bunch of awkward conversations later. And now everyone thinks you got a call about your grandfather. So it all worked out."

"I don't care what people think." And that was maybe the biggest difference between them. She had to get back to Gramps and Dottie. "We'll have to chat about this later." She started to turn, but he caught her shoulder.

"You're still doing the scene tomorrow, right?"

Was he seriously asking her that when she stood in a hospital hallway after a horrible ordeal with her grandfather? "I don't know, Royce. It's been kind of a long night. I'm not sure I'll be up for performing in front of a bunch of cameras tomorrow. And Gramps will probably need me at home."

"I know you've been through a lot but having you in that scene is critical for the café." He rubbed his hand up and down her arm, probably thinking she found that reassuring. "Gramps can come with you if you want. He can watch. You *have* to come."

She wasn't sure what choice she had. Just yesterday Jerry had texted how great a movie scene would be for business. "I'll try to be there. But only if Gramps will be all right." Her grandfather likely wouldn't feel like going out but Brando would probably be able to stay with him. "See you then." She quickly walked away before he tried to kiss her or something.

Sylvie shook her head all the way back to Gramps's room. She met Dottie and Tilda right outside the door.

"The doctor is here," the woman told her. "And not a moment too soon for your grandfather, I suspect."

Disappointment flooded her. She was already leaving? "I hope he wasn't too much of a bear." Sometimes it took a little effort to get past her grandfather's surly exterior.

"Not at all. I thoroughly enjoyed our conversation." Was that a blush on Dottie's face?

"Maybe you'd like to consider having another conversation with him sometime." Sylvie hated to meddle, but she couldn't let this woman walk away without asking. "I mean, Gramps loves talking fishing and I know nothing. I've never even been. So I'm sure he'd really appreciate having someone to talk to about it. Over coffee. He loves coffee." Oh, dear. She was coming on a little strong. But she couldn't seem to rein it in either.

"I enjoy a good cup of coffee myself." Dottie patted Sylvie's arm. "You tell him he can call me anytime if he wants to talk to someone."

Oh, she'd tell him all right. Maybe Claire was rubbing off on her. Sylvie told Dottie goodbye and walked into her grandfather's room. He was gingerly putting his arm through the sleeve of his heavy flannel overshirt.

"You're sure he's good to go?" Sylvie asked the doctor, who was typing into the fancy computer on the built-in desk in the corner of the room.

The man looked amused. "I don't think there's any stopping

him." He stood. "But yes, I'm confident he's going to make a full recovery. As long as he takes it easy. Here are the signs to watch for if there are any changes. You can call this number with questions or concerns." He handed her a printout.

"Thank you so much." She shook the man's hand and then he rushed off to see other patients.

"Can't tell you how happy I am to be out of that lumpy bed," Gramps muttered, easing himself down into a chair to put on his boots.

She almost went to help him, but her grandfather had never appreciated being coddled. "Well, you still need to rest and let yourself heal."

"I'll get more rest at home than I got here, that's for sure." For someone who had a couple of bruised ribs, her grandfather sure moved swiftly.

Before he could walk out the door, a nurse appeared with a wheelchair. "Ready to go?"

Gramps kept his distance. "I think I'll walk, thank you."

"Hospital policy," Sylvie informed him, nudging him toward the chair.

Scowling, he sat in the chair and grumbled about hospitals these days. Sylvie walked next to him as they made their way down the hall. "I forgot to text Brando to come and pick us up." They'd be waiting a good half hour for her brother to arrive.

"I tried to call him but he didn't answer." Gramps reached out and hit the elevator button repeatedly. "So I called Abe. He'll be here any minute."

She wasn't surprised he hadn't tried Claire, after the lecture her sister had given him about climbing ladders last night. "You called Abe before you saw the doctor?"

He looked at her sheepishly. "I called him while you were sleeping earlier. Told him to be here by ten."

The elevator doors finally rolled open, and the nurse wheeled him in while Sylvie stepped in behind.

"And what if they hadn't released you by ten?" she demanded. "Then what?"

"I would've walked out on my own." Her grandfather hit the button for the main floor. "I'm ready to be rid of this smell."

Sylvie turned to apologize to the nurse, but the young woman laughed. "You get used to it."

After a short ride down, they exited the elevator together. "So, um, Dottie seems really nice, huh?" Sylvie tried for a casual tone. She had to tread lightly here, lest he think she was turning into her sister.

"She's one hell of a fisherman, I'll tell you that."

Sylvie followed the nurse outside. Once the chair stopped, Gramps quickly stood, likely proving he could walk on his own two feet just fine. Sylvie thanked the nurse, and they walked to the edge of the sidewalk to wait for Abe.

"I talked to Dottie in the hallway before she left. She said she really enjoyed your conversation." She peeked at his face, wondering if she'd said too much, but his eyes were intently scanning the parking lot. "She even said she'd love to have coffee with you sometime to talk about fishing."

That drew his attention away from the cars pulling into the parking lot. "She said that?"

"Yep." Okay, so maybe Sylvie had suggested it first, but who was keeping track, really?

"That might be fun," he mused.

Be cool. Sylvie nodded, straining against her urge to squeal and jump up and down. When was the last time Gramps had used the term *fun* to describe anything? "I'll leave her card on the entryway table," she said when she was sure she could safely open her mouth without releasing an exuberant cheer.

Before her grandfather commented, Abe's truck pulled around the circular drive and stopped.

"Finally." Gramps led the charge, and Abe met them on the sidewalk with Crumpet nestled into his arms.

"Yip!" Her dog squirmed to get to her.

"Crumpie!" She stole him from Abe and covered his head with kisses. "Hi, sweetums. I missed you, yes I did. I missed my boy."

"He missed you too," Abe assured her.

"No, he didn't, if that picture you sent was any indication." But she was glad her baby had made a new friend.

"Looking good, Walt." Abe opened the passenger's door for her grandfather.

"Feeling much better now that I'm on my way home." Gramps nudged Sylvie toward the passenger's seat. "You sit in front. I think I'll be more comfortable in the back seat."

Abe helped her grandfather climb into the back seat and weirdly Gramps let him. He got situated, grumbling and groaning the whole time.

The drive back to her house passed quickly with Abe entertaining them by telling stories about Bambino and Crumpet's evening of bonding. When they arrived, Abe subtly helped Gramps into the house. As he went to leave, Sylvie stepped out onto the porch behind him, still holding Crumpie. "Thank you for everything." His presence had made this whole ordeal more bearable.

"I like being there for you, Syl." He'd said those same words before, but this time he said them softer, with tenderness. "I'd be happy to keep Crumpet at the farm for a few more days, so he's not under your grandpa's feet while he recovers. If that would help. I took extra food and his bed when I picked him up last night just in case."

While it pained her to think about sleeping in her bed without her real live teddy bear, she nodded and handed Crumpie over. "That would actually help a lot. We can't risk Gramps falling right now."

"Bambino will be thrilled." Abe donned that roguish seductive grin she'd come to know and love, holding her gaze with his. "You can come visit him anytime you want."

"I'd like that. Visiting Crumpet." She peered up at him, adding a few bats of her eyelashes for good measure. "And I'd like to visit *you* too." She made sure her tone conveyed that she'd like to do more than visit.

He leaned a shoulder into the doorframe, moving into her personal space. "How about you visit my place for dinner on Christmas Eve night? Say six o'clock?" His low, suggestive tone strummed all the right internal chords.

"Six o'clock," she repeated breathlessly. Even though that seemed like a long time to wait.

Twenty-Two

SYLVIE PAUSED OUTSIDE THE CAFÉ'S BACK DOOR THE NEXT morning, shifting her hideous Christmas barmaid costume to the other arm so she could lean closer and hear what was going on in there.

Too many voices clattered for her to identify who was who, but one thing was clear: The movie crew had officially taken over and closed the café for filming. On the other side of that door, her warm and cozy space had been reduced to chaos.

She could still run. Get in her car and drive to Jackson, where no one would be able to find—

The door flung open. "Sylvie . . ." Seth appeared in front of her and there was no hiding now. "There you are. What are you waiting for? Get in there." He stepped aside. "We have a lot of work to do. I was just going out to get the rest of my gear."

"Great." She tried to fashion a smile that would serve her for the rest of the morning, but it faltered. Stepping into the kitchen only made the hard knot in her stomach pull tighter.

There were so many people—most of them she didn't even recognize. Except for Teagan. The waitress was so excited about the filming, she'd asked for special permission to be there when they were setting up. Sylvie wished she could share her enthusiasm but the chaos only made her slightly nauseous. It seemed the kitchen had become something of a staging area for equipment and costumes and crew members. Someone had taken the liberty of making coffee and setting out the coffee cakes she'd baked last night after she'd finally managed to perfect Grams's Peppermint Mocha Cake.

"Sylvie?" Some man she'd never met approached her with a clipboard. His green eyes were sharp, and he had a carefully groomed triangular goatee. "Good. You're here. Costume goes over there." He pointed to a rack near the pantry. "First up for you is makeup. We've got you scheduled for an hour in the chair."

"An hour?" That seemed a little excessive.

But the clipboard man was already off to the other side of the room, barking at someone else.

Easing out a slow, determined breath, Sylvie hung up her costume on the rack and trudged to the makeup chair, which had been set up in front of the stainless-steel island where she usually prepped her food. Long mirrors were propped up on the counter and a special light on the other side of the island was pointed directly at the chair.

When she sat down and looked in the mirror, that light seemed to accentuate every little line and wrinkle. Yikes. And there was a pimple too.

All around her, people were talking, checking lights and cameras and papers. She assumed things were even more chaotic out in the main dining room, where they were setting up the scene. That must've been where Royce was too. He'd texted her an hour ago to make sure she was still coming. She was surprised he hadn't shown up at her house to drag her out of bed this morning.

"Okay, my dear." Seth lugged what looked like a huge toolbox onto the counter next to the mirrors. He stood in front of her and removed a small bottle and cotton pad from one of the pockets on his leather apron. "Let's get started. First things first, we need to begin with a clean slate."

He murmured something about minimizing pores as he squirted an earthy-scented liquid onto the cotton and then went about gently sponging her cheeks and forehead and nose. "So, are you excited about your big screen debut?"

"Not exactly." Sylvie wrinkled her nose. That stuff made her skin tingle.

"I don't blame you." He stood in front of her frowning as he conducted a visual examination of her face. "I like to stay behind the cameras myself."

"Me too." She preferred to stay away from these lights, away from the tingly face stuff.

Seth was still frowning at her. "Is that a hair on your chin?" The man whipped a magnifying glass out of his magic apron and held it up to her chin. "That's definitely a hair. Have you ever considered laser hair removal?"

"No," she snapped. "Because I don't look at my chin with a magnifying glass." She spent all of two minutes looking in a mirror each day. She had more important things to do with her time.

"Hold still," Seth instructed, pulling tweezers from his apron. Without fair warning, the man plucked the chin hair with gusto.

"Ouch!" Tears pricked her eyes.

Seth slipped the tweezers away. "Beauty is pain," he informed her.

"Which is why I've never aspired to be beautiful," she remarked sullenly.

"Come on now. You're a pretty girl." He dug in his toolbox and squirted some tinted goo on a makeup pad and then slathered it on her face. "Trust me. I've worked with some not so pretty people in my day." While he continued working on her face, Seth told her stories about some of the movie stars he'd worked with and the lengths he'd had to go to make them "camera ready."

He had just finished brushing on her mascara when someone tapped her shoulder. Teagan leaned in close and whispered, "We need to chat."

"Now?" Seth demanded. "We're running out of time."

"Yes, now." Teagan's serious expression lured Sylvie out of the chair.

"I'll be right back," she promised. They had to be almost done anyway. How much more makeup could her face possibly hold?

"What's up?" She followed the girl to a quieter corner near the extra refrigerator.

"There's something you need to see." Teagan held out her phone and started scrolling through a whole reel of pictures of Sylvie and Royce from the various dates they'd gone on.

"What is that?" She watched the images pass in front of her. There had to be ten pictures of them. "Where did you find those?"

"They're all posted on this entertainment blog." The girl closed out the pictures and showed Sylvie the title of the article. WHO IS ROYCE ELLIOT'S NEW LEADING LADY? "Did Royce ever tell you he was having pictures taken?"

Sylvie's heart started to thrum. "He was *having* pictures taken?" Like he set her up or something? "No. I'm assuming photographers were just sneaking up on us." He couldn't have—

"I'm pretty sure he had the pictures taken. I mean, look at how posed these are." Teagan zoomed in on the image of Sylvie and Royce at the movie theater, sitting close and staring into each other's eyes while they smiled. "Was anyone else in that theater that night?"

"No." Her lungs churned out furious breaths. "Not that I know of. I mean, one of the employees had to be up in the booth running the movie, but they couldn't have taken a picture at that angle."

"And look at this one." The girl scrolled to the picture of Sylvie and Royce about two seconds away from kissing in front of her door. Both of their eyes were already closed. "It looks like someone took this on your porch."

She examined the image closer. Yes, whoever took that picture had to have been standing just around the corner on her wraparound porch . . .

"Sylvie! Yoo-hoo!" Seth waved her back over. "We have to finish up so I can move on to my next victim."

"Coming," she squawked.

"I'm so sorry." Teagan pocketed her phone and rested her hand on Sylvie's shoulder. "Maybe he's doing it for publicity for the movie or something. Either way, I saw it this morning, and thought you deserved to know."

Oh, she deserved to know all right. In fact, she deserved to know that she was some pawn in a publicity scheme a long time ago. Her forehead burned underneath all those layers of makeup. "Will you send me the link to that blog, please?"

"Sure thing." The girl tapped on her phone.

"And don't tell anyone else about this." Though everyone else likely already knew. Everyone here was probably in on his little ruse. Poor naïve Sylvie. She'd be an easy target to use for publicity.

"I won't say a word," she promised.

Sylvie marched back to the makeup seat, sure that all of the powder and foundation Seth had applied was going to melt off her skin.

"Everything okay?" Seth pursed his lips while he brushed on her lip gloss.

She made a noncommittal sound, trying to hold still. Everything was not okay. She was sitting here preparing to wear the most ridiculous costume she'd ever seen and as much makeup as Sally Bowles in *Cabaret*, all so she could play a poorly written part in a movie she had no interest in even watching, let alone being in.

What the hell was she doing? What the hell had she been doing for the last few weeks?

"Perfection," Seth declared, setting her free from the chair. "Now be careful you don't mess anything up when you get your costume on."

She should've been careful, all right. She should've seen the signs that Royce was playing her. She should've known. Sylvie went into the bathroom to change and then sat in the hairstylist's chair, mentally replaying every moment she and Royce had spent together. Every moment he'd been pretending. On some level she'd known he wasn't genuine but she'd still given him the benefit of the doubt. And look where that had gotten her.

She wanted to be mad at herself for not recognizing the

signs but she *had* recognized them. Like when he'd given her a movie line. The truth had been right in front of her. She'd simply chosen to ignore it. And what really got to her was that, if she was honest, some part of her had felt special when she spent time with an actor. Maybe she was no less shallow than anyone else in this town.

After her hair had been fashioned into a loose bun on top of her head, Clipboard Man told her to wait by the door to the dining room. Someone had already set her peppermint mocha masterpiece on the counter nearby. She was busy inspecting the perfect layers when she heard Royce.

"Hey. You look incredible."

Instantaneous anger writhed in her stomach at the sight of him. "What is this?" She pulled out her phone and waved it in front of his face. "All of these pictures of you and me? Where'd they come from? How did the press get them?"

The nervous twitch of his mouth betrayed his casual shrug. "You know how photographers are."

"You expect me to believe that these were random?" She found the image on her porch. "The paparazzi doesn't follow you around, Royce. You're well known, but you're no A-lister."

"Not yet. But I will be." His eyes narrowed defensively. "This movie is going to go big, Sylvie. This is my chance. My big break."

"Oh. My. God." So this wasn't even about publicity for the *movie.* "You paid a photographer to follow you around so you could get publicity for yourself?"

"Everyone does it." His camera-ready smile had disappeared. "All the big names in Hollywood."

"No—the ones who can actually act."

"Come on." The man's tone became patronizingly gentle.

"Don't be upset, Syl. You said you wanted publicity for the café. And look what we've done. This place is taking off."

"You're right. I did say that." She'd lost herself in the midst of all this. She'd lost her whole sense of purpose—the whole reason she'd started baking in the first place. Simply to bring other people joy. To help them celebrate their special occasions and relationships. She didn't do it for money or notoriety or so she could end up being an extra in a movie.

"Maybe I should've told you about the photographer, but the photos needed to look authentic," Royce said demurely. "It's all working out. I've never been on that blog before. And the café is going to thrive now. You'll be able to keep your job. So it's a win-win."

"I thought you actually liked me." Her laugh came out borderline hysterical. "I thought all of those thoughtful things you did—the movie and the sleigh ride—were because you *liked* me."

"I do like you. But surely you didn't think this would turn into anything serious—"

"Royce," Clipboard Man called. "We need you in place."

"It's go time. We'll talk later." Royce opened the door to walk into the dining room, but then paused. "The photographer's still here for another week, so if there are any shots you want to set up, let me know. We could do a really great date in the café."

Oh, no. This was over. She was going to find her own photographer and end this now. Sylvie surreptitiously waved Teagan to join her. "I need you to follow me and take a video."

The girl's eyes went wide. "Oh my God, what're you gonna do?"

"Something that will get Royce more publicity than he ever could've dreamed." A few weeks ago, Teagan had told her she had to do something epic to go viral. And Sylvie had the perfect thing in mind.

"Sylvie, you're going to enter the dining room with your tray on my cue," Clipboard Man said.

"I'm ready." She'd never been so ready to make a point in her entire life. Grinning at Teagan, Sylvie picked up the tray that held her beautiful Grams-inspired cake. When the man pointed at her, she pushed through the door, hoping Teagan was right behind, and beelined straight for the table where Royce and his costar sat.

Instead of following the script, she set down the tray, picked up the dessert, and dumped the layers of cake and gooey whipped mousse over his head.

Silence fell over the room as Royce sat there in shock, picking pieces of mocha cake stuck in peppermint frosting away from his eyes.

"How's that for a publicity stunt, Royce?" she asked when he looked up at her. "Not as fun when you're the one who's surprised, is it?"

"Cut!" someone yelled nearby.

Sylvie didn't know who. She didn't care. She simply marched away from the mess to where Jerry stood in the corner watching the scene unfold. "I quit."

"What?" Panic scrambled his features. "What're you saying?"

"I'm saying go enjoy your retirement, Jerry. Sell the café. I'm not going to run the place for you." She would find a way to do what she loved, to bake and to bring people together in the spirit of Christmas all year.

But she would do it on her own terms.

Twenty-Three

SYLVIE STARED UP AT THE CEILING ABOVE HER BED, NOTING the peeling paint in the corner.

At least that would give her something to do now that she was officially unemployed. She'd have time to paint every ceiling in this house . . . and maybe the crown molding too. Of course, she wasn't sure how she would afford to buy paint when she had no income.

Yesterday, in her righteous indignation, she'd neglected to consider that quitting on the spot would mean cutting off her cash flow. She had savings, but with virtually no job prospects on the horizon—and almost nothing available in Silver Bells— she would have to be careful and stretch every penny.

Throat tightening, Sylvie lifted the picture of her and Grams off her bedside table and studied it. Brando had taken the picture of them sitting in front of the Christmas tree like a couple of little girls the Christmas before they'd lost Grams. They'd been wearing their PJs, of course. The two of them had always organized the presents under the tree first thing in the morning together. They'd done so much together, and now her grandmother wasn't here to help her pick up the pieces anymore.

"Oh, Grams." A sigh eased the pressure in her chest. "What am I going to do? I lost it. I lost our favorite place." The place that held so many of their memories. The place where Sylvie had found herself. The place that had given her refuge when she'd had to say goodbye to Grams too soon.

She couldn't quite picture a walk down Main Street without the Christmas Café. The place had been the heart and soul of everything Silver Bells stood for. It had been her heart and soul.

Her phone buzzed with an incoming text. Sylvie set the picture back down and picked up her phone, glancing at the screen. It was from Jerry. One simple sentence. *Need you to clear your stuff out of the kitchen and pick up your final paycheck so the new owners can get started with renovations right after Christmas.*

Dread washed over her anew. How was she going to face cleaning out her space? Packing up all of the trinkets and signs and décor Grams had bestowed on that kitchen?

A knock on her door made her want to pull the covers over her head.

Gramps didn't bother waiting for her to invite him in. "Time to get up, beautiful girl," he announced, marching straight to her curtains and throwing them open. "Look at that sunshine. It's just waiting for you to get out there and enjoy the day."

"I have nowhere to go." That wasn't exactly true. She had to go pack away the life she'd built. She turned her head to gaze at her grandfather. *Wait one minute.* Sylvie sat up straight. "What're you wearing?" She had to blink a few times to make sure she wasn't seeing things. "You haven't worn your bowtie in ages. And a sweater vest?" She narrowed her eyes. Why was he so dressed up? Did he have a funeral to go to? "Where are you going?"

"Out." Gramps plodded out the door.

Oh no he didn't. Sylvie dragged herself out of bed and followed him down the hallway. "Out where?"

Gramps handed her a fresh cup of coffee, steam still curling off the top. "If you must know, I'm going to Denny's."

"Denny's? The mediocre breakfast restaurant? All the way over by the hospital?" Gramps rarely ventured outside of Silver Bells unless it was for fishing.

"That's the one." He went to the sink and rinsed his empty mug. He was still moving gingerly from the bruised ribs, but there also seemed to be a distinct bounce in his step this morning.

"But why are you going there?" she pestered. "And why are you all dressed up?" Hope had already started swirling through her, giving her heart a lift.

"All right. Fine." He lumbered past her to the coatrack by the front door and slipped on his old bomber jacket. "I'm meeting someone at Denny's. You happy?"

Sylvie gasped with excitement before he cut her off.

"But don't you go making a big deal about this, understand?" Did he realize that he didn't sound nearly as gruff as he probably wanted to? "Dottie and I are only friends. I told her I would bring some of my flies to show her. She thinks she might like to tie a few flies herself."

"You *called* her?" It was all Sylvie could do to keep her feet firmly grounded instead of jumping up and down. This was huge!

Gramps wound the bulky red scarf Grams had given him around his neck. "I wanted to see what stretch of river that guide took her out on last summer. That's all."

And he just had to know that right now? When he couldn't even fish until spring? "And then you asked her out to coffee?"

"We got to talking about flies and she wanted to see some of mine," Gramps muttered. But a smile was starting to sneak through his surly expression. "So I suggested we meet at Denny's. No big deal."

It was a very big deal, but Sylvie pinched her lips together. There would be no squealing right now. None. Not even a little squeak. "I could give you a ride if you want." Forget her self-pity. Gramps was going on a date!

"I'm perfectly capable of driving myself." The man snatched the keys to his truck off the hook by the front door. "You heard the doc. He said I'm cleared to drive."

"I know. I was just offering." Spying on Gramps and Dottie sounded a lot more fun than going to the café to clean out her stuff.

"Unless I miss my guess, you have a new life to get on with too," her grandfather said gently. "You know what your grandmother always said . . ."

"When one door closes, a better one will always open." They recited the optimistic mantra in unison.

"It would seem the doors are a little limited around here, though." And she had no desire to move away from Silver Bells. Not away from Gramps or Brando or Claire. Not away from her cozy little house. And not away, she had to admit, from Abe.

"Then you're going to have to build a new door for yourself." Gramps laid a hand on her shoulder, his brown eyes resolute. "If anyone can build something new, it's you, honey.

I'm real proud of you, Syl. You know who you are and what you want. And you weren't afraid to stand up for yourself with that damn actor."

He had a point. The fear that had gripped her earlier started to release its hold. "Standing up for myself took me a while, but yeah. I guess it was kind of empowering to dump that cake over Royce's head."

Gramps chuckled. "I still wish I coulda been there to see his face."

"I can show you the video later." Teagan had sent it last night, but Sylvie hadn't had the guts to watch it yet. According to her friend, though, well over three hundred thousand people had already watched it.

Brando came cruising down the hallway, already geared up in his coat and hat. "Wow, Gramps. Lookin' sharp. You got a hot date or something?"

"Or something," their grandfather mumbled as he quickly shuffled out the door. He probably didn't want to answer any more questions.

"What about you, Syl?" Brando got a glass out of the cabinet and then went to the refrigerator and poured himself some orange juice. "What d'you have going on today?"

Sylvie was too stunned to answer for a second. He'd actually poured the orange juice into a glass! She felt like she should hand him a certificate welcoming him to adulthood. "Um, I have to go clean out the café's kitchen and pack up my stuff," she said instead. But the prospect already didn't seem as daunting as it had an hour ago. Painful, yes. But Gramps was right. She could start something new.

"You did the right thing." Brando chugged his juice and then swiped his mouth with the back of his arm.

So maybe he wasn't quite ready for that certificate.

"I don't know where I'm going to work, Brando."

"You're really talented, Syl. Something will come along." Her brother actually put his glass in the dishwasher. "I need to run some errands but I'll come by the café to help you out in a little bit."

"That would be nice." She'd need help loading all of the boxes into her car. She bid her brother goodbye and then took her coffee back to her room, where she pulled on some of her extra comfy sweats and wound her hair up to clip it on top of her head. She found some collapsed boxes in the back of her closet. If Gramps could go on a date, Sylvie could march into that café and take back what was hers and then step into a whole different life. It was time to build her own new door to walk through.

Even with the internal pep talk, her heart got heavier and heavier as she drove through town.

Instead of parking in the back alley, Sylvie drove around to the front of the restaurant. The lighted marquee sign had gone dark, and Jerry had posted a hand-written cardboard sign to the door. PERMANENTLY CLOSED. The sight tore at her heart. Carrying the few boxes she'd brought, she used her key to let herself inside the Christmas Café one more time.

The vacant dining room practically echoed with memories. This had been her favorite place to go with her grandparents when she'd been a little girl. Her favorite table had been that one right there, by the farthest window, where you could look out and see all of the Christmas decorations lining the street. She sat at the table one last time, remembering what it felt like to anticipate that tray of goodies that would arrive any moment. Sometimes Grams would be working her shift, and Sylvie would hang out in the kitchen with her, learning and laughing and discovering more about herself.

Since those days, she'd seen kids' eyes light up when she brought out their cookies and cupcakes and muffins. She'd seen countless people gather here in this dining room, celebrating and laughing and living—really living. Because wasn't the whole point of life to be together with the ones you love? That's why she couldn't have kept working at the café— constantly under pressure to make enough money to keep Jerry happy. She didn't want to rush the food or the people. She wanted everyone who walked in through her doors to feel free to stay as long as they wanted to. To sit and enjoy a happy, peaceful space.

She inhaled deeply, standing back up. So how could she recreate that magic somewhere else? Maybe she could get a business loan. But she'd still have to find an affordable space.

Sylvie walked into the dark kitchen and flipped on the lights. Out of habit, she went right to the coatrack, where all of the aprons Grams had made for her hung and chose the red and white one that read *I'm working on my Santa bod.* It had always been one of her favorites.

Sure, she didn't need to wear an apron to pack up, but it was the closest she could come to having Grams with her for this.

If she had been there, Grams would've turned on some Christmas music and danced her way around. Nothing had ever gotten that woman down. Not change or endings or new beginnings. She'd hummed and danced her way through every challenge—even when they'd found the cancer, even when her body had grown weaker and weaker. Days before she'd passed away, she and Sylvie had a dance party in Sylvie's kitchen . . . Grams had grooved with her walker, and Sylvie had grooved with the broom.

So that's what she'd do now. Sylvie turned on some music

and danced in honor of Grams, who was still inspiring her with her legacy of hope and optimism and faith in what was to come.

No matter what, Sylvie had to keep the faith.

She got to work, humming and cleaning and packing. Honestly, it was more fun than she'd expected.

"How dare you start the party without me?"

She whirled. At some point, Jen had walked into the kitchen. Seeing her friend brought on the tears. "I'm sorry. I'm so sorry." She threw her arms around the woman, hugging her and crying. Because of her, Jen had lost her job too.

"I was kidding." Her friend patted her awkwardly on the back. "You can party anytime you want."

"No, I'm sorry I lost our jobs." She slumped down onto a stool. "I'm sorry I made a scene and dumped that dessert over Royce's head and told Jerry off." At least they would've had one more week here. They would've had a little time to look for a job . . .

"Are you kidding?" Jen pulled out the stool next to her. "Royce and Jerry deserved it."

"But now we have no work right before the holidays, and—"

"Come on." Jen stood and tugged on her arm. "I have something to show you." She led Sylvie through the swinging doors.

"Whoa." She took one step into the dining room and halted. It was packed with people. The whole space. Claire and Brando and all of the familiar faces who'd visited the café regularly. "We're closed," Sylvie mumbled dumbly. What were they all doing here? She had nothing to feed them!

"We know, silly." Claire came to stand on one side of her and Brando moved to the other.

"No one in this town wants to see the Christmas Café go," her brother said.

Murmurs of agreement went around the room.

"So we've been out collecting donations from everyone in town all morning." Claire showed her a check from the local bank. "You may have rejected being Miss Christmas, but every single person we talked to said you are what made the Christmas Café special. You are what makes it a warm and welcoming place."

Sylvie looked down at the check, her hands shaking. "I don't know what to say . . ."

"Say you'll start a new Christmas Café," Jen called out.

"The check should be enough to get you started," Brando added.

Applause started, and the sound of it—of all these people showing up and helping her made her eyes burn. The tears spilled over and she was helpless to stop them, helpless to do anything but stand up there in front of them and cry.

When the claps died down, it was clear everyone was waiting for her to say something. She'd never been good with words but she cleared her throat anyway. "This is . . . well, it's amazing. And I can't thank you all enough for the gesture. I guess now all I have to do is find a space and—"

"I have a space."

That was Abe's voice! Sylvie frantically searched the room and then everyone parted and he came walking up from the back of the crowd, holding Crumpet nestled against his chest. His smile beat out every other smile in the room, beaming at her like he couldn't be prouder.

"I have a space at the farm I'm not using," he said, gazing at her like they were the only two people in the room. "You should check it out. Maybe you could open a Christmas goat café."

Sylvie laughed and a few more tears spilled out. "I love that idea." She reached for him because he was still too far away, and when her arms came around his shoulders, a chorus of *awww*s rang out all around them.

Crumpie seemed to enjoy the embrace too. Wedged between them, her doggo showered both of their faces with kisses. But at this moment there was only one man she wanted to kiss. And she didn't even care who saw. Perching on her tippy toes, Sylvie went for it, touching her lips to Abe's for a kiss that sent shockwaves all through her.

Somehow he managed to shift Crumpet to one arm and his other hand caressed her cheek.

Within seconds, a round of catcalls and whistles serenaded them.

Sylvie uttered a disgruntled sigh. She really needed to get this man alone. And soon.

Abe pulled back slightly, his eyes still locked on hers. "We'll have to pick up where we left off tonight."

She kissed him once more before answering because she couldn't help herself. "I can't wait."

Twenty-Four

SYLVIE SIGHED A HAPPY, DEEP SIGH AND LET HER HEAD sink into the inflated pillow that was suction-cupped to the side of her clawfoot bathtub. Soaking her packing-weary muscles in a nice hot bath seemed like the right thing to do. At least it would kill some time before the date that felt like it might never come. The anticipation still simmering from that interrupted kiss earlier had made every hour until six o'clock seem more like a year. Tonight, though, there would be no interruptions.

The thought made her impatience flare again. Would it be wrong to show up two hours early for a date?

The doorbell chimed distantly but she let it go. Brando had secured a photography contract with the fancy ski resort near Jackson, so he was off doing special Christmas shots today. And Gramps, who could believe it, was still off with Dottie somewhere.

The doorbell chimed again and then again.

Oh, for Pete's sake. Sylvie hauled herself out of the tub, dried off real quick, and then threw on her fleece bathrobe.

A series of knocks sent her hurrying down the hall. "Who is it?" she called through the wood.

"It's Royce."

Ruh roh. Sylvie's first instinct was to run. He was probably so angry with her for the whole peppermint mocha cake incident. But where would she go? Ultimately she had no place to hide. Panic hammered her ribs. "Um, what do you want?" Her voice creaked.

"I brought you a Christmas present."

She tried to get a look at him through the peephole but there must've been a layer of ice covering it. Was he messing with her so she'd open the door?

"Come on, Sylvie. I only want to give you a present and talk to you for a minute. And there's no photographer. I promise." His voice sounded sincere, but she'd thought that before too. "I won't go away until you talk to me."

"Fine," she grumbled. "Just a minute." She couldn't exactly greet Royce in her bathrobe. Tearing down the hallway, she pulled on her Grinch sweats and then raced back to the front door, opening it only a crack to peek out. Sure enough, Royce held a silver gift bag.

This made no sense. She opened the door all the way and left him standing there while she marched to the corner of her wraparound porch to make sure there were no lurking photographers nearby.

"Relax," Royce said with a chuckle. "I gave Mitch the day off."

She crept back to where he stood but didn't take the gift bag from his hands. "I can't figure out what you're doing here. Why you're giving me a gift." Unless this was some sort of practical joke. Maybe she'd open that bag and spiders would crawl out. "The last time I saw you, I dumped an entire cake over your head." So a revenge stunt could be warranted. Especially because Teagan had posted the footage online. It was so cringe-worthy, Sylvie spent the whole night dreaming about all of the ways Royce might take revenge.

"Yes, I seem to remember the cake." Royce's expression was more amused than smirking. "It was delicious, by the way." He was joking around. So he sure didn't seem upset with her.

"Well, you can understand why I would be a little nervous about opening a gift bag from you after our last interaction." Maybe he was wearing a hidden camera.

"I'm not mad at you, Sylvie." Royce's tone was quieter than usual. "I actually came to apologize."

"Really?" She couldn't seem to step out from behind her shield of skepticism.

"Really." He shrugged. "What happened was on me. I should've been up front about what I was doing. Trust me. Jun let me have it after you walked out on the scene. And she was right. Tricking you into those photographs was a stupid thing to do." A grin hiked up one corner of his mouth. "But in my defense, I seriously thought it would be a win-win for both of us."

Sylvie continued to gape at him, lips parted, eyes narrowed. He was seriously letting her off the hook for humiliating him?

"I promise I only came to apologize to you. Without any cameras." He held up the bag again. "And I wanted to give you a peace offering." He handed her the gift. "It's obvious that you're really happy with who you are. You're not trying to be someone else. And that's refreshing. Ultimately I think I learned a thing or two from you. So thank you."

"You're welcome." She almost stopped there but then

added, "Maybe I learned a thing or two from you too." Mainly that if something looks too good to be true, it probably is.

Royce nodded to the bag. "Open it. Trust me. You'll like this gift."

"The suspense is killing me." Sylvie carefully removed the tissue paper and peeked inside. She had to laugh. "My missing shoe." She withdrew the red ballet flat that had flown off her foot during her hasty retreat from the Christmas ball.

"I thought you'd like to have the set back together." Royce was chuckling.

"I do love them." She slipped the shoe onto her bare foot and held out her leg to admire it. "You've got great taste."

"In the interest of full disclosure, my assistant picked them out," he admitted sheepishly. "*She* has great taste."

"Well, either way, thank you. I love them. They really fit *me*."

"I'm glad." Royce stepped back but then hesitated. "I hope you won't look back at the last couple weeks with any regret."

"I don't. The movie . . . the sleigh ride . . . it was all fun." Even if it had been for show. And who knew . . . maybe if she hadn't spent time with Royce she never would've recognized Abe's feelings for her. "So what's going to happen with the movie scene I ruined?"

"We have plans to refilm it in Jackson right after Christmas." He didn't appear too disappointed.

"Tell me the truth . . ." She glared into his eyes. "Is that why you wanted me to be in the movie so badly? For more publicity?"

"It would've made a good headline—'Actor Has Secret Affair with Miss Christmas.'" His raised eyebrows prompted a laugh.

"Only in your dreams."

"Touché." Royce stepped back. "I should get going. We've got a production meeting."

"On Christmas Eve?" What kind of Grinch made their employees work the day before Christmas?

Royce grimaced. "We're already a little bit behind on our production, thanks to me driving you away."

Sylvie felt a twinge of sympathy for him. Only a twinge. "Do you have to work on Christmas too?"

"Nah." He walked down the porch steps. "Jun gave us all a day off."

"Well, you should stop by then." It was Christmas, after all. No one should have to get takeout on Christmas. "Gramps and I are making dinner for whoever can come. So if you'd like to have a home-cooked meal, you know where to show up at four o'clock."

"I'll keep that in mind." He glanced back at her, and his real smile wasn't quite as sparkly as the one he wore for everyone else. "Thanks, Sylvie."

She waved and then shut the door, smiling to herself. Wonders really did never cease. On the way back through the living room, Sylvie glanced at the clock.

Abe! She had to get ready. Not that he'd ever mind her messy hair and Grinch sweats, but for today—tonight—she wanted to put in a little more effort. Instead of obsessing over what to wear, she went right to her closet and selected her stretchy jeggings and her comfy gray sweater. She decided to keep her hair tied up on her head—so it stayed out of her way—and then completed the outfit with her brand-new, overly expensive red ballet flats.

Minutes later, she drove onto Abe's driveway extra slowly so she could admire all of the decorations. She drove past Jed and Loretta's house, and parked her car in front of Abe's garage, anticipation simmering.

He answered after one knock as though he'd been looking forward to this moment as much as she had.

"Come in." He took her hand and led her through the door, where she was immediately accosted by her favorite little wiggle butt.

"Yip! Yip!" Crumpet leapt for joy, trying to land himself in her arms.

"Hi, baby." Sylvie knelt and showered him with kisses. "Have you been a good boy?"

"He's been great," Abe assured her. "He and Bambino are best friends."

The baby goat had wandered over too, eyeing Sylvie curiously.

"Well thank you for babysitting this little fur ball." She gave Bambino a pat on the head too and then stood back up, holding Crumpie in her arms. Now that she could get a good look around, she found Abe's great room to be warm and unpretentious and inviting.

On the farthest wall a beautiful stone fireplace with a crackling blaze drew her gaze. On either side, large picture windows gave a glimpse of some of the yard decorations bringing color to the dark night outside. An impressive kitchen made up the other part of the room, with rustic hickory cabinets and dark stone countertops. Every square foot of the space, from the worn furniture to the cluttered bookshelves, looked well lived in and she instantly felt at home. "I love your house." And she loved seeing Abe in his house, dressed in his usual jeans and a simple wool sweater, his hair slightly unkempt. Who wouldn't want to run their fingers through that hair?

"Thanks. I renovated right after I came back." He walked into the kitchen and ladled what had to be hot apple cider from the stove into a mug and brought it to her. "It's cold out there. I thought you could use a warm drink."

It was cold outside, but the minute she saw him every part of her had started to melt. "Thank you." Sylvie let Crumpet down and her pup scampered off, elated to be reunited on the floor with Bambino. The two of them were so funny together—nudging each other with their noses, chasing each other around. She watched them and laughed while she sipped her drink.

"Dinner isn't quite ready." Abe set his mug on the counter. "So before we take off your coat, I thought we'd take a walk down to see the potential space for the new Christmas Café."

Yes, then they could get that business out of the way before getting down to other kinds of business. "I'd love to see it." Looking past him, she watched her dog try to play tug-of-war with Bambino. The poor goat didn't seem to understand. He simply kept dropping his end of the knotted rope and bleating. "Think these two will be okay for a few?"

"We'd better bring them with us." Abe put on his coat and then captured Bambino in his arms. "The other day, I discovered that they both have a thing for toilet paper. I went upstairs for two minutes and when I came down, they'd pulled a whole roll out of the bathroom and T.P.-ed the entire living room."

"That sounds like Crumpet." She stooped to pick up her dog. "Were you a naughty boy?" she asked gravely.

He licked her nose.

Abe opened the door and the four of them set off down the well-lit driveway. "I liked having him around. The house gets too quiet sometimes."

"There's no such thing as quiet when he's around." She snuggled her pup into her coat. "But I wouldn't have it any other way."

Abe cozied up next to her. "Watch this part of the driveway." He slipped his arm around her waist, drawing her in close, and close to Abe was the best place in the world to be. The wind whipped around them, blowing the snow in swirls, but being tucked into Abe's side kindled the inner fire that made her warm all over.

"Here we are." He unlocked the door to a small red barnshaped outbuilding. "Mom and Dad used to do the milking in here." He flipped on a light switch and gestured for her to walk into the space first. "But then we got new equipment and had to build a bigger facility. So it's been sitting empty for a couple of years."

Sylvie walked in, already picturing what could be. "The kitchen could go over here." She set Crumpie down and sailed to the other side of the large empty space. Oh, it would be beautiful. All new appliances but still rustic for that farmhouse feel. "And then the tables over there." She moved as quickly as her snow boots would let her to the opposite corner. "And maybe we could put in some of those special garage doors, so you could have a cute patio available for seating in the summer."

"That's a brilliant idea." Abe joined her. "We could string lights up everywhere too—" He stopped abruptly. "I mean, you could. If you wanted. I'm not trying to take over your vision or anything."

Sylvie turned to face him, her blood thickening to honey. "Lights are a fabulous idea." She moved a step closer, pulled in by the intensity of his gaze. "And I like the sound of 'we.'"

He appeared to swallow slowly and inhale deeply and the fact that he was so nervous only made her like him more. "I like the sound of 'we' too."

They stood there staring, the air between them humming, Sylvie's heart trilling because she knew he was going to kiss her again. But she wouldn't rush things. This kind of anticipation was something she'd been waiting to feel for her whole entire life—her knees softening and her lungs full of that good ache and magic swirling from the lowest, deepest places in her, all the way to her heart. She hadn't even known anticipation could be this good. This powerful.

Abe smiled at her, all lopsided and unguarded, and she liked to think that he was feeling the same kinds of things happening in his body and soul, that the magic was swirling in him too. His hands found hers, and their palms fit together, and Abe started to lower his face closer, his eyes staying with hers the whole way. Their lips were so close to touching . . .

"Bleat! Bleat!"

"Yip! Yip!"

Sylvie cracked up. She couldn't help it. Bambino and Crumpet were suddenly having a singing contest somewhere behind them.

"Well, this is romantic?" Able said through his laughter.

"It is, actually." Sylvie smoothed her hands over his shoulders, lacing her fingers behind his neck, peering up at him with that fire smoldering inside. "I'll have you know that this, Abe DeWitt, is the hands-down most romantic moment of my life."

His eyes brightened then. They were so full of light. And when his lips touched hers, that light seemed to shine right into her and illuminate every dark corner.

Abe's arms held her close, and he finally kissed her, firm and insistent but tender too, lulling her into a rhythm that opened her heart. Now she knew what all the fuss was about, how the entire world could turn upside down in a matter of seconds.

Breathless, she pulled back. Only for a second. "I didn't know," she whispered. "I didn't realize you had feelings for me." But maybe that was because she hadn't had the confidence to see him clearly.

Abe leaned his forehead against hers, light still beaming from his eyes. "I fell for you in fifth grade when you did that book report on the cookbook."

"*Baking with Julia.*" A giggle slipped out. That had been her favorite book at the time. And Mrs. Wilson had said they could report on any book they liked. When she'd gotten up there to discuss one of Julia Childs's classic cookbooks, their poor teacher hadn't known what to do with her.

"Yes." Abe's palms held her cheeks. "That's when I fell for you. And that's why I bought you that rolling pin for Secret Santa. But I knew I could wait until you fell for me too." His lips grazed hers again before he pulled back once more. "I'd have waited as long as it takes."

Sylvie stood on her tiptoes and murmured, "I have a feeling you won't be waiting any longer," right before she kissed him again.

Twenty-Five

"GRAMS WOULD'VE LOVED THIS."

Sylvie inhaled the tart and savory aroma of the citrus and herb turkey that had been roasting in the oven all afternoon. She continued washing the mixing bowl she'd used for the fig and rosemary cranberry sauce and peered out the window over the sink.

"The kitchen was your Grams's favorite place to be on Christmas." Gramps stirred the sliced onions that had been caramelizing on the stove in butter and olive oil for a good forty minutes. Though he was still recovering from his accident, he seemed to be moving around with a new energy today, and she wondered if it had anything to do with the fact that Dottie would be joining them for dinner.

Every Christmas was special, but this one seemed especially perfect. Sylvie stilled herself for a second, taking it all in—the fat snowflakes floating lazily to the ground outside, the faint hum of "Winter Wonderland" coming from her record player in the living room, the smells and sounds of the holiday feast she and Brando and Gramps were whipping up for the crowd that would be arriving soon.

As for his part, Crumpie was currently sitting directly in front of the stove, sniffing the scent wafting through the vent while he whined every so often. Her pup was obsessed with turkey.

"Can I be done mashing the sweet potatoes?" Brando held up the antique wooden-handled potato masher that had belonged to Grams's Gram. "No one uses these things anymore. Get me the hand mixer."

"That's cheating," Sylvie informed him. "Grams always used the hand masher for the sweet potato casserole and we're not breaking with tradition now." They would do everything the way Grams had done it, and they'd feel her warm sunny presence around the table with them.

Her brother scowled but he also knew he wouldn't win this argument. Sylvie's kitchen, Sylvie's rules. That was the mantra she'd already invoked a good five times today.

"Can't say I ever remember you helping us in the kitchen," Gramps said to Brando. He set down his stirring spatula and sipped on his homemade eggnog.

"What can I say? I've turned over a new leaf." Her brother went back to mashing the sweet potatoes, grunting dramatically. "Though if I'd known it would be this good of a workout, I might've helped more."

"See?" Sylvie dried her mixing bowl and placed it back in the cupboard to preserve counter space. "Kitchen work is good for you. All these years you've been missing out. You could've been toning your muscles instead of just eating the food."

"Next time I'll know better than to reject potato duty." Her brother held out the pot for her to see. "Does this meet your approval?"

Sylvie frowned at the lumpy potatoes. "You need to keep mashing, I'm afraid. They have to be silky smooth.

"Okay, turkey and stuffing are almost done, sweet pota-toes are getting close, cranberry sauce is in the fridge, green beans are boiling, onions for the green beans are almost suf-ficiently caramelized . . . Oh! And the pies are in the warmer." She'd made a gingerbread-spiced pumpkin, Grams's special fruitcake pie, a chocolate chess, and a coconut macaroon pie for good measure.

She'd quite literally been in the kitchen all day, but in her opinion there was no better feel than that ache in your feet after hours of cooking and baking.

"I think I've earned a *whole* pie." Brando held out the pot of sweet potatoes again, and Sylvie wished she had a gold star to give him.

"See? You didn't even need a mixer." She took the pot to the counter and then used a spatula to smooth the potatoes into her casserole dish.

"My forearms are sore." Brando poured himself a mug of eggnog and added a splash of brandy. "But it will all be worth it."

"That's right." Sylvie sprinkled on the pecans and marsh-mallows and used her kitchen blowtorch to scorch the top. "You can finish setting the table for me." It was almost time!

"Where are the paper plates?" her brother teased.

"Grams's china is in the cabinet. Forks on the left with the napkins and spoons and knives on the right," she informed him.

"Yip!" Crumpet barked at the stove, his tail sweeping the floor. "Yip! Yip!"

"You, mister"—Sylvie swept him into her arms—"need to wait to eat with the rest of us." She set him gently in his bed. "Bambino will be here soon." And Abe. Her heart sighed. "And you need to be a good boy—"

The doorbell sent her dog into a yipping frenzy.

"Hello?" Claire stepped inside, followed by Manuel, and they set their armloads of packages on the bench in the entryway.

"Merry Christmas!" Sylvie hurried to greet them both with hugs.

"I can't believe how good it smells in here." Manuel handed her a basket of his homemade dinner rolls, all wrapped up and still warm. "This is our humble contribution."

"I love your dinner rolls," she assured him, setting the basket down on the table. His great-aunt's recipe, they were chewy and divine.

"It smells like Grams is in the kitchen." Claire carted the presents they'd brought to the Christmas tree in the corner of the living room.

"We made all of her traditional dishes." Sylvie added another log to the fire in her little stone hearth.

Claire froze with a hopeful expression. "Even coconut macaroon pie?"

"Even the pie." Sylvie was about to walk over to the warmer to reveal a sneak peek, but the doorbell rang again. She opened the door with that anticipation blitzing through her and found Abe and Royce both standing on her porch. "Oh. Hi." Was this awkward? Should it be awkward?

"Merry Christmas." Abe held Bambino under one arm, and he also somehow had secured a box of what looked to be presents and some kind of side dish in the other.

"Merry Christmas!" She refrained from going straight for a full-on kiss—because last night was not enough kissing. She could never get enough kissing when it came to Abe—but she probably didn't need to go right for it in front of everyone, so she simply brushed a quick one across his cheek. Then she turned to Royce. "So glad you could make it."

"Thanks for the invite." He handed her a bottle of fine wine, and she had to giggle at the contrast between the two men standing on her porch—Abe in his worn jeans and faded denim trucker jacket holding a goat under one arm . . . and Royce in dark slacks and a wool coat offering a bottle of wine with a label she couldn't pronounce. But it was Christmas and all were welcome and appreciated. She stepped aside. "Come in, come in."

Brando appeared behind her and took the box from Abe's hands.

"All right, Bambino." The man set down the goat. "You behave yourself now."

The goat went right to Crumpet, nosing her dog's shoulder.

"They'll be fine." Sylvie squeezed his hand, which would have to be enough for now because the doorbell rang again.

"I'll get that." Gramps nudged Sylvie out of the way and made a beeline for the door.

Sylvie shared a smile with Brando as they listened to their grandfather greet Dottie.

"Come on in." Gramps ushered the woman into the living room, where everyone else was mingling. After he made the introductions, Dottie came right to Sylvie in the kitchen. "I know Walt told me not to bring anything, but I simply had to." She held out the dish in her hands. "It's Brussels au gratin. My mother used to make them, and I've made them every year on Christmas since she passed."

"How special." Sylvie took the dish from her and found a place for it on the table. "It looks divine. There's nothing better than family recipes."

"They help bring back memories of the ones you miss," Dottie agreed. "I'm so grateful that you invited me to join you.

I was supposed to drive to Denver to visit my daughter, but with all the snow between here and there, it would've been a bit too treacherous."

"We're thrilled to have you." She squeezed the woman's hands. Dottie couldn't possibly understand how thrilled. She'd come into their lives at just the right time, a true Christmas gift.

"This table is incredible." Dottie admired the spread. It had taken two leaf extensions to fit everyone and everything. "Can I help with anything before we eat?"

"I don't think so." But Sylvie loved her for asking. "Everything's under control—"

The doorbell rang again.

"I'll get it," Abe called.

A few seconds later, he walked back into the kitchen with his parents and they all traded hugs.

"I think we're ready to sit down," Sylvie said after the new introductions. She signaled for Gramps to cut the turkey that Brando had pulled out of the oven at some point when she'd been greeting guests. She clapped to get their attention. "Everyone! Go ahead and find a seat—wherever you want." While the chaos of everyone deciding where they were going to sit ensued, she helped Gramps arrange the turkey on a platter.

She brought the platter to the table and found the seat next to Abe open.

"I saved it for you," he murmured when she sat down.

Sylvie held his hand under the table.

Gramps took his seat at the head of the table, and it had been a long time since she'd seen such a big smile on his face. "Look at this crowd," he mused.

"We couldn't be happier to have you all here on Christmas," Sylvie added. Grams had always felt strongly that anyone and everyone would be welcomed to her table so no one would ever have to be alone for the holidays. That meant they'd always had a neighbor or someone's coworker or an acquaintance from the gym join them. Back then, their table had been full. But the last few years—with her father and mother in Florida, and Brando passing through, and the grief both she and Gramps had battled, Christmases had gotten smaller and quieter. Until now. She looked around the table, happy tears glistening, and she knew Grams was with them as well. "Here's to gathering for the holiday." She raised her glass.

"To Sylvie and Gramps for cooking this wonderful meal," Manuel added, raising his glass a little higher.

"Hey, what about me?" Brando demanded. "I want everyone to focus on how silky smooth those sweet potatoes are."

"To Brando." Claire tipped her glass toward him. "And his mashed sweet potatoes."

Laughter went around the table.

"Thank you." Her brother stood and bowed.

"And to your grandmother, and your dearly departed wife." Dottie squeezed Gramps's hand and then held out her glass. "She must've been truly extraordinary."

"She was," Sylvie managed to murmur even with emotion jamming her throat.

"To Silver Bells." Royce joined the toast, and Sylvie couldn't get over the fact that he'd opted for a mug of eggnog over his fancy wine. "Where the spirit of Christmas truly lives."

"Hear! Hear!" everyone else agreed before clanking their glasses and sipping.

"To Sylvie and Abe," Loretta sang.

"I knew it!" Claire clinked her glass against Sylvie's. "I totally knew he liked you."

"I do like you." Abe stood and raised his glass. "To the lovely and talented Sylvie, who has always brought people together the way she's brought us all together today—with food and love. And to the very bright future of the Christmas Café."

"To Sylvie!" rang out all around her. She stood too, and she kissed Abe for all to see, and then she clinked glasses with everyone who sat around them.

Many more toasts were made during dinner—to Brando's new photography work, and to the fact that Claire and Manuel had turned in their adoption paperwork. To Dottie and Tilda, who'd spent Christmas Eve visiting patients at the hospital who didn't get to go home for Christmas. To Gramps's swift and speedy recovery. To Jed's new Parkinson's treatment program. At the end of dinner, everyone complained about how full they were, but that didn't stop them from demolishing the pies she'd made.

After dessert, everyone lounged in the living room, and they opened the presents under the tree while her parents video chatted wearing matching flowered Hawaiian shirts. Everyone received their very own small block of herb-encrusted goat cheese from Abe. Royce had brought gift cards for everyone. Brando—always the delinquent—had gotten the entire group their very own Pooping Pooches calendar, since everyone seemed to love dogs so much, he said. But that was okay because Sylvie had bought him bulk laundry detergent and wrapped it beautifully.

When the presents were opened and the fire had lain down into a bed of flickering red-hot coals, everyone started to stretch and yawn. Claire and Manuel left first since she had to be at City Hall early the next morning. Then Jed and Loretta started yawning and eventually made it out the front door. Royce took off next, saying he had a video call date with his family back in California.

"You know what?" Brando smiled at Sylvie. "I'm going to do the dishes. Consider that my real present to you, Sis. The Pooping Pooches are just a bonus."

"That would be the best gift ever." She was still tucked on the couch with Abe, along with Bambino and Crumpet, both of whom were snoring.

"And I'm going to make sure Dottie gets home okay." Gramps reached out his hand and helped the woman out of his favorite chair.

"And come in for a cup of coffee, I hope?" she asked somewhat shyly.

"A cup of coffee would be grand." The two of them bundled up and walked out the door chatting easily, and Sylvie was once again overcome with gratitude.

She and Abe were finally alone. Sylvie leaned her head on his shoulder, letting out a contented sigh.

He slipped his arm around her and brought her in closer. "I got you another present, by the way. But I couldn't bring it inside."

Sylvie turned her head to peek up at him. "Really?"

"It's in the back of my truck," he said mysteriously.

Curiosity was enough to lure her out of her warm, comfy spot next to him. "Well, what are we waiting for?"

Laughing, Abe stood up too. He took her coat off the rack and helped her slip into it, brushing a kiss across the side of her neck as he drew close.

The glow from that kiss stayed within her as they walked

down her porch steps hand in hand. When they reached his truck, Abe hopped up on the tailgate and flung off the blanket that lay over something bulky.

The streetlamp above illuminated a sign lying in the truck bed. No, not only a sign. *The* sign. The beautiful marquee sign that read *The Christmas Café*.

A cloud rose from her mouth with her delighted gasp. "How did you get that?"

"I bought it off Jerry." Abe hopped back to the ground, standing close to her. "It's not like he's going to need it. I figured you might want it, but if you don't—"

She silenced him with a kiss, her arms coming around him. "I love it." She could only whisper because this man stole the power right out of her lungs every time he touched her. "It's perfect. It's a piece of the history that will be the perfect complement to our new future." She squealed happily and touched her lips to his again when suddenly her boots were off the ground and he was holding her tightly against him, kissing the breath clean out of her.

When her feet came back down to earth, Abe kept his arms around her and gazed into her eyes. "Merry Christmas, Syl."

"Merry Christmas," she murmured, letting her head fall back so she could peer up at the beautiful diamond-studded sky. This really was a wonderful life.

ACKNOWLEDGMENTS

First, I want to thank every reader who has picked up this book. What a joy it is to share Sylvie's story with you! Writing this story would not have been possible without help and support from so many wonderful people. I especially want to thank my agent, Suzie Townsend, for pointing me in the right direction. You told me to write Christmas and here we are. Thank you to the Hedrich family at LaClare Creamery for educating me all about goats. I appreciate your time more than I can say and absolutely loved the tour of the creamery and kid barn. Everyone really must visit www.laclarecream ery.com and try some of their divine cheeses. (Or, if you're in the area, stop in for some goat yoga!) To the creative and talented Amanda Cupcake—I am so happy our paths crossed. You are the sweetest! Thank you for collaborating with me on an epic holiday dessert recipe. Keep sharing your art with the world and making it a brighter place. To my new team at Putnam . . . all I can say is wow. I feel blessed to be working with you all. Kate Dresser, editor extraordinaire, thank you for choosing Sylvie's story. You are the one who truly made it shine. As always, a huge thank-you to my guys—Will, AJ, and Kaleb. You truly teach me more about love every single day.

Gram's Peppermint Mocha Mug Cake

Recipe by Amanda Cupcake
https://www.amanda-cupcake.com/

This peppermint mocha mug cake—filled with marshmallow cream buttercream, dripping in chocolate ganache, and swirled with peppermint whipped cream mousse—is a holiday dream. The cake is candy cane red, painted with a buttercream stencil, and the mug handle is a jumbo candy cane. The many pieces to this recipe are open to the baker's creativity and inspiration. The buttercream on the outside of the cake can be made in any color. Try a stencil using any craft store design—or make fondant holiday cutouts to place on the cake instead. The peppermint whipped cream mousse on top of the cake can also be used as a filling.

CHOCOLATE CAKE

(makes one 6-inch, 3-layer cake)

¾ cup unsweetened cocoa powder

1 teaspoon baking soda

1 tablespoon instant espresso powder

½ teaspoon salt

1 cup boiling water

2 large whole eggs, plus 2 large egg yolks

1¾ cups fine granulated sugar

½ cup light brown sugar

¾ cup vegetable oil

¼ cup butter (regular or goat butter), melted

2 cups all-purpose flour

1 tablespoon vanilla extract

¾ cup sour cream

⅓ cup milk (regular or goat milk)

OLD-FASHIONED "MIRACLE" PAN RELEASE

Baking spray with flour

Vegetable shortening

Flour or cocoa powder

6-inch cake boards

PREPARE AND BAKE THE CAKE

1. Preheat oven to 325°. Prepare three 6x2-inch round cake pans with old-fashioned "miracle" pan release: Spray with the baking spray. Grease with shortening. Dust each pan with flour or cocoa powder. Shake off excess.

2. In a stand mixer and using the whisk attachment, mix the cocoa powder, baking soda, espresso powder, and salt. Pour the boiling water over the dry ingredients. Let cool for approximately 5–10 minutes.

3. In a small bowl turned on its side, whisk the eggs and egg yolks until well combined.

4. Add sugars, oil, melted butter, eggs, and vanilla extract to the cocoa mixture. Alternate adding the flour, sour cream, and milk to the sugar/cocoa mixture. Using the whisk attachment, beat at medium-high speed until all ingredients are combined and batter is smooth and shiny. Scrape down the sides of the bowl with a rubber spatula and mix again to blend if necessary.

5. Pour the batter evenly into the prepared pans and bake until a toothpick inserted comes out clean, approximately 30–40 minutes.

6. Cool the cake layers in their pans on a wire rack for 10 minutes. Remove from pans and let cake layers cool to room temperature on the rack. Level the layers using a serrated knife or cake leveler. Store cake layers on cake boards in ziplock bags or plastic wrap until you're ready to decorate the cake.

TIP: If there is any leftover batter, make cupcakes! Line cupcake tin with cupcake wrappers. Using an ice cream scoop, fill cupcake wrappers two-thirds full. Bake at 325° for 24 minutes or until the cupcake springs up when touched lightly. Let cool before decorating.

Frosting Recipes

MARSHMALLOW CREAM BUTTERCREAM

13–14 ounces marshmallow cream, such as Marshmallow Fluff

16 ounces (1 pound) store-bought buttercream, softened

1 tablespoon vanilla extract

6–8 cups confectioners' sugar

Super red gel paste food coloring

With a spatula, scrape marshmallow cream and buttercream into the bowl of a stand mixer. Using the flat beater attachment, mix until fluffy and well combined. Gradually add vanilla extract and confectioners' sugar until the frosting reaches desired consistency—the creamier, the better. Add a few squirts of food coloring.

TIP: For cupcake frosting, use a little more sugar for swirling consistency.

Note that gel paste colors darken the longer they sit on your frosted cake or cupcakes. So even if the color looks a bit light in the mixing bowl, it will brighten up on your cake the longer it sits.

CHOCOLATE GANACHE

⅓ cup semisweet or milk chocolate chips

½ cup heavy whipping cream

Measure chocolate chips into a deep microwave-proof bowl. Microwave cream in a small microwave-proof bowl until boiling, approximately 1 minute. Pour cream over the chips and whisk until smooth. Let the ganache cool for about 10 minutes before using.

MINTY WHIPPED CREAM MOUSSE

4 tablespoons white chocolate or vanilla instant pudding mix (in dry powder form)

4 cups heavy whipping cream, chilled

½ tablespoon peppermint extract

White gel paste food coloring (optional)

Combine pudding mix, cream, and peppermint extract in a stand mixer using the whisk attachment. Whip the ingredients until mousse reaches stiff peaks, approximately 5–7 minutes. Refrigerate the mousse until it is time to decorate the cake.

TIP: For a whiter mousse, add 3–4 drops white gel paste coloring.

DECORATING TOOLS AND INGREDIENTS

Small and large frosting spatulas

Mini holiday-themed fondant cutters

White fondant

Craft or cake stencils

Disposable piping bags

Vegetable shortening

A few small sewing pins

Jumbo candy cane, broken in half

Large open star frosting tip

Andes chocolate mints

Mini marshmallows

Edible sparkles

Peppermint stick

8- or 10-inch cake board for display

Cake turntable

ASSEMBLE AND DECORATE THE CAKE

1. Set aside half of the marshmallow buttercream in a covered bowl to use for filling and stenciling the cake. Mix red color gel paste into the remaining buttercream.

2. Fill and stack leveled cake layers with white marshmallow cream buttercream. Let the cake chill in the refrigerator for approximately 30 minutes. Once the cake has chilled, frost with the first thin crumb coat of red buttercream. Let the cake chill for 10–15 minutes. Cover with a second layer of red buttercream and smooth with the frosting spatula until desired consistency is reached. Add a third layer of red frosting if desired. Chill frosted cake in the refrigerator for 30–60 minutes before decorating.

3. Cut out mini fondant trees or other mini fondant holiday details. Let dry.

4. Stencil the cake. You can make a stencil yourself or use any stencil from a craft store or cake decorating supplier. The print for the stencil on this cake is from a Fair Isle sweater pattern. For beginning bakers, the larger the stencil opening, the easier it is to stencil a cake. Cut a small hole at the end of a disposable piping bag and fill the bag with white buttercream frosting. Use shortening to lightly grease the side of the stencil that will touch the cake, rubbing the shortening on with a paper towel. Using small sewing pins, pin the corners of the stencil so it is flat on the cake. Pipe buttercream frosting onto the stencil details and use a small frosting spatula to spread the buttercream over the stencil. Make sure the buttercream is leveled over the stencil. Remove the pins and carefully peel the stencil off the cake. Repeat the stencil technique as often as desired. Using buttercream frosting as glue, place the mini fondant tree cutouts and whimsical holiday decorations around the cake.

5. Use the halved jumbo candy cane for the mug handle. To make the candy cane easier to attach to the cake, sharpen the broken edges with a knife first. Carefully insert the broken candy cane into the side of the mug cake. Chill the cake before proceeding with the remaining steps.

6. Prepare the ganache and let it cool to slightly warmer than room temperature. Using a spoon or a spatula, spread the ganache over the top of the chilled cake. Spoon drips of ganache just slightly over the edge of the cake. Chill the cake until the ganache is set.

7. Cut a hole at the end of a disposable piping bag large enough to fit the open star piping tip. Fill the piping bag with the whipped peppermint mousse. Pipe peppermint mousse frosting swirls on the top of the cake in small circular motions, inspired by whipped cream swirls on top of a peppermint mocha.

8. Decorate the rest of the cake as desired, using the remaining frosting as glue for the festive holiday treats. Add Andes chocolate mints and mini marshmallows, then sprinkle with edible sparkles. Place a peppermint stick on top of the cake as the straw. Display on an 8- or 10-inch cake board on top of a cake turntable.

ABOUT THE AUTHOR

© 2022 Will Richardson

Eliza Evans pens heartwarming holiday rom-coms. When not writing, Evans can be found teaching Pilates or exploring the great outdoors. A lifelong mountain girl, Evans lives with her husband, two sons, and two fur babies. *The Christmas Café* is her debut novel.

www.elizaevansbooks.com

⬡ @Booksbysaraandeliza
🐦 @saraelizabooks
ⓕ @booksbysaraandeliza